# THE **TROUBLE** WITH **FRIDAY**

# THE **TROUBLE** WITH **FRIDAY**

*An Emily Blossom Mystery*

BLANCHE RENARD PUTZEL

iUniverse, Inc.
Bloomington

**The Trouble with Friday**
**An Emily Blossom Mystery**

*iUniverse books may be ordered through booksellers or by contacting:*

*iUniverse*
*1663 Liberty Drive*
*Bloomington, IN 47403*
*www.iuniverse.com*
*1-800-Authors (1-800-288-4677)*

*ISBN: 978-1-4759-5289-6 (sc)*
*ISBN: 978-1-4759-5290-2 (ebk)*

*Library of Congress Control Number: 2012918311*

*Printed in the United States of America*

*iUniverse rev. date: 11/01/2012*

To my dearest Lei, who always asks for one more story

# Illustrations

# *Chapter One*

"Emily? Emily, is that you?" Daisy Blossom's voice usually resembled the soft cooing of her turtledoves, but today she sounded frightened and desperate.

"Well, of course, dear," Emily said. "Whom did you call?"

"I called you," the voice on the telephone quavered.

"Well, that's a good thing, Daisy, because it's me you're speaking to. Why are you calling so early? You know Charlie likes to sleep in on Sunday mornings."

Emily sat in her nightgown on the edge of her bed. She steadily stroked her cat, Charlie, who slept undisturbed on the pillow. Unlike his owner, he did not appear to be especially bothered by this early morning phone call. Nevertheless, Emily lived in constant fear of provoking his anger. He did not easily forgive her trespasses.

"Emily, it's Friday. He's chewing on a hand!"

"It's Sunday, Daisy, not Friday. Stop and think for a moment."

"I am thinking. It's *my dog*, Friday—Friday, my dog."

"I told you that was a confusing name for a dog."

"He's chewing on a hand," Daisy continued, refusing to be put off by Emily's scolding.

"I thought you didn't like pork," Emily said, now firmly convinced her sister-in-law had finally lost her mind.

"No, you don't understand. not a ham—a hand, a human hand! Friday the dog is chewing on someone's hand!"

"I told you long ago, that dog has no manners. You should train him better. Who's he biting? Tell him to let go."

"You don't understand," she repeated.

"I understand perfectly well, Daisy Blossom," she replied coldly. "You're not making any sense at all, even if it is Sunday morning."

"Listen to me. There is no person attached to the hand."

1

"Get a hold of yourself. You sound perfectly hysterical. You're beside your wit's end."

"I'm not beside my wit's end; I'm at my wit's end."

"That's what I said," Emily repeated. "You're loony."

"Emily, listen to me for once."

Emily sighed deeply and audibly to emphasize the long-suffering sacrifice she was making. To have been wakened this early to listen to gibberish was asking a lot of her generally good nature. Everyone knew Emily was not her best in the mornings. She preferred to waken slowly, meander downstairs at leisure and have a lovely cup of tea before she tackled the challenges of her day. This call from Daisy had interrupted her routine. Therefore, she felt quite obligated to explain the lack of communication in no uncertain terms.

"Daisy Blossom, let me repeat your words back to you, and you see if it makes any sense at all. You said Friday the dog is eating someone's hand, but the hand is not attached to a person. That can't be."

"That's it! That's it. You need to come down to the farm right away—before he eats all the evidence."

"Evidence. The dog's eating what evidence?"

"The dog is eating someone's hand! Someone who is no longer with us . . . someone who's been murdered! Don't you see?"

"Murdered? Did you say 'murdered'?" Emily finally comprehended what Daisy had been trying to tell her. "Take it away from him, Daisy!" Now she acted as if she had known the dire significance of a hand-eating dog all along. She also realized that, of course, Daisy was calling her, Emily Blossom, for help—not because she was her sister-in-law Emily Blossom but because she was the *famous* Emily Blossom, the most uncommonly clever sleuth who previously had great success solving her town's only murder mystery.

"I'll find Pete Picken and ask him to give me a lift down to the farm. We'll be there in a jiffy. In the meantime, put on a glove before you handle the evidence. You don't want to destroy the fingerprints."

"Fingerprints? Wait just a minute." Daisy put the phone down. The turtledove cooed in the background until she returned. "It's okay; he's gnawing on the wrist. The fingers are still intact as far as I can see."

"Daisy, take it away from him!" Emily shrieked. "Don't touch anything until we get there."

"Hurry then, or he'll eat the whole thing before I can convince him to give it up."

"We'll be right there."

Emily gently replaced the receiver. She tiptoed from the bed so as not to disturb Charlie, who sleepily yawned and stretched before he curled up again into his nest to resume his catnap.

Then she began to skitter, first this way and then that way, trying to decide how best to proceed. Clothes? Phone the police? Tell the neighbours? Go find Pete Picken? She put herself into motion before she knew what she planned to do. All the possibilities of what she should do first became muddled in her head. She caught a glimpse of herself in the mirror—a reflection of a little body rushing back and forth, nightgown flowing, arms flailing and hair sticking up in all directions.

"Wait, wait, wait a minute," she called out to herself, coming face-to-face with her image. "We need a chat. Slow down and get a hold of yourself. Just because you've been called on as Detective Emily Blossom, doesn't mean you fly off the handlebars in all directions. You know you're not good at split-second decisions. You get yourself into trouble that way.

"Take your time. No need to call Inspector Allard until you know what's actually going on. No need to spread the news you don't have. Get dressed and find Pete. Then get down to Daisy's and figure out what to do from there. There . . . that's the plan."

Staring back from the mirror's reflection was a slim, elderly woman with wispy hair that refused to stay in place. Emily snatched at the wayward lock, which always strayed over her eyes in spite of her best efforts to keep it tucked behind her ear. Her eyes were grey and sparkled like water. Her eyebrows perched high on her brow, giving her the look of constant wonder, or maybe a bit of confusion, depending on the circumstances. Wrinkles mapped an accumulation of frequent smiles and frowns gained over the years.

"Now let's start all over again. Start with what you're going to wear."

Denim slacks and a long-sleeved pullover would be the most practical to wear to the farm. Early spring in eastern Ontario might be balmy or positively chilling. The weather could never make up its mind whether it was March, coming or going like a lion or a lamb. In any case, better to be prepared.

"With all those animals down at Daisy's farm, you never know whose fur you'll be wearing home," she muttered, glancing in the mirror again to make sure she looked appropriate. "I just hope I don't look dotty."

She experimented with different facial expressions by raising her brows and cocking her head ever so slightly. "A lady, especially a detective, must look convincing to be taken seriously.

"Should I wear a hat to present a look of mystery and allure? Perhaps not . . . for the more casual, caught-by-surprise-but-never-off-guard impression."

She chose a simple broad-rimmed hat, with her signature peacock feather perched in the hatband at a flaunting angle. She cocked the brim jauntily over her left eye. Then she knit her brow to give herself the allure of a serious, concentrating sleuth.

"No, too premature. I might scare Pete away by looking too specific. He's uncomfortable with too much intensity. And besides, we don't really know if this is a false alarm. Who knows? The mutt might just have come across a doll in the garbage."

She replaced the hat among her collection of hats of various styles and colours. Her hands smoothed her tidy clothes against her stomach and hips as she reassured herself she had not gained too many extra pounds over the winter.

"Funny how a person can look so like a stranger to oneself, even after all these years of staring at one's own reflection in the mirror. At least I'm not like some of those ladies who spend hours eating pastries at the Country Kitchen. You can practically tell how old they are by how much weight they carry on their hips."

Then, remembering her mission, Emily hurried herself along, navigated the stairs and grabbed her plaid jacket from the coat rack.

She was just about to slip out the door when the phone rang again.

"Maybe I won't answer it."

The ringing persisted.

"Oh, all right, all right, I'm coming."

She picked up the phone in the living room.

The voice at the other end was desperate. "Emily, you haven't phoned the police yet, have you?"

"No, Daisy, I haven't phoned the police yet."

"I'm afraid they'll put Friday in a cage. He hasn't ever been away from home, since he was a little puppy."

4

"He's not a puppy anymore. That dog's a monster."

"He would be terribly homesick if they put him in a kennel. They won't take him away, will they?"

Emily refused to pander to her sister-in-law's sentimentalism. "Calm down. Don't be hysterical. The police are not in the business of espionage. If anyone's going to come for Friday, it'll be the local dogcatcher."

"Dogcatcher? Oh, please don't phone anyone until you and Pete get here! I couldn't bear to lose Friday."

"I'm on my way, Daisy. Don't worry. We'll sort it all out when we get there."

Since Emily discovered that she had a penchant for being a detective, she had made a conscious effort to develop a mental handbook, a guide for herself to describe a detective's way of thinking. She studied by reading all the detective novels she could find. She imagined speaking, as if in italics, to direct her actions in situations which required particular investigative acumen. Daisy's telephone call prompted her to remember the correct procedures when faced with a mysterious occurrence.

*Detectives wait until they have all the facts before rushing into action.*

Thus reminded of the basic tasks at hand, Emily set out to initiate her plan.

\*

When she stepped outside, Emily was greeted by a crisp spring morning, like the kiss of a child on her cheek. The day was fresh, bright and soft, all light and enthusiasm.

The weather on Emerald Hill was unto its own. Down in the valleys, the mists would linger; snow accumulated in drifts; the rivers ran deep. On top of the hill, the weather showed a different side of its character. The sun seemed to shine more brightly; storms raged and pelted rather than dumped, and the winds swept over the crest with extra vehemence.

In this pocket of eastern Ontario, prevailing winds brought weather from the west. Sometimes the Hill would be spared a good storm. Either the north winds would sweep, cold and biting, down the Ottawa River and push the grey ominous clouds right past the Hill, following the Gatineaux rolling into the Laurentian Mountains on the Québec side; or from the Southwest, winter storms would dump snow along the valley of the St. Lawrence, south of the US-Canadian border heading for New England.

However, when winter covered all the countryside with blankets of snow, the village of Emerald Hill gathered drifts around its cluster of Victorian brick houses like a mantle against the brutal cold Canadian winters. Hill residents hunkered down and endured the winter months, much like the skeletal maples lining the streets. Once spring arrived, Canadians emerged from their toques, mittens and parkas as buds burst forth into tender spring leaves.

The trees in the village had been waiting all winter for such a shiny day. Buds had begun to test the air, poking their little green tips just beyond protective husks, waiting for the sun's warmth to tickle them out of their shells. Each bush and the three maple trees along Pearl Street were tinged with a spray of tender green. At the roots, the remnants of last week's snowstorm refused to melt. Little blades of grass clustered at the dirty edges of ice crystals, sipping from the melting snow. Bartons and Cecil Cass would be tapping the trees by now. Below-freezing at night and warm, sunny days produced perfect weather for making maple syrup.

Such a lovely spring morning might draw hibernating groundhogs from their winter dens and Emerald Hill inhabitants from the warmth of their homes, but not this early on Sunday. Nearly everyone would be sleeping in, except for the most determined souls who refused to retreat.

English sparrows, pigeons and Pete Picken were in this category. The sparrows twittered and chattered in the eaves of the Victorian houses. All winter long pigeons cooed and cuddled in the belfry tower of the Presbyterian church.

Pete Picken inhaled coffee and the sports news for early breakfast at the Country Kitchen on the Hill, no matter what the weather. Emily knew just where to find her reluctant cohort.

# Chapter Two

The Country Kitchen on the Hill was a tiny restaurant that specialized in homemade meals and fresh baking. Clients were greeted with smells of hot bread from the oven, hearty soups and delectable desserts. Ilsa Jacob and Maria Josa were partners in cooking and hospitality. Maria's specialty was Hungarian food; Ilsa kept track of serving the customers. They knew most of their diners by name.

Their red and white aprons matched the plaid tablecloths. Fresh cookies and muffins filled wicker baskets lined with plaid muslin, displayed on wooden shelves behind the counter. Tea cups and European baking dishes decorated glass shelves in the windows hung with red and white plaid curtains.

Sundays were usually quiet, until after church services. Pete Picken, the only customer, sat at a small round table in a bright corner bathed in morning sunlight. His legs were propped on a chair beside him, his cowboy boots scuffed and scarred, with mud on the soles. His face was hidden behind the sports page. Rough hands crinkled the paper, shuffling pages held just beyond his nose, so he could decipher the scores without glasses. His handmade-leather, wide-brim hat sat on the table beside an empty coffee cup.

"Ilsa, I need a refill," Pete yelled from behind the newspaper.

Ilsa stood at the doorway to the kitchen with her hands on her hips. She silently scolded Pete by squeezing one side of her mouth into a frown. She clucked her tongue against her cheek as a commentary on his bad manners.

"Now, now," Pete said from behind his paper. "Don't go getting all huffy. All I asked for was a refill.

Ilsa disappeared into the kitchen and reappeared with steaming coffee pot in hand.

"Do you want to drink it or wear it?"

"Aw, Ilsa," Pete said, finally putting down his paper and setting his feet on the floor. "Life's too short to be so mean so early in the morning. All I asked for was a refill."

"Pete Picken, you're lucky your mother didn't chuck you out with the bathwater."

He grinned, eyes twinkling, cheeks red and rosy. His wild hair stood out in all directions except for the thin spot on top of his balding head. His moustache, stained from pipe smoke, curled around his lips and crept into a smile at the corners of his mouth.

"That's because I'm so cute."

Ilsa poured the coffee. She extracted two containers of cream from her apron pocket and deposited them on the table. Then she stood with hand on hip, waiting.

Pete emptied the cream into his already-overflowing cup, added sugar and stirred vehemently, sloshing the steaming liquid into the saucer. When he noticed Ilsa very obviously tapping her foot in front of him, he innocently looked up at her, eyebrows raised.

Without saying a word, with eyebrows raised, she continued tapping and waiting.

He grinned again. "Thanks."

She sniffed, turned and returned to the kitchen.

"How about a cinnamon bun?"

Ilsa reappeared, hands on hips. "Did you wish to make an order, sir?"

"With lots of icing."

"You mean the ones guaranteed to make you complain they're not big enough?"

"The biggest one, hot out of the oven."

She waited again with her hands on her hips.

"Please."

She disappeared into the kitchen again. Pete resumed perusal of the sports page until she returned with his breakfast. As he dug into his breakfast, he became aware of her watching his every mouthful. He stopped gobbling down his cinnamon bun and put down his fork.

"What are you staring at?" he said.

"Pete, are you hanging around with some shady characters these days?"

He looked up at her, icing dripping down his moustache. "Why? What do you mean?"

8

"A strange man was looking for you yesterday."

"Strange man?"

"Yes. I never saw him before."

"You know everyone in town."

"I never saw this man before. Frankly, he gave me the creeps."

"What did he look like?"

"Well, let me put it like this: I'm not one to judge right off the bat, but, let's just say he wasn't a local. That's for sure."

"What do you mean?"

"He was pretty rough looking. Made me nervous."

Pete waited.

"He was dirty. His clothes were torn, and he had mud on his boots."

Pete became a bit self-conscious. He wore a tattered, red-checked jacket and faded blue jeans. He shortened his jeans by cutting off the hems to fit his shorter than average stature, leaving a fringe of loose threads for cuffs. His boots, propped on a chair next to his place, were caked with mud and left dried clumps on the floor.

"Lots of farmers come in here looking like that."

"This guy wasn't a farmer. He wore a Harley Davidson motorcycle jacket, with long hair pulled back into a ponytail halfway down his back. I'm sure he had tattoos where you wouldn't even want to imagine. He had earrings in his ears, lots of them."

"Lots of ears?"

"Cut it out, Pete. You know what I mean. Even his lip was pierced. His tongue kept poking at that ball thing when he talked."

"What did he want?"

"Said he was looking for you. Needed to get hold of you. Heard you came in here a lot."

"What did you tell him?"

"I said I'd pass along the message that he was looking for you."

"Did he give you his name?"

"That's when he got really scary," Ilsa said in a quivering voice. "His eyes got all shifty when I asked him to write down his number. Said he didn't have a phone. Said he'd come by again when your truck was outside."

"Thanks for the message, Ilsa."

"I hope he doesn't come back," she said. "A man like that in here is not good for business."

"If I find him, I'll tell him you said so."

"Don't you dare," she said quickly, rising to his bait. "He's the sort to burn down the place."

"I'm sure he's not that bad." Pete tried to soothe her ruffles. "Probably just some guy acting tough."

Ilsa let the subject drop and wandered to the window and rearranged the display of tea cups and dried flowers. She scanned the street for prospective customers.

"It's quiet this morning," she said over her shoulder.

"The dragon ladies will be in soon," said Pete. He had the habit of introducing references, which challenged his listeners to guess at his meaning just to see if they were listening. He also liked to goad Ilsa's curiosity. He succeeded in provoking her.

"Who is that, exactly?"

"Most of them are related to Attila the Hun's mother-in-law."

"Who do you mean?"

"You figure it out," he said. "She comes in every morning to check up on the gossip."

"C'mon, Pete, you could be talking about any number of ladies who come in here."

"When some people arrive, everybody's happy; when some people leave, everybody's happy." Pete refused to make it easy for her to guess.

"I give up."

When she failed to continue the guessing game, he changed the subject.

"By the way, are you going to be open on Parade Day?" he said. "Business should be good then."

"What day is that again?"

"St. Patrick's Day."

"There's no Irish folk in this town, Pete Picken."

"Everybody's Irish on St. Patrick's Day. You wait and see. Emerald Hill will be full of green-clad leprechauns."

The sweet aroma of freshly baked muffins reminded Ilsa of her duties in the kitchen. "I imagine we'll be open. Maria will make sure to serve up some good Irish stew and Cornish pasties."

She picked up his empty plate and left him to his coffee.

Before Pete could resume his scrutiny of the sports scores, the bell at the door announced a customer.

"Oh no, here comes trouble," he said under his breath.

Emily Blossom wasted no time homing in on his table. As she sat down, she bumped the table, spilling Pete's coffee from the saucer onto the tablecloth.

"Emily, watch what you're doin'," Pete said as he grabbed for a napkin.

"Good morning, Pete," Emily said in her cheeriest voice, designed to engage even the most reluctant participant. She took the napkin out of his hand and proceeded to dab at the expanding coffee stain in front of him.

"What's so good about it?" Pete asked. "You're here, aren't you?"

"Yes, and you should be pleased as pitch that it's me and not someone less charming and more nosy, who shall remain nameless."

"Punch . . . pleased as *punch*," Pete corrected. "And I'm not sure who I'd rather see first thing in the morning."

"Punch, yes, that's it. I knew you were pleased as punch to see me too."

"Can't a guy just have a peaceful cup of coffee in a place without you messing everything up? Leave me alone. That's enough of that." Pete yanked the soggy napkin from her hand and threw it onto the next table over.

Emily pulled her seat to the table and asked Ilsa for a cup of coffee.

For a few moments, Pete continued to hide behind the paper, while Emily practiced just how delicately she could hold the cup with her little finger extended—enough to demonstrate her prowess at grace and etiquette and not so much as to draw attention to herself, were she to have had an audience.

Pete's retreat behind the sports page was clearly ineffective.

"I need your help," Emily said without apology or introduction.

"No."

"Please, Pete. I know you won't turn down a request from a lady."

"No."

"You don't even know what I'm asking for."

"I don't want to know. The answer is No. N. O. No."

"A gallant and brave man like you, turning down two damsels in distress? That's not like you."

"Two?"

"Two," Emily repeated with a smile that twinkled in her eyes.

"No and no," he repeated. "That's two nos: one for you and one for her, whoever she is. What part of 'no' don't you understand?"

"Daisy, Daisy Blossom, my sister-in-law."

"Triple no," he said quickly.

"C'mon, Pete. All I'm asking is that you drive me down to her farm. She's got a little problem. She's beside her wits."

"At her wit's end," Pete corrected

"That's what she said. Daisy's at her wit's end, and she called to ask for some help. It's not a big favour I'm asking," Emily crooned.

"You drive yourself."

"You know I've never had a license. I count on my friends when I have to leave the village."

"Well, call your friends then."

"You're my friend, Pete. Please. Just drive me down to the farm. It won't take long."

"Look, the last time you asked me for a little favour, it turned into a really big deal. You almost got killed, and I almost ended up in prison. So the answer is no. I'm not interested in your little schemes."

Emily tried another approach. She quietly placed her coffee cup on its saucer, placed her hands in her lap and turned to stare out the window.

"All right, if you want to be like that," she said softly. "You'll miss a good chance to buy some pretty fine antiques, and then you'll be sorry. Daisy's house is full of good Canadiana. She started collecting way back when a diamond point was a real pine cupboard with carved doors and six-inch crown moulding in original paint—none of this fake wood and applied decorations. She's got at least six armoires from heritage farms around here. She's got a sideboard made down in Glengarry by Cameron MacDonald in 1865. Her kitchen table is seven feet long with a two-board top and stretcher base. You might miss a chance to buy something you could make money on, just when she gets around to selling."

Emily sniffed and sighed at the same time, gazing vacantly at the empty street while she watched his expressions out of the corner of her eye.

"I know all about Daisy Blossom's antiques."

Emily seized on the opening. "You know her house, the old stone farmhouse down at Blossoms' Corners, with the original beams running the length of the building and windowsills four feet wide."

"Perhaps you've forgotten; I've probably known Daisy longer than you have. Unless something's changed drastically in her life, she's not about to sell anything out of that house anytime soon."

"She makes a mean lemon meringue pie."

Pete hesitated.

"It's not far. It won't take any time at all for you to drive me down there."

Emily held her breath, pretending to be interested in anything but him.

"Did she tell you she had pie?"

"She didn't have to. Daisy always has pie."

"All right, then. It's been a while since I've been down to Blossoms' Corners."

"Fine, let's go."

"It's your turn to pay for the coffee."

Emily happily paid. She knew Pete was not averse to a little icing on his cake. "The way to a man's heart is in his stomach."

"Through his stomach," Pete said.

"Yes, yes, that's what I said," Emily said with a smug grin. "The way to a man's heart is through his stomach."

House with Gingerbread

# *Chapter Three*

Pete rarely parked in front of wherever he happened to be. Emily was prepared for the search. He told her once that he didn't like other people to know exactly where he was. He didn't like to fuel gossip either. In a small town like Emerald Hill, everyone wanted to know everything about everyone else. He had said, "I prefer to keep my business to myself, and my private life private. The whereabouts of my truck keeps people guessing."

Emily happily played the guessing game. She followed Pete when they left the Country Kitchen. They had to walk halfway down the block and around the corner to reach his truck.

Emily spotted the truck rack first, overhung by an upside-down canoe, a pine turned-leg kitchen table, a green trunk missing one hinge and a child's cradle with broken rockers. The club cab was filled with a smattering of antiques. The rear seat had no room for passengers. Emily identified various objects: an elaborate mask, possibly carved by the indigenous people of Western Canada, but more probably of Indonesian origin; pieces of a formerly elaborate bronze candelabra; a cast iron stand for a glass table, the top of which was carefully stowed, wrapped in antique coverlets to avoid breakage; and hand-tinted photogravures of people, long-since forgotten, now torn and water-stained portraits in gold-painted frames. Emily couldn't imagine what else was packed into boxes and trunks stuffed underneath the seats.

Emily clambered into Pete's truck by hoisting herself onto the running board and grabbing a handle above the door to pull herself onto the seat. Her feet barely touched the floor, which was a good thing since the floor was cluttered with empty coffee cups and papers; discarded receipts; a screwdriver and wrench; several screws and broken pieces of antique furniture. Pete used the dashboard as a shelf for pipes, his glasses, auction announcements, and photos of an icebox and three cupboards, for sale to his clients in Toronto. Emily had the odd sensation she was not the only passenger in the truck, although her traveling companion was mute:

behind her, a seamstress's mannequin reclined on a child's toy box; the featureless face stared blankly at the back of her head.

Once established in the passenger seat, she surveyed the street with a satisfied grin.

Pete settled into the driver's seat with the relaxed pose of one who spent more time here than anywhere else in the world. The large fingers of his right hand curled around the steering wheel, directing the truck from its parking place with ease, while his left hand held the essential, smoking pipe. His hat dipped over his eyes, screened by sunglasses that he wore with the allure of mysterious secrets, hidden behind the reflection of daylight in dark mirrors.

The furniture rattled and banged as the vehicle swung onto the street.

The air of the village was spring-like. However, the truck smelled far from fresh. The odour of stale cigars mingled with pipe tobacco, ashes and spilled coffee.

Emily tried not to say anything about the cloud of smoke in the cab produced by Pete puffing on his pipe. She opened the window and took a deep breath, but she choked on the cold, biting breeze.

She quietly rolled up the window and said, "Would you mind opening your window, please?"

Without hesitation, he did so.

The truck moved down Main Street as if it owned the pavement.

"Do you always drive down the middle of the street?"

"You asked me for a lift, didn't you? I'll do the driving. You navigate."

Emily had to think for a moment. Pete knew the countryside like the back of his hand. How was she supposed to explain to him where they were going?

"You go down the hill for a while, turn off after the big tree and keep going until you're there."

Pete guided the truck along the block lined with stores comprising "downtown" Emerald Hill: the post office, two banks, a clothing store, gift shops, a hardware store and the offices of the Hill *News*. After the one stoplight in town, they descended the Hill's residential section of Victorian brick homes and apartments.

From the passenger seat, Emily had a fine view of the village, with its brick houses with decorative architectural gingerbread on the porches as they sped by the window. The town was usually neat and tidy. The residents took great pride in their properties. At this time of year though, when spring was barely on the horizon, the countryside looked stark and drab from the ravages of winter. Dirty snow patches smudged the shady corners of porches and underneath trees. The grass had not yet rejuvenated itself. The tender shoots were barely a green tinge around the yellow, dry weeds, which lay like a blanket on the earth, protecting little creatures hibernating underneath. Frost smothered the countryside. The trees were delicately fringed skeletons with spring buds ready to burst into blossoms.

As they left town, Emily recalled the phone conversation she'd had with Daisy that morning. Her mind began to race, anticipating several scenarios playing out in her imagination: the possibilities ranged from finding a large dog playing with a toy, to discovering a real-live, dead murder victim to encountering Inspector Allard already on the scene of a gruesome crime.

To disguise her excitement, Emily began to chatter. "We do live in a wonderful country. We Canadians are very strong. We're hardy. We come out of hibernation, from underneath our blankets and our sweaters and our long johns when the sun starts to warm the earth. We're very resilient, you know. We like challenges, the challenges of the seasons. It's what we are. We rise to it. We hide from it. Well, not really so much, I mean, over the winter, we get out; we make do; we live through the cold. We actually like the challenge of a winter's storm. We like to prove that we can make it through the drifts and shovel the snow. We especially like the warmth of our cozy houses, but come spring, everybody is itching to get out."

Emily paused to catch her breath.

Pete continued to puff on his pipe and agreed with a humph, without saying much of anything.

In a rare spark of insight, she surmised that his lack of response might mean something.

"You're not sulking, are you, Pete?"

"I can't believe you actually convinced me to leave the sports pages behind. I missed the results of last night's hockey game, and I didn't even finish my coffee."

"I'll make it up to you, Pete. Who knows, maybe I'll buy tickets to the hockey game sometime."

"That'll be the day," he said. "Don't make any promises you have no intention of keeping."

"I wouldn't do that. You know me better than that."

"Yes I do . . . and yes you would."

The buildings and the homes of the village thinned beyond the brow of Emerald Hill, with the descent into the valley. In the distance, the blue and purple hills of Quebec rose on the north side of the invisible Ottawa River, known as La Rivière Outaouais in La Belle Province.

Emily searched for neutral ground to avoid an argument.

"Snow covers a lot of evils. In the spring, all sorts of junk appear from underneath the melting drifts. Garbage has been hidden until now, but all of a sudden we can see all the stuff we've been throwing out, the stuff the wind has blown across the countryside. You see remnants of winter's trash. You can never tell what you're going to find. It's the worst time of the year for that."

"The garbage men will come and pick it up," he said. "When they have the 'big trash day,' the whole countryside will turn into one huge trash pile until the trucks come and take it all away."

"Oh, I know, I know. And it'll be warm soon. Then the sun will be hot, and the buds burst open, and inevitably we'll forget—we always forget what it was like when everything was white. Pretty soon our memories fade; the leaves come out; the birds start to sing; the flowers, especially the crocuses, begin to bloom. I have crocuses next to the brick wall. They're in such a hurry to display their flowers. I hope they don't get frostbitten. I know spring's coming, but it can never make up its mind to get here soon enough for me. Winter hangs on forever, like it's got claws in the earth and won't let go."

"No sense being impatient. Before we know it, we'll be complaining it's too hot."

As they drove down the hill, the land flattened into black, ploughed fields in the bottom land. Farm houses with long laneways cropped up among the skeletal forests. Blood-red dogwood bushes lined the ditches. Pussy willows polka-dotted the edge of wetlands.

"From the top of Emerald Hill, you can see where you are. The mountains are such a deep purple in the distance, and you can see where the sun is," Emily said. "But when you come down the hill, you're lost in the valley. Up on the hill, we know where we live. Down here, you can't tell what's around the corner. You never know which road leads where."

"It's not so bad if you know where you're going."

Emily was not to be put off, even though she rarely paid attention to directions. She relied on her driver to get wherever she wanted to go. Still, she never missed a good chance to complain about the ways of the country folk when she had an opportunity.

"The names of the roads don't help much because the directions change depending on where you're going. If you're heading to Emerald Hill, you take the Emerald Hill Road; that's easy enough. But then if you're going down the same road toward McAlpine, you take the McAlpine Road; if you're going farther, all the way over to Routhier, the Emerald Hill Road heading east becomes the Routhier Road, heading west. If you happen to be going down to Barton's farm, you're on Barton Road. Heaven forbid if you haven't been here long enough to know who used to live where fifty years ago, because all the houses are named after the people who used to own them, not the people who live in them now. Newcomers get lost if they don't know the names of the old families. You have to know who lived in a house two generations ago in order to know how to get to a place."

Pete began a running commentary on the passing countryside. "That's where the two Warren sisters used to live. One of them was herding turkeys with a whip and it snapped back and took out her eye. Everyone called her Buckeye after that.

"That's the old schoolhouse where 'Old Man' Duval used to live. He'd sit on his porch all day waving to everyone who drove by. Used to say, 'When you do as much waving as I do, you gotta get up early'."

Emily said, "It also helps to know the history of the place. Never mind that sometimes you'll get directions to 'cross the tracks' at the corner, only to find out that the railroad tracks were torn up ten years ago, and now it's a bicycle path. Or someone tells you to go down the dirt road past the yellow house, only to find out the road's been paved and the house has been painted blue."

"It's just the way people are around here. They know where they're going," he said.

"Precisely. They might know who lives where, but I find it very confusing."

"That's because you don't drive."

"I do drive," said Emily. "I just don't."

"That's what I said."

"Pete, you've been in this area for a long time. Have things changed a lot since you first came here?"

"Used to be that when somebody bought a house and moved in, the neighbours would drop in with some jam or cookies to say hello and find out who the new people were. Usually they'd know who bought the place; how much they paid for it; how many kids were in the family; and what the guy did for a living, all before the buyers even signed the offer to purchase."

"The grapevine worked that well?"

"Yep. You could be dead and buried before you even knew you were sick. Sometimes people got it wrong, but not too often. There's usually some truth to the rumours somewhere along the line. These days, though, it's hard to keep up with who's living with whom, and who married somebody else's wife or whose husband is sleeping with whose ex. People don't seem to stay together so much anymore the way they used to. It's hard to keep up with the bed swapping."

"So what about Daisy?"

"What about Daisy?"

"How would you describe how to get to Daisy's place?"

"Let's see. That'd be something like this: Come down off the Hill, past where the moose almost hit Diane's car when she was pregnant with Jordan, past the Bartlett farm, which used to be Seguin Road—now it's Alton's Road—turn in the middle of the curve, where you used to go straight ahead but now it's a turn off the main highway onto a side road, which used to be a concession road. Turn to the right over what used to be the railroad tracks and is now a skidoo trail; continue to the corner where there's a stop sign, which used to be just a bend in the road, with a steep hill, where the Parson boys used to jump their trucks off the crest of the hill to see how far they could fly before hitting the gravel. Daisy lives in the old McDonald house, which was originally owned by the Stevenses, and after that by the Newmans, before Newman's wife took up with the next door neighbour's son, left her husband and moved in with the younger lady."

As they approached Blossoms' Corners, Emily began to wiggle. She could hardly contain her excitement. *Detective Emily Blossom, about to arrive at the scene where gruesome evidence was discovered by . . .* She paused to consider the sound of her own narrative . . . *by a dog*

She frowned. *The dramatic denouement lacks a certain* je ne sais quoi.

"Well, I appreciate your taking me down here, Pete. I know you're not—"

"Not a taxi service."

"That's not what I was about to say, but I do appreciate this very much. Daisy will be so glad to see you."

"I'll believe that when I see her."

"Once in a while she'll sell one of her antiques." Emily chose to believe she was prone to exaggerating the truth rather than blatantly lying outright. "Of course you remember all the furniture that's been in her family for years. She's sitting on a fortune."

"I doubt whether Daisy sees things in those terms."

As they approached Daisy's farm, the hay fields along the road were small, undulating and impractical. In contrast to the rich farmland of the Ottawa River Valley, where crop land stretched in tidy rows for miles upon flat miles, this homestead was divided into pieces by wayward ditches, straggling forests and swamps. The farmhouse snuggled close to the road, with sheds and the barn clustered around the corner. Nineteenth-century settlements of Eastern Ontario had been established before the original carriage roads provided a network of transportation between dwellings. Buggy tracks, which once led to each farm, eventually became worn and well-travelled when cars replaced horses, and paved highways superseded gravel lanes.

The Blossom house had been constructed with stones from the surrounding fields. An attached brick addition was built fifty years later, intended as a summer kitchen. A shed, built on angle from the original house, was once a carriage shed and granary. The old barn dominated the farmyard. Every structure looked slightly out of place, not quite square or planned. The settlement just squatted on Blossoms' Corners as if huddled there, in the crook of the road, for warmth and comfort.

When they turned Blossoms' Corners and approached Daisy's farm, Emily felt a little twist of conscience. She had never approved of Daisy's lifestyle, even when she was first married to Daisy's brother, Don. She preferred not to visit too often. Whenever she did, she was overwhelmed by the contradictions between Daisy's rustic ways and her own comfortable standard of living. Nothing was orderly, according to Emily. Even the vines, which grew up the side of the house, annoyed her.

"Those vines are not good for a house. They're supposed to look like an old English cottage, but they're just messy. I don't know why she can't clean up this place and make it neat and tidy. It always looks so . . . so uncombed."

"Kempt . . . unkempt."

"Yes, yes, that's the word . . . not quite straight. There's no trees in a row; nothing's straight. Plants just grow up where they want to, Manitoba maples all over the laneway. You can't even see into the yard from the road. And there's no pretty flowers, no gardens . . . Well, she has gardens, but they're full of weeds. I don't understand why she lives on this farm all by herself. It's such a struggle to keep things going. I don't know how she manages to make ends meet."

"Does she?" Pete asked.

"Well, she's lived here for years and years, so she must have some sort of income."

"Takes a lot of work to be a farmer."

"Oh I know, but Daisy's quite versatile. She can do all sorts of things. But I never know exactly what she does or how she spends her time. I really don't know how she copes. Everything is so helter-shelter around here."

"Skelter," Pete said. "Helter-skelter."

"Yes, yes, that's what I mean . . . helter-shelter . . . helter-skelter . . . helter . . . helter, whatever . . . you know what I mean. Up on the hill, where we live, everything seems much clearer. You can see around you, and you know what's going on. You can see farther. You have a view. Down here, you get down off that hill and nothing is obvious. You can't see where you're going; you can't see who your neighbours are. You can't even see past the trees. It's all hidden. There are secrets."

"Are you telling me Daisy has secrets?"

"No, no, not Daisy . . . Daisy, Daisy! She's the salt and the pepper."

"You mean the salt of the earth?"

"That's what I said. She's straightforward. You know who she is and where you stand. She doesn't slice her words."

"Mince . . . she doesn't mince her words."

"That's what I said. She tells you what she thinks. Usually I disagree." Emily paused, as if to reevaluate what she was saying, but then she continued, convinced of the truth of her assertion. "Of course usually I'm right, and she's wrong, if you ask me."

"Does she ask you?"

"Well, no, no. I'm just her sister-in-law, you know. We rarely actually agree on anything. She's always got that bit of sadness about her that . . . it bothers me . . . well, frankly, she bothers me. That's all there is to it. I believe you should live your life and be happy . . . not always dwell in the past. Daisy likes her memories and wishes and regrets. She's always sorry with the way things turn out."

"Is she really?"

"There's something about Daisy that makes me uncomfortable. The minute you're near her, you kind of sense there's a lot more there than what you see."

"I thought you said she was straightforward."

"She is, but all the ends are loose. Nothing is ever finished. She begins things, and then she never finishes them. She never lets go."

"That so?"

"Yes, yes, now, I'm not going to say any more. Here we are, and well, Pete, ah . . . oh, you'll see . . . you'll see . . . you'll know . . ."

"Know? Know what?"

\*

Pete had his own ways of finding out the truth about other people's business. Emily's methods of inquiry tended to be devious but focused; Pete considered himself more circumspect. Actually, he was quite familiar with Blossoms' Corners; however, he preferred to keep his social life private.

He didn't like the way Emily was fidgeting in her seat. Her eyes were darting around the farmyard. He wondered what she was looking for. He knew Emily well enough to know that she was hiding something, and he also knew he probably wouldn't like what that "something" might be. He didn't know what it was, but he already suspected he didn't like it.

The minute he saw Daisy rush out of the house, he realized this was not a place he wanted to be. So he said, "Well, um, I . . . I . . . I just remembered . . . I'm supposed to be somewhere. I have an appointment with someone. I'm going to drop you off. When do you want me to pick you up?"

"No, no, no," Emily said, "I need your help. You can't leave me here all by myself. I mean . . . I mean . . . you know Daisy."

"Ah, yes. I do know Daisy . . . well enough to know that . . . you know what? I have a meeting with a man about a horse."

"You do not. You don't even buy horses," Emily said. "I can see through you, Pete Picken, and you're not going anywhere."

At this point, Pete and Emily were sitting in the driveway. Pete had the truck running. He had his hand on the gear shift, and he was ready to put it into reverse as soon as she left his truck. He leaned over in front of her—a very uncharacteristic movement, since it brought him into close physical contact with her.

While exaggerating a smile, he opened the door. "Goodbye, Emily. I'll pick you up in an hour."

Emily smiled back at Pete with a disarming grin. Then, quick as a wink, she reached over, turned the truck off, and pulled the keys out. "Pete," she said, holding the keys up where he could see them clearly, "you're staying with me."

Pete's face turned purple. He was not accustomed to being told what to do, and he didn't appreciate it. Emily immediately realized her mistake, and, hardly taking a breath, she dropped the keys into her bodice. Then she jumped out of the truck as if she was a teenager.

Pete glowered from under his hat. He sat with both hands on the steering wheel, his fingers thumping. When he looked up, he was dismayed to see Daisy Blossom's face close to his on the other side of the window. She was beaming; her soft blue eyes were misty. That familiar look he had once known so well had never left her face. He gulped and blushed. Then he quietly put his hand on the handle and opened the door.

"Hi, Pete," she said, "I'm so glad you came down. Thanks for bringing Emily. I really need her advice."

"You do?" he said, beginning to realize he had walked smack dab into the middle of a trap. "Emily said you had antiques to sell."

Daisy tut-tutted, glanced at Emily and shook her head, indicating she knew Emily's ways.

"Well, I am so happy to see the two of you, you can't imagine. I have a problem that's much bigger than anything I can solve by myself, and I'm glad to have the two of you to help us—me and Friday, that is."

Pete stared at Emily, and Emily threw a self-satisfied grin back at him: here was *the* Emily Blossom of detective fame come to the rescue. Pete recognized the look and felt immediately ill. He had been taken in by Emily's tricks before. He knew he was in for big trouble.

At this point, Daisy began to chatter. "You must come in. You must come in. Emily, I did what you told me. I did what you told me. I took away Friday's present. He wasn't too upset. He thought he had found a most wonderful treasure, and he wanted to share it with me. I hope he doesn't jump on your nice clean clothes . . . I have what he found . . . I put it in a bag . . . it's in the kitchen. I put the tea on. I knew you'd want a cup of tea. We have to discuss. We have to figure out what to do."

"Who's 'we'? White Man?" Pete asked.

"Don't make racist remarks," Emily whispered at him as if he were a naughty child.

Pete rolled his eyes and raised his voice just to annoy her.

"It's a figure of speech, Em. Get over it. Don't you remember the Lone Ranger and Tonto?"

"Still, you shouldn't say things like that."

The two of them carried on their quibbling, while Daisy continued to chatter.

"We, you know. We . . . we're all in this together. You'll see, Pete, and you'll see why I need your help. I know you'll never say no to a woman in distress. As much as you'd like people to believe that you're . . . that you're . . . well . . ."

"I'm what?" he asked.

"Well, you know . . . you know . . ."

"No, I don't know."

Emily finished Daisy's sentence. "She's telling you that people think you're a grouch."

"I'm not a grouch. I don't want people to think I'm a grouch, and being a grouch has nothing to do with it," he said. "Don't call me names."

At that, Daisy stepped in and diffused the situation by saying, "Come in. Come in. You'll see. You'll see what it is, Pete, and you'll see why we needed your help."

**Daisy's House at Blossoms' Corners**

# Chapter Four

Just as they were about to enter the house, a jangle of dog tags announced the arrival of a very large dog from behind the shed. The hound looked like a mix between a bull mastiff, a golden Labrador retriever, and maybe a St. Bernard somewhere in his distant lineage. He appeared to grin from ear to ear, although he could just as well be showing his fangs to warn off strangers. His golden eyes shined brightly.

Pete stood stock still and let the dog sniff his pants.

"He can't decide if he's glad to greet visitors or if he recognizes hot human dinner being delivered to his door. I hope the wagging tail is a good indication that he remembers his old friends."

Emily, walking quickly toward the house, dodged behind Pete to keep him between her and the dog.

"Friday, these are the people I told you about." Daisy spoke to the dog as if he was fluent in English. "They came to see your treasure. You'll be so pleased to show it off, even though I know you'd be quite happy to keep it all to yourself. Be a good dog now. Don't soil Emily's clothes. I told her you wouldn't bother her.

"Pete, Friday recognizes you," Daisy continued. "He doesn't often grin with such enthusiasm."

At this point Pete couldn't resist reaching down and scratching the dog behind his ears. The dog continued to wiggle from side to side as hard as he could, with his tail whipping back and forth.

True to her word, Daisy had the tea kettle on, and it was whistling loudly as they entered the kitchen.

"Oh my, oh my. I keep telling myself I shouldn't put the kettle on when I'm not in the house. But I'm so discombobulated today. I just can't possibly think straight, and I did want you to have a nice cup of tea when you came in. I know, Emily, how much you like tea. Pete? Coffee, I think, double, double."

"You remembered?" Pete asked, forgetting to disguise the surprise in his voice.

"Of course," Daisy said, bustling about the preparations for her visitors. "I'll get everything ready. But, here, come here, you must see what we're talking about."

As soon as Pete laid his eyes on the table, he felt an immediate urge to throw up.

In a plastic bag in the middle of the kitchen table was a human hand: pale, olive-coloured, fingers flexed as if it were holding the air, yet frozen, immovable, in a gesture of despair.

Emily rushed to the table and picked up the package.

"Oh my goodness, my goodness, my goodness, my goodness!"

She repeated her exclamations, at a loss for more words to describe her excitement.

*Detective Emily Blossom arrives on the scene and immediately recognizes evidence of a brutal crime. Her intuition is impeccable.*

"This is surely a sign of a murder." She practically sang with delight. "You're right, Daisy, Friday didn't eat the evidence."

She poked at the fingers through the plastic wrap, examined the tips in the light of the window.

"There are almost perfect fingerprints on this hand. Oh my, oh my! And look! There's a tattoo . . . and . . . and . . . oh, I'm sure we're going to find out lots just by having this complete specimen. Imagine! Imagine! Someone must have cut the hand off the body. It's quite . . . it's quite . . . the root of it, at the wrist, is quite smoothly sawn, except where Friday was chewing on it. They must have cut it off after the body was already dead."

"And frozen," Pete added.

"Yes, yes, of course," Emily said as if it had been her own observation. "There's no evidence of blood. The hand was already frozen when it was decapitated."

"Don't you mean amputated?" Pete asked.

"Yes, yes, that's what I said. Who could possibly have done this? And where did it come from?" Emily was so excited, she couldn't contain herself. She clutched the packaged hand to her bosom and wandered around the room, gazing at the ceiling as if trying to pick up clues by conjuring an image of some gruesome reality.

Pete rolled his eyes, trying to look anywhere else to not encourage her enthusiasm.

"Have you called the police?" asked Pete, afraid of the answer. "Emily, get a hold of yourself. This isn't a game. Daisy, you did phone the cops, didn't you?"

Daisy busied herself with making tea and avoided looking at him.

"Well, I was waiting for you to arrive before I did anything rash," she said. "I don't want them to blame it on Friday. Emily said to wait until she got here before I called. You wouldn't want anything to happen to Friday, would you, Pete? You know he didn't do anything wrong."

While she was speaking, Daisy laid out the cups, retrieved milk from the fridge and produced a bowl of sugar from a potted plant in the centre of the table.

"Did you find anything else, Daisy?" Emily asked, interrupting Pete's questioning and ignoring his nervousness as if he were being picky.

"Oh no! Friday wouldn't tell me where he got it. He usually goes out first thing in the morning to do his business. He wasn't there when I came out this morning. Normally he greets me at the door when we go to the barn to do the chores. The next thing I knew, he brought me his treasure. He'll always bring me things that he finds, just to ask if he can have it or not. The garbage man is always bringing him things to distract him while he picks up the trash cans. I don't know, maybe the garbage man brought him this. But it's Sunday morning, and they don't pick up the garbage until Thursday.

"Friday is very polite. He brought me the hand to ask me if he could eat it. He'd already tasted just a little bit. He couldn't resist, you know. But he's a very good dog, and when I asked him to give it to me, he let me have it right away. He was quite disappointed, but then, he thought I'd make a stew of it. I do that when the garbage man brings him a hunk of meat. I'll cut it up and I'll make him a stew. He thought he might have a feast for a few days. He didn't know that there was anything wrong with his surprise. He thought it was a perfectly fine treat."

"Oh my goodness, look at this tattoo," Emily said breathlessly, barely listening to Daisy's explanation. "Why would anyone want a ring tattooed on his or her finger? Left hand . . . ring finger . . . I wonder if that's significant. It's a small hand; it's a gentle hand; it's not a working hand; it must belong to a young woman. There are no calluses, and the nails are so short, she must have been a nervous type. Funny she didn't wear any nail polish.

"Oh dear, oh dear, oh dear, what are we going to do?"

Pete had managed to extricate himself from the conversation by disappearing into the other room. Although he could hear their discussion clearly from the other room, he did not feel obliged to participate. He was intently scrutinizing a magazine from the comforts of a plush wing chair in a dark corner of the living room.

"Pete, Pete, come and get your coffee," Daisy cried. "You'll feel better. I know you're feeling a bit out of your element, but it's okay; we won't hold it against you. I admit, this is a very difficult problem."

The kitchen was large but filled to capacity. The kitchen table was piled high with papers and dirty dishes. All the walls were hidden behind old cupboards that held dishes and food. Daisy cooked on a cast iron stove, decorated with pink and green tiles and a chrome towel rack. In the middle of the room, the stove chucked out heat with the smell of wood smoke, sweet and acrid at the same time, comforting yet choking. The room was cozy and almost too warm. Savoury soup boiled on the stove, while the tea kettle whistled and the coffee pot percolated. A white cat was curled up asleep under the oven.

In the corner on a chair was a box heated by an old brass desk lamp with a hooded bulb. A little chick in the box peeped, busily scratching and gathering food, discussing with itself how warm and toasty it was in this lovely kitchen. A ring-necked turtledove perched on top of the refrigerator. There was no bird cage in sight, and apparently the dove was free to fly wherever it pleased. The bird punctuated Emily's "oh my goodness" with a sound resembling cheerful laughter, as if whatever she said was quite funny.

Daisy filled a cup with steaming coffee for Pete. She added cream and sugar without asking.

"Emily, I've got some lovely English Breakfast, or Heather tea from Scotland, or maybe you'd prefer Lapsang Souchong, although I guess that's a little too strong for this morning."

"Anything would be fine, anything . . . just a good hot cup of tea. I'm definitely in need of a good hot cup of tea right about now. Give me my favourite cup, please—you know, the one with the blue flowers on it, the one that I love so much. That would be just lovely."

"I have to think. We have to think. We have to come up with a plan."

"A plan?" Pete asked. "The best plan is to get on that phone and call the police. In the meantime, I'll be on my way, like I said. Emily, if you would please give me my keys back? When Inspector Allard gets here, he won't find me or my truck here.

"Allard will no doubt be the one heading up the investigation, and I'd sooner not meet him under these circumstances. We met before when Emily was playing detective, solving the first murder in town. He wasn't fond of me then, and I don't think his opinion would have changed much since. We wouldn't want to distract him from solving the crime he's investigating. You can tell him you took a taxi down or that your ride left. Give him some plausible explanation that does not include me."

"Oh, Pete, you don't have to leave quite so soon. It's all right. We'll come up with a plan. All of us together will come up with a better plan than any one of us separately."

"Oh yes, oh yes," Daisy said, "I would just love suggestions. I don't want them to take Friday away. He just found the evidence, but he didn't do anything wrong. I just don't want them to do anything awful. I'm afraid they'll put him away in a kennel. He'd hate to be penned up. It wasn't his fault."

"We have to find the rest of the body," Emily said. "That's the clue. It must be somewhere around here."

"I did ask Friday to show me where he found the hand, but he just ran around in circles. He didn't go in any one direction. Pete, maybe you could convince him to show us where he found it?"

"Me?"

"Well, he does like you quite a lot," Daisy said.

"Emily, just give me my keys."

Emily feigned a look of innocence, as if she'd forgotten what she had done with them.

Daisy piped in. "Emily, give him the keys. He was nice enough to drive you down here, wasn't he? Don't torture the man."

"I have a spare set in the truck anyway," Pete said as he stood by the door with his hand on the knob. His voice had an edge to it, making his meaning quite clear. "I've had enough of your games."

"Oh, all right," Emily said, turning her back as she retrieved the keys from her bra. She plopped them into his outstretched hand as if somehow she was the slighted party because her little joke had been misunderstood.

Then she turned back to her tea, which Daisy was in the process of pouring, piping hot, from a huge, well-used pot.

"I'll wait for the police with Daisy. We'll phone 911 right away." Her voice was sticky sweet, her tone subdued, planning her next manoeuvre, but Pete was in too much of a hurry to be suspicious. He couldn't get into his truck fast enough.

*

As his truck disappeared down the driveway, Emily turned to Daisy and said, "He doesn't fool anyone with his tough-guy attitude. Deep down he's just a softie."

"There are worse traits in a man. He means well. You don't have to embarrass him though, by treating him badly."

"Bad? Bad? Look who's talking. I never strung him along the garden path, only to show him the door."

"Let's not discuss that now, shall we? We have other things to attend to." She picked up the phone and handed it to Emily. "You call. I don't know what to say."

# Chapter Five

Pete always felt better in his truck. The cab was his cozy living room, office and den all in one. Here he could be himself. He sighed with relief as soon as he pulled out of Daisy's driveway. His half-smoked pipe beckoned from the ashtray. Once smoke filled the air he immediately felt safer, out of the danger of Emily's finagling and Daisy's complications.

He was trying to figure a way out of his own problems. He was surely into something deep. As an antiques dealer, he tried to avoid suspicion as to the origins of his merchandise. He was quite wary of any sign of police or crime. He also had a particular aversion to anything dead, and this, surely, was something dead. He loved to quote from the old western movies about cowboys and Indians that he had watched when he was a kid.

"Best to get out of Dodge while the gettin's good."

His destination was Sauvé's Gas Bar. In addition to cheap gas, he could catch up on all the upcoming auctions posted on the bulletin board at the gas station. Plus, Nick Sauvé had good cigars. Catching up with Nick's news of the community would be a pleasant way of taking Pete's mind off the events unfolding at Blossoms' Corners.

When he turned his truck onto the side road leading back to the Hill, the gas gauge showed empty. With the price of gas rising daily, filling the tank was an increasingly painful experience. So he had avoided spending the money and let the tank run dangerously low. Now he was in a bit of a predicament. He could drive the long way back to town and hope he arrived before it completely ran out, or he could take a chance on a shortcut that would save on mileage but would add wear and tear on his truck.

He decided to take the shorter lane cross country, where a sign warned "Road Closed. Proceed at Your Own Risk." This section of road was not travelled this time of year. The snowploughs did not keep it open during winter, and the surface was barely firm enough for traffic. Nevertheless,

Pete noticed that at least one other vehicle had already passed ahead of him. He followed its lead. The deserted boundary road would get him to town quicker and, with any luck, without running out of gas.

Trees lined the narrow lane as the road led through a swamp in the valley. The wetland willows were the first shrubs to show signs of spring bursting. The poplars along the edge of the hay fields would leaf out in a couple of weeks, depending on the weather.

Pete scanned the bush for pussy willows, white polka dots against the shadows of red dogwood twigs, his favourite harbinger of warm sunshine and lengthening days. He heard the songs of red-winged blackbirds above the motor of his truck as he passed through low-lying swamp. The calling Canada geese overhead heralded the break-up of ice on the Ottawa River. Soon the countryside would burst into brilliant, vibrant greenery, and all thoughts of winter's desolation would fade into distant memories.

Pete noticed that someone had dumped two garbage bags by the side of the road. With annoyance at some people's careless disregard for the beauty of nature, Pete pulled his truck to a stop. He threw the bags into the back of his truck box and continued on his way to town. He would put them at the end of his neighbour's driveway for pick up on garbage day.

He proceeded into town and easily manoeuvred his truck up to the gas tanks at Sauvé's One-Stop Shop Depanneur and Gas Bar. He waited at the self-serve station until the attendant spotted his vehicle and turned on the pump. The price was now well more than a dollar per litre, and a fill-up didn't take long to reach one hundred. Pete wondered how long he would be able to afford to drive around town, much less continue trucking to the big city to sell antiques. However, he could not imagine life without a truck, and he quickly put the thought out of his mind.

As he entered the store, a bell rang announcing customers. The smell of over-brewed coffee and stale cookies wafted on the warm, musty air of a crowded store. Shelves were lined with convenience items: greeting cards opposite common spices; cat food next to breakfast cereal; thumbtacks and scotch tape in the section with white flour and sugar. Ten different kinds of potato chips and pretzels crowded the counter next to Lotto tickets and lighters. Several rows of candy bars next to the cash register encouraged impulse buying.

Nick Sauvé leaned on the counter as if part of the merchandise displayed on the shelves around him. The shopkeeper had abundant white hair, neatly parted on the side. His grey eyes were punctuated with smile wrinkles, and his forehead expressed surprise as a matter of course. A neat set of white, even teeth clicked prematurely whenever he opened his mouth to speak. He wore a red-checked shirt and blue suspenders.

"Got a good cigar for me?" Pete asked.

Nick reached under the counter and produced a Cuban special. Pete nodded from under his hat and gingerly peeled the cellophane wrapper off the hand-rolled stogie. With careful attention to a ritual known only to himself, Pete went about preparing for a good and proper smoke. He extracted a knife from his pocket, nipped off the butt and placed the cut end neatly underneath his moustache in a gap between his teeth, testing its weight and balance. He licked the cigar with a moist, pink tongue, rolled it several times between his lips, spat out a leaf tip onto the floor and replaced the moistened end in his mouth. Striking a match, he tipped his head sideways just enough so as not to burn the brim of his hat as he lit the tip. His large hands practiced the art of cupping the flame just enough to light the cigar without setting his moustache on fire. The tobacco flared with each puff as he sucked the flame with hollow cheeks through the sparking leaves, sending clouds of smoke into the air around his head. The acrid smell of strong, unfiltered cigar smoke filled the room.

Nick never objected to the smoking ritual Pete indulged in with obvious relish.

"Got any interesting listings on the board?" Pete asked, producing a garble of words winding their way around the cigar. "Auctions should soon be starting up again."

"I put up your poster," Nick said, indicating with a nod the parade announcement.

**Come to the St. Patrick's Day Parade and**
**Celebrate the Luck o' the Irish!**
**Green Beer and Poutine.**
**All Floats Welcome.**
**Emerald Hill, Ontario**
**Parade starts at 1:00 p.m.**
**The Parade Route will be published in The Hill *News***

"Thanks," Pete said. "I hope we get a good turnout."

"These days it all depends on the weather. This time of year you could get anything from sunshine and twenty degrees to a snowstorm with six inches of snow."

"Don't remind me," Pete said, puffing on his cigar.

"You announcing the parade again this year?"

"Yep. Got any good Irish jokes I can use?"

"None you could repeat in public."

Pete slouched against the counter, contemplating the smoke patterns rising from his cigar.

Nick sat on a stool leaning on his elbows, as he had been doing for years while serving customers, passing the time of day, catching up and spreading the news of the neighbourhood. "How is the antiques business these days? Do you still get pretty good prices for stuff?"

"Sales aren't the same as they used to be," he said between puffs. "Nobody wants junk anymore. Middle of the road doesn't sell. Only high-end pieces, and those are harder and harder to come by."

"Where do you find the right stuff? How do you know what's going to sell?"

"You never know for sure what people will pay for. Most of the time I've learned to listen to my gut feelings. It's always a gamble."

Pete was usually quite careful not to reveal too many details about his business, but he couldn't resist a bit of bragging now and again. "Last month a guy offered me a cupboard, two doors, four panels, original paint, pretty good condition, but the price was high. I told him I'd get back to him. So I phoned one of my customers and sold the piece before I bought it. That's the best way to do business, but you can't always pull off a deal, sight unseen. Sometimes you just have to take a chance."

"Who do you sell to mostly? People around here?"

"Oh, no. A person can't do business where he lives. Everybody thinks you're out to screw them. I put together a load of antiques and then drive to Toronto every couple of weeks and sell to a few dealers down there. They know me pretty well. I've been picking for years, and they know they get what they pay for. I don't try to fix stuff up and hide the defects. I sell it all in the rough. That way they know what they're getting."

"How do you know what you're buying is legit?" Nick asked in a tone of voice that finally made Pete suspicious.

"Legit or hot?" Nick leaned a little too heavily on his arms on the counter for Pete's comfort; he seemed to study Pete's reaction a little too closely. "Ever happen that somebody wanted to sell you something you knew was stolen?"

"Why do you ask?" Pete asked, finally understanding that Nick had something specific in mind.

"There was a guy in here looking to sell some furniture," Nick said. "He said it belonged to his grandmother, but I had my doubts."

"A guy in a motorcycle jacket, long hair and tattoos?"

"Yeah, that's him. Do you know the guy?"

"Not that I know of, but Ilsa at the Country Kitchen told me somebody was trying to get in touch with me."

"He looked more likely to be selling drugs than antiques," Nick said.

"Lots of people figure they've got valuable antiques when they're short of cash. Usually turns out, guys like him have some piece of junk they want to get rid of in a hurry."

"I told him about you," Nick said. "I thought you might be interested in what he had for sale."

"Thanks, Nick. I appreciate that." Pete tipped his hat. "That explains a lot."

Both men relaxed, having cleared the air of uncertainty between them. In a village like Emerald Hill, rumours were often larger than facts, and innuendo could substantiate suspicions as easily as truth. A stranger asking questions in town would be more than sufficient cause for comment among the locals. Stories could easily get out of hand and were likely to spread faster than wildfire.

"For your information," Pete continued, even though Nick didn't ask, "I never buy anything I'm not sure of. I might be dumb, but I'm not stupid."

Nick's eyebrows flickered, and his grey eyes twinkled with understanding.

"If something turns up missing," Pete said, "I'm the first guy they look for. I don't take those kinds of chances." He stubbed out the cigar on the bottom of his boot, careful to grind the ashes into the mud on his sole. "And contrary to public opinion, I don't deal in drugs either."

He reached into his jeans back pocket for a worn wallet and produced a wad of wrinkled bills. He meticulously peeled off one fifty-dollar bill, two twenties, a ten and a five. Then he emptied his pocket of a few toonies, loonies and loose change.

"That's too much," Nick said. "There's a hundred bucks on the gas."

"Keep the change," Pete said. "Where else am I gonna get another stogie as good as this one? The Indians at Caughnawaga don't even have cigars like that. Thanks again."

Nick nodded, still leaning on one elbow as if attached to the counter as part of the décor.

Pete paused with his hand on the knob before opening the door. "I'll let you know when I find out who the guy is . . . Interesting to see if he's got anything worth buying."

"If I were you, I'd be careful."

"Thanks for the advice," he said as he set off the bell signalling the door opening. "Hope you can make it to the parade."

# Chapter Six

Pete consulted his radio clock. *I've got plenty of time to catch a short snooze before returning to Daisy's to pick up Emily,* he thought. *I want to give the cops plenty of time to complete their initial investigation and then give Emily plenty of time to come down off her high horse before I turn up.*

The high school parking lot was empty on Sunday. He parked so the sun beamed into the cab. Placing his boots on the dash in front of the passenger seat, he stretched out, cradling his head against the door. He pulled the broad brim of his handmade leather hat down over his eyes, crossed his arms over his faded jacket and snuggled down behind the steering wheel. Preparations for a nap were familiar and automatic.

Eventually Pete's stomach felt the first twinges of hunger; snores merged into snuffles and coughs. The soles of his boots disappeared from behind the windshield. His moustache and bushy eyebrows emerged from under the hat when he sat up.

Pete glanced at the clock, which was always set twenty minutes fast: 12:52. Surely the police would have finished at Daisy's. Automatically he turned the key, and the truck roared obediently into action.

"Maybe Emily will buy me lunch, unless Daisy has some soup on the stove. I'll take any excuse for a good homemade meal, especially if I don't have to pay for it."

As he rounded the Blossoms' Corners, he was relieved to see the farmyard clear of vehicles, except for Daisy's 1966 Case tractor and her Chevy truck.

*Couldn't have timed it better,* Pete thought, feeling quite smug. *Averting potential disaster is always a good plan.*

Friday greeted him as soon as he pulled into the driveway. The dog's huge jowls folded into a wrinkle, revealing white fangs and pink gums. One could interpret his greeting as an exuberant grin of happiness or a life-threatening sneer.

"If you're snarling at me," Pete said to the dog, "I could be in big trouble."

However, the white tip of the mastiff's tail waved like a flag of truce, and his golden eyes sparkled in canine pleasure. When Pete offered to pat his broad forehead, the dog leaned against him as if offering a hug.

"Yes, I see you're a nice dog," Pete said. "Now let me pass. I'm on a mission."

However when he tried to move past the beast, Friday gently took Pete's hand in his mouth like a host leading his new guest through a maze of strange surroundings. He escorted him to the house in no uncertain terms: this was his prize, the offer of a gift to his owner.

Pete was relieved to see Daisy at the door.

"There you are, Pete. See how much Friday appreciates you! Now, now, Friday, be a good dog. Leave him go. I'll look after him from here."

Reluctantly Friday opened his mouth and released Pete's hand from the grip of his teeth. Pete scooted through the opening past Daisy, attempting to avoid any physical contact with the large woman who held the door only wide enough for two to pass through. The dog's head remained in the doorway, tail waving cheerfully, as he surveyed the kitchen in the hopes that he would be invited in.

"Friday, you can stay by the door if you're good," Daisy said. "If you lie down and be quiet, you can stay in for a visit."

Walking into Daisy's kitchen was like settling into a nest. One immediately felt comfortable and safe. As Pete entered, he was greeted by the sounds of cheerful chattering and animal noises: peeping, cooing and purring. A mélange of wood smoke, fresh bread and the vague odour of barn filled his nostrils when he inhaled.

"Emily, if you want a ride back to town—"

"Don't go back to town for lunch," Daisy said. "Have lunch here with me. I've got a lovely soup. I have homemade soup with lots of vegetables."

"Vegetable soup?" Pete said.

"I didn't mean that. I know what you eat. This is a delicious soup you'll like."

"I don't eat vegetables."

"I know, I know, I know. I've got some lovely chicken soup. Chicken soup it is. I've got some fresh bread hot out of the oven, and . . . and I've got lemon pie."

Emily contributed her version of persuasion. "Besides, this is a lovely cup of tea. While Daisy puts the soup on, we'll tell you about the police visit. We were just talking about Inspector Allard. He seems so down to earth. Pete, you would have been impressed to see him in action."

"I doubt that," said Pete.

"They're very good at what they do," Daisy said. "And they were very thorough. Unfortunately, we couldn't provide them with a great deal of information, since Friday is the only witness, and he's not talking."

"So what did they say? What happened?"

"Well, Allard was so glad to see me here," Emily said.

"Yeah, right," said Pete, without trying to hide his sarcasm.

"He said he was."

"Yeah, I'm sure he did," Pete said, raising his eyebrows and nodding vehemently, mocking her naiveté. "What did he say? Something like, 'Oh, Mrs. Blossom, how were you so very clever as to wheedle your way into this incident'?"

"Well, he didn't say it right off the bat, but he did want to know what brought me down to the farm on just such an important morning, especially when Daisy was involved in rescuing the evidence from Friday."

"I hope you didn't mention my name," Pete said.

"That was when you reminded him of it," Daisy pointed out.

"Of what, exactly?"

"Well, I just had to tweak his memory a little bit," Emily said. "I told him about how helpful I had been in solving Emerald Hill's only murder on record, the only murder that has occurred in the village—ever—in people's memory."

"Did you mention my name?" Pete repeated his question.

"Well no, not really. It wasn't really relevant."

"I'm glad of that," said Pete, feeling quite relieved, but not convinced that he was actually off the hook so easily.

"Emily, you always make it all sound out to be such a game," said Daisy, who was prone to taking life very seriously.

"Well, life is a game. If you don't make it into a game, what's it going to be like? Life would be rather dull, wouldn't it?"

"Well, my life isn't dull," said Daisy.

"Yes it is."

"Now don't you two go getting into that," Pete said, interrupting. "I'm hungry. Daisy, if you're going to put the soup on, put the soup on. I'm famished."

Emily continued the conversation about the police, while Daisy set the table.

"They definitely suspect murder, by the way. Allard said he couldn't say for sure, but the evidence is very suspicious."

"Tell me that you didn't jump right in and tell him you were investigating a murder."

Pete's sarcasm fell on uncooperative ears. She changed the subject.

"Did you go to town, Pete? Has the word gotten around yet?"

"I'm sure if you go to the Country Kitchen, everybody will be talking about Daisy and Blossoms' Corners and Daisy's dog."

Daisy said, "I was so worried they were going to do something about Friday, but he was very well behaved. I told him he had to be a good dog when the police were here because otherwise they might take him away. But they were very understanding and there was nothing really they could do anyway, because there's no proof . . . there was no indication that Friday did anything other than find a treasure."

"So where are they now?" Pete asked, suspiciously looking out the window and down the driveway.

"They've all gone off, doing whatever it is they have to do. They took a report, and they wrote everything down, and they put us down as witnesses. Well, they put Daisy down as a witness. I'm not a witness. I just happened to be here . . . totally coincidental, you understand," Emily added with a wink.

"Yeah, right," he said. "And Allard believed every word you said."

"Soup's on," Daisy piped in, cheerfully changing the subject. "Pete, go wash your hands. You can sit at the head of the table."

A red-checked tablecloth covered the length of the kitchen table. Daisy had removed a pile of papers from one end and set three places. A loaf of fresh bread still warm from the oven begged to be cut in thick slices and slathered with butter. Steam wafted from broth the colour of daffodils in blue-glazed soup bowls.

Daisy's soup was more like hearty stew. Chicken legs swam in thick gravy full of carrots and onions and dried garden herbs. Meat fell off the bones in chunks. Knives were superfluous. A bowl in the middle of the table was intended for the skeletal remains of the chicken. Soon the room dissolved into sounds of slurping and lip smacking as they concentrated on the task of devouring every last drop. Even Emily forgot her manners when it came to swabbing her plate clean with chunks of bread.

"I'm sure Johnny Aimer, the gun dealer, had something to do with this," Emily said, dabbing the corners of her mouth daintily. "I'm just sure."

"Don't go jumping to any conclusions," said Pete. "You could get into a lot of trouble. You should stay out of it."

"Inspector Allard told you to stay out of it," said Daisy.

"Well, how can a person stay out of something when a person has been murdered? I can't bear . . . I just can't bear not to try to get involved in . . . in changing the world. This is my chance. This is where I shine."

"I'm not sure you're shining all that much," said Pete.

"I think you're rather taken up with yourself," said Daisy.

"Now, Daisy, don't you say that. You're always too conservative. You never get involved. You always stay in the background. You're comfortable here, and you go about your chores, and you don't even know what goes on in the world."

"Stop talking about me. I know perfectly well what I need to know in my life, and I don't need to go beyond my farm. I'm living a life of good principals. I respect the environment. I respect nature—"

"Oh, I know all that. I don't mean anything by it," Emily said. "Everyone has to justify their way of thinking. You know what I mean, don't you, Pete?"

Pete cleared his throat. "How does a person who sells antiques justify his existence?"

"Oh, that's recycling," Daisy said.

Emily said, "That's an appreciation of great art. As an art collector, I know all about the importance of collecting antiques."

"Back to the subject of this murder investigation, how about if we discuss possible suspects? Pete, we need your input. I say we should visit the local gun dealer. That's at least a place to start."

"Oh yeah, right . . . You're just gonna walk up there and knock on the door and say, 'Johnny Aimer, I'm here to talk to you about dealing guns'."

"No, no, of course I wouldn't do that," Emily said. "This is my *modus vivendi.*"

"I believe modus operandi is the proper Latin idiom," Pete said in an unusual display of intellectual prowess. "I was very good in Latin at school."

"That's what I said." Emily refused to be put off track. "Strategic planning. I've always suspected Johnny Aimer of dealing with criminals. Who else would buy all those guns? I've always been curious about a man who gets away with manufacturing and selling guns in public. I've been dying for an excuse to go up there and snoop . . . I mean . . . look around."

"You had it right the first time. You're going to waltz in there and start snooping."

"I corrected myself . . . I meant to say 'investigate'."

Pete refused to let her evade his interpretation of her motives.

"Snooping without an invitation. He's hardly going to give you a guided tour, especially if he suspects you're looking for trouble."

"I know his house is for sale. I'll pretend I'm looking for a place to buy in the country. What if Johnny Aimer has something to do with the murder? Inspector Allard would never pick up on it."

"Why should he? There's no rational connection except your imagination."

"Institution, Pete. I have a detective's institution."

"Intuition? You're trying to tell me you've got intuition, when really you're just nosy and bored."

Suddenly there was a commotion in the corner behind a rocking chair by the stove. Scratching, clawing and scuttling punctuated the crackling of the wood fire and steaming kettle. A second later, a white cat emerged with a mouse firmly clutched in her jaws.

"Sweetie, what a good kitty," Daisy crooned. Her soup-filled tablespoon barely hesitated on its way to her mouth. "I've been trying to catch that mouse for days now."

Pete saw the tiny feet still struggling, even though the rest of the mouse's body was engulfed in Sweetie's mouth. He felt an immediate urge to depart. He watched in morbid fascination as the cat's eyes scanned the room, assuring herself she had no competition threatening to steal her prey.

Emily, however, continued to daintily sip her soup. Her little finger was poised in the air, a token of the ancient ritual she had learned was the unwavering sign of good breeding.

Friday lay by the door, watching the cat with his head on his paws, without interfering. Only his eyes followed the hunt. His tail thumped once on the kitchen floor.

"Poor thing," Daisy said between sips of soup, "She has no teeth . . . finds it hard to convince the mouse to give up its fight."

"I would too, if I had no teeth," Pete said.

The little legs wiggled, and the cat released its grip. The tiny creature sped under the table, across Pete's foot, with the cat in hot pursuit. Pete yelped and pushed his chair over backward as he stood up and jostled the table. Soup splashed on the tablecloth. Emily, Daisy, and Friday didn't react.

Pete glanced around, realizing that neither of the others was going to stop the cat from devouring its prey or desist from enjoying the delicious dinner. He sat down again and tried to resume eating his meal.

The cat retrieved the struggling mouse, which succumbed to its fate with one last weak waver of a paw, as if to say goodbye to the outside world. Sweetie proceeded to mouth the body into a mush and eventually tear it into bite-sized pieces that she could swallow.

"That's one thing I'm not very good at," Daisy said. "I find it so hard to find a good mouse trap. I won't use the ones that snap their heads off, and when I catch them in a live trap, I have to take them outside and release them in just the right spot . . . far enough from the house that they can't find their way home, and I make sure the weather's not too cold so they won't freeze to death. I worry about taking them from their snug, little homes and releasing them into the cold, cruel world. It's such a dilemma for me. I find it much easier if Sweetie looks after the problem. Only trouble is, she's old and can't catch them all. Now that it's spring, I'm afraid they'll all be having babies, and we'll be overrun by cute, little furry tyrants."

"What about poison?" Pete asked, engaging in a conversation he would prefer to avoid.

"That would never do," Daisy said. "Too dangerous for the cat if she catches a dying mouse with poison in its blood."

"It's the chain of command," Emily said.

"Chain of command?" Daisy and Pete said at the same time.

"Yes, you know: who eats whom and all that."

"You mean the food chain," Pete said.

"Yes, yes, that's what I said. The food chain. Mice are at the bottom."

"That girl was at the bottom too," Daisy said sadly.

"What girl?" Pete asked.

"The one who belonged to Friday's hand. The evidence the police took."

"Being murdered is about as low as you can get, I'm afraid," Emily said.

"Stop talking like that," Pete said. "You make me nervous."

Daisy's Recipe For
Chicken Soup
or
a Boiling chicken
onions
carrots
peas
potatos
salt and pepper
green herbs from the garden
dried (or fresh if possible)
Thyme
oregano
chervil
marjoram
bay leaf
maybe a little curry powder

- Put chicken in soup pot
- Cover with water
- Add vegetables
  (dice and fry them in butter
  until edges are crunchy)
  then add to soup pot
- Boil then simmer until
  chicken falls apart
  (5-10 hours depending on
  age of chicken)
- If you don't have a wood stove
  you can use a slow cooker
- Add fresh herbs ½ hour before
  serving

Dumplings
  slice of butter (¼ cup)
  an egg
  cup of flour
  pinch of salt
  enough milk (about 6 tablespoons)
    to form balls
  DROP INTO Simmering soup 10 minutes
    before serving.

Daisy's Recipe for Chicken Soup

# *Chapter Seven*

At that moment, Friday let out a sharp bark of warning. A police car appeared in the driveway outside the window.

"Oh no," Pete said with a groan, which sounded like a long, low moan of pain.

"It's okay," Daisy said. "They've been very nice so far."

"They're probably back to tell us what they've discovered in the course of their investigation," Emily said.

Before they had a chance to leave the table, a loud knock at the door barely preceded an announcement.

"Police! Open up the door. Pete Picken, come out with your hands up! *Ouvrez la porte immediatement!* Open up immediately."

Friday emitted a menacing growl and assumed a spring-loaded crouch. Daisy grasped the dog's collar and called out loudly to the strangers at the door. "Why are you shouting? Come in! Come in!"

"They must think we're in danger," Emily said.

"Do as they say," Pete said. "They're not fooling around."

Slowly, Emily and Pete put down their utensils and stood up from the table just as the door burst open, and an armed officer burst into the room with a pointed gun.

Friday lunged toward the intruders and almost pulled Daisy off her feet. Pete froze.

Emily bravely approached the officer. "Now, now, Constable, there's no need for violence. *Il n'y a pas de problême ici.* There's no problem here."

"Put your hands up!" he shouted, poking the gun in the air, and waving Emily back from his sights. "Pete Picken, you're under arrest!"

Pete felt his head swimming, as if he were standing outside his body watching the blood drain from his cheeks.

He heard Emily's response from a distance. "Don't be ridiculous!"

*

Inspector Alain Allard brushed past the officer with the gun. His hand rested on the barrel pointed at the group of three and then pushed the weapon aside. "Wait for me outside!" he commanded, leaving no room for argument. The officer lowered the gun and disappeared.

Allard was a tall man, more than six feet, and his presence filled the overcrowded kitchen to capacity. He had dark hair and thick eyebrows, but his eyes had a softness that betrayed his gruff demeanour. As the chief officer of the OPP detachment to Emerald Hill and surroundings, the inspector enforced the law but tempered his official role with a sympathetic understanding of the locals.

He sauntered into the room with careful abandon.

"Pete, we investigated the contents of those garbage bags in the back of your truck. What do you have to say in your defence?"

"Garbage bags?" Pete asked. "What garbage bags?"

Emily and Daisy stared at him in amazement. Emily, for once, was speechless.

"The ones in the back of the truck."

He suddenly remembered. He hunched his shoulders and showed empty palms to the air. The cock of his head queried, as if he were trying to decipher the answer to a trick question.

"I picked up some garbage on the way back to town this morning. On the back boundary road, the one they don't plough in the wintertime. It's open now. I took the shortcut because I was low on gas. It's a deserted road, so some jerks dumped their junk where nobody will see it littering up the countryside. I picked the bags up to bring them into town to put out on garbage day. Some people are real pigs."

"What time was this?" Allard asked, slowly wandering the room, surveying the kitchen as if to discover new clues he may have overlooked earlier.

"A couple of hours ago, around ten this morning," he said. "I dropped Emily off here and went back to town for some gas."

"What's this all about, Officer?" Emily piped in, unable to contain her curiosity any longer. "Have you found more evidence concerning the murder victim?"

"The body's in pieces in the back of Picken's truck," said Allard. "Two garbage bags full of frozen body parts. Doesn't get much more obvious than that!"

"Now look, Allard," Pete said.

"Inspector Allard."

"Yes, yes, Inspector Allard—sir," Pete said. "I didn't look at what was in those bags when I picked them up out of the ditch. Take my word for it. I might be dumb, but I'm not stupid. Do you really think I'd be driving around the countryside with frozen body parts in the back of my truck if I'd known what they were?"

Allard's eyes narrowed as he listened, trying to pick up any slight indication of a lie. He looked down from his height onto the top of Pete's head, which was thinning with wild hair growing in all directions.

"I'll have to take you down to the station for questioning just the same," Allard said. "We might have to impound your truck."

"Impound the truck!" Pete cried. "You can't do that. That's my livelihood! I didn't do anything wrong. I was just picking up garbage, doing a good deed, looking after the neighbourhood."

"Officer." Emily stepped up to Allard and faced him down. She was even shorter than Pete, but she drew herself to her full height. Eye level brought her to Allard's chest, so she stood on her tiptoes to get closer. "Pete's done you a favour."

Allard paused just long enough to show signs of wavering.

Emily continued relentlessly. She lowered herself to stand squarely in front of him with one hand cocked on her hip. Then she glanced over her shoulder at Pete, winking as if she was privy to secrets that no one else knew.

"Don't you see?" She turned back to Allard in frank confrontation. "He found the rest of the evidence. Where would you be if he hadn't been alert and conscientious? Body parts would be spread all over the countryside. You owe him a vote of thanks, not a warrant for his arrest."

Her scolding seemed to have an effect. Allard raised his chin and shrugged. He looked past the top of Emily's head. "Take Mrs. Blossom home, Pete, and come down to the station afterward for questioning. Where did you say you found those bags?"

"We'll take you there," Emily said before Pete recovered his composure. "It's on the way back to town anyway. That's what you said, eh, Pete?"

Pete nodded willingly, knowing enough to keep his mouth firmly closed in Allard's presence. He let Emily do the talking.

\*

Emily scuttled after Allard, chattering at his back. "Oh, Inspector, aren't you so very glad that we've found the rest of the body? Now we can really get down to the gritty nitty of our investigation."

"Thanks for the soup," Pete said to Daisy as he retrieved his coat from the chair by the door. "Nitty-gritty," he said to Emily as he escorted her to the passenger side of his truck.

"Yes, yes, that's what I said. The nitty-gritty of our investigation, the real guts, you know!"

Pete nodded his pipe up and down as he opened the truck door for her. She offered her arm to him, and he gently guided her slight figure into the passenger seat.

Emily happily installed herself, neatly folded her hands in her lap and surveyed the landscape from superior heights.

"I'm resisting the urge to dote," she said when Pete took his place behind the steering wheel.

"Gloat, not dote, gloat," he corrected her.

"Yes, of course, that's what I meant."

"You can gloat if you want to."

"No, no. No need for thanks," she said. "I realize you have me to blame for getting you into this whole mess in the first place."

He glanced sideways at her as he lit his pipe before pulling out of the driveway.

"I'll make it up to you," she said. A smile curled around the edges of her trim mouth and wrinkled her cheeks just enough to highlight her eyes sparkling in the sunlight.

As Pete pulled out of the driveway, the constable driving the police car pulled out behind him and turned on the lights and siren for effect. Pete's truck led the convoy down the road through the bush bursting with signs of spring.

# Chapter Eight

At the window, Daisy watched them all pull out of the driveway before she turned to the task of clearing the table.

"It's been quite a morning," she said to the animals, whose eyes followed her every move. "Whoever said living in the country was boring?"

The cat surveyed from underneath the stove, warm and full of hot meat dinner. The ring-necked turtledove sat on a curtain rod above the sink. She scanned the room by nodding her head each time she refocused her carnelian eyes on a new subject. The chick in the box looked at Daisy with one eye and then the other hoping for fresh grain and water. Friday was scratching on the outer door.

"You have to stay out, Friday. You're too big. Every time you come in, your tail manages to sweep something off the table. You've broken too many good dishes lately."

Daisy's kitchen at the best of times looked rather much like a hurricane had passed through. There were papers and boxes strewn on the floor; slippers, long since separated from their partners, cluttered around the furniture feet and several coats were heaped around the base of an overloaded hat rack in the corner. On one side of the counter piles of unwashed dishes waited for washing; on the other side, a wire rack was storage space for clean plates and tea cups. An endless cycle of dishes and cutlery moved from one side of the sink to the other without ever spending time in the dish cupboard. A variety of cast iron pots and pans lived on the stove and received a token swipe from time to time between meals.

Three antique cupboards stood in the shadows like sentinels, one on each wall, lending the room a comfortable air of security. An assortment of paintings hung on the walls. An oil painting of a young man with startling blue eyes and a soft smile commanded a view of the kitchen. An aerial photograph of the farm, taken twenty years ago, held time in place, as if defying any changes in the landscape.

The dark walls had never been painted, and layers of varnish had aged into an alligator patina. Tongue-in-groove boards formed a diagonal pattern bordered by a sturdy chair rail and wainscoting. The ceiling, formerly white, was now the colour of smoke, except for one patch in the corner. In a fit of unusual enthusiasm for housecleaning, Daisy once had attempted to wash the slatted boards. However, an ailing ewe in the barn had distracted her attention, and she never got back to the job.

Small details of the room were like time hesitating: a drawer hung open until Daisy found what she was looking for; a barn jacket hung on a chair waiting for chores; dried flowers from the past summer were faded, standing in an empty vase; chairs stood away from the table, as if someone invited for a meal was yet to sit down. The shelves were cluttered with containers, pitchers, teapots, vases and bowls, all empty and covered with dust. Books, papers and unopened mail overflowed every available surface. The kitchen appeared to be full of life waiting, ready for any occasion still to come.

"I should be washing dishes, cleaning up or going to the barn to do some work, but I think I'll just sit here by the fire for a spell."

Friday's scratching at the door persisted until Daisy let him in. Then she sat down, and the large dog stretched out at her feet. As soon as Daisy settled into her favourite rocking chair by the stove, the white cat jumped into her lap, and the turtledove flew down from its perch and landed on her shoulder.

The stove radiated soothing warmth. Daisy gave up trying to contemplate the events of the morning. Her eyelids drooped. Soon she and the other occupants of the room were all dozing peacefully, as the morning sunlight drifted into noon.

She had no idea how much time had passed when a loud knock interrupted her snooze. Friday's huge bark brought her fully awake with a start. The cat jumped off her lap and disappeared under the stove. The bird flew back to its perch over the window.

As she approached the door, she caught a glimpse of herself reflected in the windowpane. Her grey hair was dishevelled. She winced at the size of the figure she saw in grubby blue jeans and chequered shirt staring back at her. She tucked her hair behind her ears and wiped her hands on her pants, as if to neaten her appearance by smoothing down the wrinkles. Then she shrugged. *What you see is what you get,* she thought.

A middle-aged man with salt-and-pepper hair and smooth skin stood in the entranceway. When she saw his pinstriped suit and shiny shoes, Daisy immediately assumed he was lost or out of gas. He was too polished. None of the locals would dress like this unless they were going to a funeral.

"Mrs. Blossom?" he asked. "Are you the lady of the house?"

"Miss Blossom," she said. "That's me. I don't know about the 'lady' part. Won't you come in?"

"Thank you," he said with a nod of his head and faint click of his heel. He entered the house as if he owned it.

Daisy would never turn away anyone in need of help. She assumed he wanted to use the telephone.

Friday growled a low, guttural greeting, and Daisy felt his head nuzzling her hand for guidance. She took his collar and patted him for reassurance. "It's okay, Friday. The man doesn't mean any harm."

The dog bristled, hair raised along his long back, tail arched, like a white-tipped flag of warning.

"You act as if you don't believe me," Daisy said to the dog. To the man she said, "Friday is wary of strangers. We don't get a lot of visitors here."

"I love dogs," he said. "I know he's just doing his job. Who wouldn't want to protect a lady as beautiful as you?" He smiled, his big teeth capped with gold. Then he winked at her as if he were letting her in on a special secret just between them.

Daisy wondered why, if she was really as attractive as he implied, he would need to pretend otherwise.

Daisy used to rely on her first impressions. She used to think she could peg someone in the first few seconds of knowing him or her. However, over the years, she had learned to mistrust herself. She had a tendency to trust a person first and ask questions later. She used to be susceptible to men with large smiles and big hugs. She thought they offered security and understanding. However, with experience, she learned to wait for her intuition to kick in, which was usually more reliable. Overly friendly fellows usually covered up for quick tempers and selfish motives. Their veneer would crack under pressure.

Daisy knew that, on the surface, she appeared to be a good mark. Single, bright-eyed and sentimental, she was often underestimated. Most people made the mistake of assuming she was sweet and kind, which she was—to her animals. In the community, she was fodder for gossip because she did not fit any mould they were familiar with. She was unmarried; she mostly kept to herself and she did not spread rumours or stories. Men often figured she was vulnerable. Women took her for a fool. Only her close friends realized she was clever and calculating. Fierce independence enabled her to survive alone on the farm. Hard work earned her an ample living, sufficient to support her simple lifestyle.

The man strode into the room, scanning its contents as if evaluating what he saw in dollars and cents. He emanated the sweet, sticky odour of a heavy dose of aftershave. His green tie made his eyes look like jade. "My name is Rocco. Luigi Rocco."

She offered her right hand for a shake and held Friday with her left. The dog growled and bristled. The stranger handed her a business card that she couldn't read without her glasses. Everything about Luigi Rocco smelled of success. He was the epitome of a man who never took no for an answer.

"This is a lovely home you have here," he said. His words were smooth as silk.

Daisy detected a clip to Luigi's sentences that hinted of an accent. She couldn't be sure of the country of origin, but English, despite his polished intonation, was clearly not Rocco's native tongue.

"Yes, thank you."

"I see you like antiques. I'm partial to them myself. However, I prefer European. The style is more ornate and sophisticated. Still, the early Canadian homestead furniture does have a certain . . . shall we say . . . charm." Rocco spoke through his nose, as if he smelled a bad odour.

Daisy bristled. "Most of these pieces were originally from this area, crafted by the early settlers who came from the old country."

"I suppose they did as well as they could with what they had at the time." He spoke as if disguising an insult beneath the compliment.

She was surprised that she took the remark personally, as if he were commenting on her taste. He implied her home was somehow inferior to his, just by virtue of its location.

She was already on the defensive when he abruptly changed the subject and caught her off guard. "I believe we have—rather, had—a mutual friend. Michel Mercure?"

Daisy felt the blood drain from her face. She released the dog and turned abruptly toward the stove to busy herself. "Won't you have a cup of tea, Mr. Rocco?" she asked hastily, trying to steady her voice. She offered tea in spite of herself. The mention of Michel's name felt like Rocco had punched her in the stomach. She needed something to busy her hands and give her a chance to regain her composure.

"Thank you."

Rocco lounged with his hands in his pockets, with a familiarity that made Daisy uncomfortable. A watch fob dangled from a pinstriped vest under his suit jacket. Everything about him reeked of pretense.

Daisy bustled to prepare the tea, setting out cups, milk and sugar. When she was fairly sure she had regained her equilibrium, she resumed where the conversation left off.

"Where did you meet Michel, Mr. Rocco?"

"I knew him in Montréal. We spent some time together over beer. You might say we were drinking buddies."

"That was a long time ago."

"Time passes in strange ways."

"Did you know Michel well?" Daisy couldn't resist pursuing the subject, painful as it was to her.

"He was a nice lad. I believe he was living out here at the time."

"Come and sit at the table. Help yourself to milk and sugar." She refrained from offering homemade cookies, even though she had a fresh plate piled high on the kitchen counter.

Rocco filled his mug with milk to the brim. Then he added four heaping teaspoons of sugar and stirred vigorously, spilling tea onto the saucer and tablecloth. He downed the contents in one swig.

When Rocco sat at the table, the dog immediately approached the stranger and began sniffing his crotch. Mr. Rocco clamped his legs together and folded his hands in his lap protectively. He continued to speak but eyed the dog. "He spoke very fondly of you."

"Michel was a good friend of mine. We were very close. However, I didn't know any of his friends from the city. He didn't talk much about that part of his life." Daisy paused to recoup, and then she continued on with a sigh of resignation. "How exactly did you know Michel, Mr. Rocco? Were you well acquainted at the time?"

Luigi shifted his eyes from the dog to the room to his tea cup. His hand brushed his cheek in an awkward gesture just before he spoke. Daisy wondered if he was lying.

"Let's just say we had some business dealings."

*Guilt*, she thought. *He's avoiding the truth.* "What kind of business did you say you were in?"

"Construction. We build things."

"Things?"

"Yes, buildings, roads, bridges. Pretty much anything you want to build, that's what we do."

"Michel never told me he knew about construction," she said. "He could hardly hammer a nail without slamming his finger."

"My company, Bella Vista, is, shall we say, very diversified. We also have a shipping business. Michel did deliveries and security, actually. We always need someone to protect our assets."

"So it's not just by accident that you happened to drop by? How did you know where to find me?"

"Well, that's a long story," Rocco said, fidgeting with his watch. "I know it's been a long time since Michel's death, but I've always meant to come out here and meet you in person. He told me that eventually you'd be interested in hearing what I might have to offer—your future, you know—he was concerned about your old age and how you would manage out here on your own."

His eyes began to shift nervously around the room as if scanning for an escape. Either the topic was difficult or it was complete fabrication. Daisy guessed he was lying again, only this time he was more transparent.

"Just before he died, he made me promise to get in touch with you. He asked me to look in on you from time to time to be sure you were able to cope."

Daisy's shock at his disclosure quickly turned to anger. She sniffed impatiently and stood up, knocking over her tea cup, and spilling her tea all over the papers piled at the end of the table. She grabbed a dish towel and dabbed aggressively at the puddle. Friday licked up the tea dripping on the floor.

Usually Daisy was exceedingly hospitable to anyone who entered her home. She would go out of her way to make a person feel welcome. Her curiosity about people and her desire to bring out the best in everyone usually led to long hours of conversation over several pots of tea. However, today was an exception.

Daisy grew more and more uncomfortable. The man's mannerisms were making her animals nervous. The chick had stopped peeping; the dove was silent; and instead of napping, the cat studied the stranger's movements from under the stove. Hackles still stood straight along Friday's back. Daisy had learned much of what she knew about human nature by relying on her animals' reactions. They did not like Luigi Rocco.

The sound of footsteps preceded a light tap announcing the arrival of a newcomer. Friday's angry fixation on the stranger in his kitchen changed immediately. His tail wagged, and his lips curled back in a grin.

"Come in, Robin," Daisy said in an overly loud greeting. As she opened the door, she added, "Mr. Rocco's just leaving."

Robin was a young woman with smooth skin and a snub nose. Her dark hair, pulled away from her face into a tight ponytail, sculpted high cheekbones and a sharp, angular chin. She wore a short denim jacket with a red shirt peeking over low slung, tight blue jeans. Heavy eyebrows and lashes accentuated flashing black eyes.

"I'm so sorry, Daisy, I didn't mean to interrupt. I just stopped by to see if you needed any help in the barn."

"I'm going out too," Daisy said. "Mr. Rocco is leaving *now*." She stressed the last word as a command. With her hand on the door knob, Daisy indicated that the conversation was over.

To his credit, Luigi Rocco received Daisy's dismissal without comment. He stood up and bowed slightly, in a gesture intended to cover his abrupt departure with a sign of respect in the presence of a lady. "It's been a pleasure, Miss Blossom," he said, exaggerating good manners.

His eyes scanned Robin's slim figure as if he could see through her clothes. Then, assuming a misplaced sort of intimacy, he leered and winked as he passed too close beside her.

Robin's answering smile was quizzical, with an uneasy grimace between pleasure and pain.

Friday followed him outside.

Daisy watched through the window as the man walked toward his car using long, impatient strides. Friday tried to take his hand in his mouth to escort him to his vehicle, but Luigi yanked back a fist and booted the dog out of his way. As he climbed into his car he threw a glance over his shoulder to see if anyone saw him kick the dog. His vehicle was long and shiny and black, without a speck of mud. Daisy didn't need to see the Quebec license plate to know he was not a local.

"Who is that man, and what did he want?" asked Robin.

"It all goes a long way back," Daisy said distantly. "Better off forgotten. To tell you the truth, he caught me so off guard that I don't even know what he wanted. I forgot to ask."

"He looked kind of out of place in your kitchen. Like a city person."

"He gave me his card, but I couldn't read it without my glasses." She rooted through the papers on her table. "Here it is."

She handed the card to Robin, who read out loud: "'Luigi Rocco, Bella Vista Social Club, construction and transport, secure deliveries guaranteed'. Sounds like a guy with a lot of dough."

"Money and influence, I figure. The kind of person who thinks he can buy whatever he wants."

"What happens if it's not for sale?" Robin asked.

"I don't think he likes no for an answer."

"Creepy."

"Yes, let's talk about something more cheerful." Daisy began to bustle around the kitchen as if she were ridding the air of a nasty odour. "Would you like a cookie? Fresh baked this morning."

Daisy offered the plate, and Robin selected the biggest one off the pile. She took a generous bite. Her tongue was pointed and delicate, licking away the crumbs gathered at the corners of her mouth. "Thanks. I came over thinking you could use some company," she said. "The news is already all over the country about Friday and you finding that dead body part. Are you all right, Daisy?"

"Yes, yes," she said, hustling around the kitchen looking for her barn clothes. She hid her expressions by hiding behind straggly hair dangling over her eyes while she laced up her barn boots. "It's sweet of you to ask."

"Well, actually, I also wanted to tell you about my new resolution. I've made a breakthrough."

Daisy loved Robin's enthusiasm. She could rely on her young friend to chatter with unending fascination, about her hopes and dreams—however unrealistic they might be.

"Your optimism is such a comfort."

"I've decided," Robin said with considerable determination, "to talk to a man."

Daisy waited. She double-knotted her laces. Surely there was a sequel. However, none seemed to be forthcoming. She sat up, hands on knees, and cocked her head.

"That's it? Do you have anyone particular in mind?"

"Any man will do," Robin said with her nose in the air and a dreamy look on her face.

"About anything in particular?"

Daisy stood up, slowly unravelling herself from the kinks in her tired muscles that tended to keep her from moving too quickly. She didn't want to startle the girl into self-conscious embarrassment.

"Every time I get near a guy, I clam up. I can't put two words together. I keep asking myself: How am I ever going to meet somebody if I can't say a word? Even 'Hello' or 'How do ya do?' I'm sick and tired of being a fly on the wall. So I woke up this morning, and made a resolution. By cracky, at least I'm going to talk to a man. That's a step in the right direction."

Daisy and Robin made their way across the barnyard, escorted by Friday, his tail waving like a beacon indicating the way. The white cat followed in their footsteps. Approaching the barn, they were greeted by a cacophony of baas, bleats, and crowings.

"What will you say?"

"More than two words would be a good start."

"They're just people."

"I know, I know." Robin could barely contain her exasperation. "But it's the fear—the 'what if?' . . . what if?" Robin had wide eyes and broad lips, innocent and optimistic like a puppy.

"Pretend they're animals. You don't have any trouble talking to Rosy the sheep or Peggy the chicken. A man's just like anyone else."

Robin blushed, "Yes . . . but no."

Daisy began her chores feeding the animals without comment.

The noise of animals increased until Robin had to shout over the din, "I will talk to a man before the year is over!"

Daisy nodded. "That's good. The new year is a long way off. That should give you enough time to work up your courage."

"Speaking of courage, do you want to put together a float for St. Patrick's Day? Pete Picken's organizing the parade again this year."

"Sure, we could decorate the old truck with some flags and streamers. It would be fun."

"There, that's settled. We'll figure out the details later this week."

The two women settled into their work. They coordinated their chores without words, each with her own tasks, going about the routine as they had every morning and every evening since Robin was old enough to come to the barn. Daisy had come to depend on her neighbour's help and her company.

# Chapter Nine

When Pete entered the Country Kitchen the next day, the restaurant was buzzing with excitement. He felt the intensity of the conversation before he even knew what was being said.

Mrs. Seguin, the would-be mayor, was holding forth from one of the tables in the corner. She spoke to her friend Marie Cartier in a voice loud enough for the whole room to overhear. Her back was turned to the door, and all eyes were on her. She commanded complete authority. "Daisy Blossom's dog chewed the hand off the victim's body," she said. "Daisy walked out into the yard first thing in the morning to go to the barn, and there was the dog, gnawing on the dead corpse."

"Imagine how you'd feel, finding that in your yard first thing in the morning?" someone asked.

The questions flowed:

"Where was the body?"

"Was somebody murdered down at Daisy's farm?"

"Who was it?"

"Who called the police?"

Everyone in the little restaurant had questions and comments. They were all talking at once, the discussion flying back and forth across the room between tables.

The would-be mayor felt it was her duty to enlighten the crowd. Her voice rang out over the murmur of exclamations. "Daisy phoned Emily Blossom yesterday morning, and Emily and Pete Picken drove over to Daisy's farm to help her search for the murderer. The dog was covered with blood, and there were guts all over the yard!"

Mrs. Seguin had embellished just a bit on the details to improve the dramatic effect for her eager listeners.

"You know Daisy lives down there on that farm all alone."

When Suzanne Duval noticed Pete standing in the doorway, she gasped and then loudly cleared her throat to alert the crowd. The chatter in the room subsided into a whisper and then faded into silence as all eyes shifted from the would-be mayor to Pete Picken.

"Good morning, everyone," Pete said. His silhouette was highlighted by the daylight of the open door behind him. His presence seemed magnified by the silence it commanded. The bell rang as he released the door to close behind him, and the resonant chime broke the spell over the dining room. Whispers resumed like echoes between tables: "He was there. He saw everything. What will he say?"

He strode to the only empty table, scraped a chair along the floor and sat down, placing his feet on the chair next to his. Pete crossed his arms and grinned. "Ilsa, bring me a coffee, please."

"Pete Picken," Mrs. Seguin said, assuming the role of interrogator after recovering her composure. "You had something to do with what happened down at Daisy's yesterday, didn't you? Was somebody really murdered?"

"Daisy's dog found a severed hand," Pete explained, speaking from underneath his hat. His dark glasses surveyed the room, reflecting the astonished and curious faces one by one. He gained considerable pleasure from the collective murmur that rippled from table to table. "The police were sure glad I found the rest of the evidence," he said. "The body was missing, you know."

"Didn't the dog drag the body home?"

"Not exactly."

"Tell us, tell us," several eager listeners said at once.

Pete happily obliged. "Well, you see, it happened like this." Pete shared yesterday's details.

"What did you find?"

"Oh, just a couple of garbage bags in the ditch down on the Boundary." Pete took a long swallow of coffee and watched their faces over the brim of his cup. His moustache dripped coffee from its edges. As his tongue meticulously licked away each drop, he savoured the suspense.

"Garbage bags? Did he say garbage bags?" Suzanne's mother was hard of hearing.

"I knew immediately they were suspicious, so I put them in the box of the truck. I figured the cops would be very interested in the contents."

"The police were collecting garbage?" Old Mrs. Duval cupped her hand around her ear and shouted, as if the words would make more sense if she repeated them loudly.

"No, no," Suzanne explained. "Pete picked up the bags for the police."

"What did the police want with garbage bags?"

Pete obliged the old lady with a carefully expanded explanation. He took advantage of her deafness by raising his voice for dramatic effect. "The garbage bags were full of body parts—frozen solid and sawed into little pieces."

Pete was enormously satisfied when the whole room erupted into uncontrollable chatter.

"I'd say that was cold-blooded murder, for real."

"A human body?"

"How did they saw it into pieces?"

"Who was it?"

"Why was it frozen?"

The would-be mayor scowled and chose to ignore the fact that she had, just a few moments earlier, misled the group with false information. "I told you it was a dead body," she asserted.

"Who was it?" Suzanne repeated for the third time.

"Why did the police put body parts in the garbage?" her mother asked.

"How much did the dog eat?" Ilsa asked. She was always concerned about one's appetite.

"You were very clever to find such good evidence," Marie Cartier said sweetly. Marie was always eager to compliment Pete. To his dismay, she took every opportunity to prove she had very special feelings reserved only for him.

"I always wanted to find a dead body," Cecilia Allen said. At twenty, Cecilia had every reason to be optimistic. "I knew, in my heart, one day somebody would turn up dead in a ditch."

"It's my fault," Cecilia's boyfriend, Burton Barton, admitted. "I told her the story of old Zephron Duval, who ended up in the ditch dead, frozen and covered with snow until spring. He was a drover and lived alone. After he lost his eyesight, he had to ride his bicycle into town. Somebody must have hit him in the night. Nobody reported him missing. Fifty people drove that road every day, and nobody ever noticed the crumpled body."

"There's so much road kill these days," Ilsa said.

Maria the cook entered the conversation from her usual refuge in the kitchen. In the Country Kitchen on the Hill, Maria was famous for two things: good cooking and unwavering pessimism. She could be relied on for finding the negative side of even the most positive situation. "I always feel sorry for the poor groundhogs who come out after a long, hard, cold winter and get splattered all over the pavement before they've even had a chance to enjoy the spring and warm sunshine."

"I saw a program on CBC last night about missing persons," Suzanne said. "Sometimes they never even identify the body. A person just vanishes, and nobody ever speaks up to report the poor soul missing. That would be bizarre, just to disappear and nobody cares enough to notice you're gone."

A welcome tinkle of the bell announced a new customer and a change in the gruesome conversation.

Emily Blossom entered as if she was walking on stage. She closed the door with a flourish and flicked her scarf over one shoulder, turning to greet her audience. Her countenance brightened dramatically when she bestowed her gaze upon her Dr. Watson, a.k.a. Pete Picken. "There you are. I figured I'd find you here."

Uninvited, Emily approached Pete's table. She lifted his boots, legs and all, off the chair. She brushed the mud from the seat and settled into place. "Ilsa, how about a lovely cup of tea this morning? I have a hankering for some Lady Grey."

Then, scanning the restaurant, she joined the communal conversation, "Has anyone seen Mr. Malarkey yet? Is there going to be an article on the investigation in *The Hill News?*"

"Maloney," Pete corrected her. "Mr. Maloney, the newspaper editor."

"Why do I always get his name wrong?" Emily asked, vaguely addressing no one in particular.

"Did you say Maloney was covering the murder investigation?" Mrs. Seguin piped in. "The news doesn't take long to get around town, does it?"

"It's called an effective grapevine," Suzanne said.

"Is someone talking about wine?" Suzanne's mother shouted. She was always keen whenever the subject of alcohol came up. "Personally I prefer sherry."

"No, Mother, we're just having tea this morning," Suzanne said.

Emily turned her attention to Pete. However she kept her voice raised so everyone could overhear what she was saying. "So, Pete, did you survive the police interrogation yesterday?"

Pete glanced around the room to see whether the others were listening. The would-be mayor pretended to arrange her hair. By cupping her hand around her ear, she could eavesdrop more effectively. In vain, he signalled to Emily that she should keep her voice down.

Detective Emily continued louder than ever. "I'm glad they didn't take your truck," she said heartlessly. "After all, you were discovered red-handed—excuse the pun—with the body parts of a murder victim in the back of your truck."

"Was Pete Picken arrested for murder?" old Mrs. Duval asked her daughter in an uncomfortably loud voice.

Suzanne shook her head and ignored the question.

Pete detected a look on Suzanne's face betraying a mix of emotions. He leaned over to Emily and whispered, "If her mother was found dead in a ditch, Suzanne might not be so quick to report her missing, either."

"Shh, Pete, that's not nice." Emily refused to whisper back.

He was trying to deflect Emily's revelations. At his expense, she had an obvious ploy to tell everyone in the dining room exactly how important she was to the murder investigation at Blossoms' Corners. Pete's efforts to distract her were unsuccessful.

"If they thought you were an accomplice, that would pretty well end your antique business, now wouldn't it?"

"Emily, you explained to the inspector it was all a misunderstanding." Pete reluctantly admitted she had played a valuable role in his release.

"Precisely, Pete." Emily smiled. "Now you owe me one."

"Emily, what are you up to?" Pete asked. He tried to whisper from under the brim of his hat. He held a finger to his lips to give her the idea that she too should be keeping her voice down. "I have the odd sensation you're up to something."

"Pete, you should know me better than that by now," Emily said, feigning a hurt expression.

"I do," Pete said. "That's the point."

"I want to do some investigating down at Johnny Aimer's place."

"You're really going to Guns 'R Us?"

"Yes, really."

"Be my guest!"

"Will you come with me?"

"I don't think so, Tim." This was one of Pete's favourite sayings.

Emily always assumed it referred to Tim Horton, the famous hockey player who owned a chain of popular Canadian coffee shops.

"I don't know why you talk about Tim as if he was your best pal," she said. "You don't even like their coffee."

"Not Tim Horton . . . Tim from the *Home Improvement* show."

"You don't even watch TV."

"It's just an expression. You're just trying to confuse the issue so I'll forget what we were talking about and agree to your crazy schemes."

"Pete, would I be like that?"

"Yes, you would, and no I won't. You don't need me to go down there and snoop around."

"What can I do to convince you to come along?"

"Em, let me remind you: the cops staged a raid there last year. Four helicopters descended on the place. Apparently they were looking for illegal weapons."

"Nothing happened though, did it? They didn't make any arrests."

"As far as we know."

"He's got some valuable antiques," she said with a bright smile that Pete easily recognized as a ploy.

"Didn't you tell me that about Daisy's?" he reminded her. "Look where that got me."

"Daisy does have some excellent antiques in her house. You can't deny that."

"No, but they're not for sale, now are they? You knew that when you tried to bribe me to take you down there. You knew, and you pretended not to. So what's different about Aimer's place? Eh?"

"A 'For Sale' Sign."

"That doesn't mean he has antiques for sale."

"Look, Pete, I have an appointment with the real estate agent this afternoon."

"Good, you go with her."

"Won't you come with me? Aren't you curious?"

"And get my head blown off? No thanks. Besides, I have another house call to make. And I know this guy *does* have antiques for sale. I'm busy."

"If I find something interesting, will you go back with me for a second look around?" Emily asked, refusing to let the subject drop.

"We'll talk later." He stood up and grabbed his coat from the back of her chair. With his pipe dangling from one side of his mouth, he yanked and tugged at the bottom of his coat. The two sides of the zipper would not line up.

Without ceremony Emily reached over, gently settled the zipper into its clip, and slipped the jacket closed over his plaid wool shirt.

"In the meantime, it's your turn to buy the coffee," he said, turning toward the door.

"It was my turn yesterday."

"Then it's your turn today too. You owe me one for yesterday."

"Pete, you're a hard man to bargain with."

"That's what they all say," he said with the flicker of a grin. "But a man has to make a living, don't he?"

# Chapter Ten

Emily emerged from the Country Kitchen to find Pete waiting for her beside his truck.

"You want a ride?"

"No thanks, Pete. It's a fine spring day. I'll walk home. Colleen Houseman is the listing agent for the Aimers' property. She tells me she's made an appointment for a visit this afternoon. You go ahead on your house call. Let me know if there are any interesting paintings."

One of the pleasures of Emily's life in the village was the short walk home from the centre of town. Walking was a healthy alternative if one did not drive a vehicle. Emily's home was situated on a side street one block from Main.

Shoots of tender green grass peeked from under the remaining crusts of snow along the sidewalks. Crocus heads ventured out of the brown earth in Mrs. C.'s flower garden. The bricks on the south side absorbed the warmth of the sun, inviting the first bulbs to defy frosty mornings.

Most of the houses on the Hill were built with Victorian brick the colour of burnt amber. The gardens were neat and well-tended. Residents took considerable pride in nurturing the historic features of their homes. Main Street was lined with buildings, serving as stores at street level and apartments on the upper floors. Balconies and porches featured decorative architectural trim known as gingerbread. The village was known as the Gingerbread Capital of Ontario.

Emily Blossom lived in a duplex that she had purchased when she moved to the Hill. Once an elegant mansion, now the house was essentially two separate dwellings under a common roof. On the outside, one side was white with brown windows, and one half was brick with paint-peeling, multi-paned windows. One side appeared modernized and plain; the other looked old and sedate with a bit of wear and tear around the edges. Inside, each apartment featured a kitchen and living/dining room area with the bedrooms and bathrooms upstairs.

This arrangement perfectly suited the widow Mrs. Blossom. She rented one apartment and lived in the other. Having a tenant enabled her to pay her mortgage. Her pension covered her living expenses. Whatever was left over contributed to her art collection.

Emily's apartment featured architectural details of former elegance: wide pine floors, decorated mouldings around the door frames and high baseboards lining the walls. The raised-panel cupboard in the kitchen was painted the original antique azure blue. A fireplace mantle graced one end of the living room. A curved banister with an elaborately carved newel post graced the stairway leading to the second floor bedrooms. A claw-foot bathtub and pedestal sink were more recent additions to the décor, since the house had been built before indoor plumbing.

Erected before the paving of the village roads, the house stood quite close to the road. The yard was the size of a mud puddle. Emily rarely had time for gardening. After walking through town and admiring her neighbours' picturesque properties, she was discouraged to see her own excuse of a lawn, with straggly weeds and dried remnants of last year's chrysanthemums.

She preferred to appreciate the stained-glass window above her front door. In the morning the coloured panes caught the light at just the right angle to cheer a dimly lit hallway. When she pushed the latch and opened the door, a beam of sunshine patterned red and green splashes on the pine floor. The curtain at the living room window rippled and fell back into place.

As usual, Charlie had been waiting for her return while sitting on the sill soaking up the morning warmth. He rubbed his fluffiness against her leg when she entered.

"Charlie, isn't it a delightful day?" Emily crooned when she spoke to the purring ball of fluff who folded into her arms. He insisted on being picked up and cuddled before she could even get her coat off. Then, after the proper ceremonial greeting, he wriggled free and ran to his bowl, meowing to be fed.

"I know, I know," Emily said, "I'm coming as soon as I can. We'll have a cup of tea and some soup before I have to go out again."

She set the table: one place setting for her and one for the cat. However, when she heard shuffling next door, she automatically added another bowl and silverware. The walls between the two apartments were paper-thin.

Both occupants could hear the activities of the other as if they were in the same room. The ring of the doorbell was hardly a surprise.

"Come in, Cassie." Emily sang her greeting toward the door without hesitating to put the soup on the stove. "It's open."

Cassie's bright smile and youthful enthusiasm was infectious. Emily had been grateful she had found such pleasant tenants. Their friendship was a bonus she never anticipated. By now she considered Cassie and Robert family.

"Sit down, dear. I've got soup and tea on. Your timing is perfect."

"Emily, I'm so glad you're home. I've got big news." Cassie's slim figure fairly danced around the room. She was dressed in tight jeans. Her hair slipped enticingly into her sparkling eyes. A frilly blouse revealed just enough of her breasts to show pride of ownership. Emily would have been embarrassed to wear such flimsy material. She did approve of the pink colour that highlighted Cassie's cheerful cheeks.

"Oh, dear, oh dear, I'm not sure I like the tone of your voice," Emily said. "Should I sit down? Can't it wait until we've had tea?"

"I'm pregnant. You're the first one to know. I haven't even told Robert yet."

Emily's heart skipped a beat, and her breath caught in her throat. "Cassie, you shouldn't do that to me. I'm not sure I like surprises like this."

Usually the Emily Blossom of detective fame was composed and self-assured. However, caught so unawares in spite of her efforts to be calm, the grandmotherly Emily Blossom felt her face flush. Rare tears welled into her eyes. "I'm much better with idle chatter," she said, trying in vain to hide her emotions by bustling over preparations for tea.

Cassie gave her a big hug, and Emily's four foot eight inches melted into weeping. She put her arms around the woman's slim waist and held tightly just for a second before returning to fidgeting over cups and saucers.

"I'm happy for you, dear," she said, wiping her eyes with the back of her sleeve. "Really I am. It's just a bit overwhelming."

"I'm sorry to burst in on you like this, but I just had to tell somebody."

Emily tended to idealize Cassie's youth. She admired the girl's confidence in the ways of the world. Cassie had once confessed that she still believed in happily-ever-after. Emily knew that, for Cassie, the possibility that anything could go wrong with pregnancy was inconceivable.

"We didn't really expect it. I've actually been on the pill, and even though we've talked about it, we never really thought it would happen like this."

Emily subdued her scepticism, but she could not blot out her inner thoughts. She imagined that the young woman, who had been murdered, whose body they found in pieces with a tattoo on her ring finger had once been as optimistic and innocent as Cassie.

*How time has a way of changing our expectations*, she thought. *Thank goodness we don't know what tomorrow brings.*

She said, "I'm sure it will be a beautiful baby. Congratulations!" She motioned to Cassie to sit down, and she placed a bowl of steaming hot soup in front of her. For Charlie, she added a generous splash of milk.

"Charlie finds the soup too hot," she explained to Cassie. "A bit of milk makes him happy. You'll be doing that soon for the little one too."

As she watched Cassie and Charlie drinking their soup, she settled into a comfortable sort of euphoria. She cupped her hands around the warmth of her tea mug for comfort.

"I'm glad I chose the Emperor's Rose Garden for tea this afternoon." Emily chose her grandmotherly, cheery tone to disguise the heaviness in her heart. She didn't want to discourage the girl in this moment of bliss and optimism. "The flowers are perfect for celebrating the prospect of a blossoming little baby on the way."

She continued, satisfied she had managed to regain not only composure but eloquence. "Tell me about your objectrition."

"Obstetrician?" Cassie suggested.

"Yes, tell me about your doctor? Do you have a good one?"

"That'll be the next step—after I tell Robert, that is."

"Will he be pleased?"

"I hope so. I'm sure the baby will look just like him. He's so handsome."

"And intelligent too, I'm sure."

"Oh, yes, of course."

The two women smiled in complicity.

The sound of the doorbell reminded Emily of the time. "Is it one o'clock already?"

She glanced at the grandfather clock in the corner, relentlessly ticking away time, as if there were an endless supply of seconds.

"That must be Miss Houseman. I have an appointment to go see a house in the country."

"You're not thinking of moving, are you?" Cassie said.

"Oh, no, no, dear! You know me, I'm always curious. It's one of my little adventures. I just want to do some exploring."

"Oh good," Cassie said. "You had me worried there for a moment."

The doorbell sounded again, followed by an impatient knocking.

"Come in. Come in," Emily sang as she hurried to open the door.

Colleen Houseman was a towering blonde dressed in white. Pink, high-heeled shoes matched a large, pink, leather purse slung over her shoulder. Her smile revealed flawless teeth decked in cumbersome braces. Bangs suitable for a Barbie doll strayed over her forehead.

Emily ushered her into the living room. "I'll be ready in just a moment," she said. "Cassie, excuse me."

She gave her neighbour a quick but honest hug to dismiss her obligations of hospitality. Then she skipped up the stairs to reconsider the practicality of her attire. She needed long pants and a warm sweater. Beige would be best to hide country dirt. Comfortable walking boots would suit for navigating snow banks. She chose nothing that smacked of money. Reasonable affluence was acceptable; careless decadence was not.

*I want to look like a prospective customer with serious intentions of buying a property in the country,* she thought as she evaluated her image in the full-length mirror. *Frankly, I consider the look of experience to be a badge of merit.*

Although her hair was more white than grey, she refused to consider herself old. The wrinkles around the edges of her mouth and along her forehead always surprised her. She never remembered that they were now a part of her character. She smiled and studied the stains on her crooked teeth. *A definite sign of character . . . detectives should never look too perfect. They need to show a touch of humanity.*

Although she repeatedly tucked her hair behind her ears, one lock always annoyingly fell into her eyes. She put the stray curl firmly in place and plunked a brown felt hat on her head just at the right angle to keep her hair in place.

Cassie called upstairs as she was leaving, "Bye, Emily. I cleaned up the dishes. I'm off. Wish me luck."

"Goodbye, dear," Emily called over her shoulder as she primped her attire in front of the mirror. "I'm sure you'll do just fine. Robert will be so thrilled. Let me know what happens."

The downstairs door slammed, and Emily hurried to gather her belongings. When she was sure the overall effect was correct, she hopped gingerly down the stairs and greeted the real estate agent as if she had known her for years.

"How nice of you to come for me," she said, offering a warm hand shake. "I'm so looking forward to seeing this house. I have a feeling it will be just what I'm looking for."

Colleen was courteous enough not to talk down to her elderly client. If she had any misgivings about Mrs. Blossom's financial wherewithal, she didn't show it. She handed Emily a folder of information about the property. "These are the details. They include the taxes, a description of the property size, a layout of the rooms and everything you'll want to remember after our visit when you're preparing your offer. You can always call me, of course, if there's anything you've forgotten. Shall we be on our way?"

Emily happily donned her coat and said goodbye to Charlie for the second time that day.

"I always feel perfectly fine when I'm heading off on an adventure," she said, happily taking her place beside her agent in the white SUV with a Dynamic Real Estate logo on the door.

# Emily's Tips About Tea

* Preheat tea pot before pouring boiling water for tea

* Choose proper tea pot for the occasion

* Select tea mug suited to your mood.
    - Red for cheer
    - Blue for thinking
    - suit yourself

* The size of the mug can shorten the conversation.
    - Serve small cups when you don't want your company to stay too long.
    - Do not offer a refill unless you want the conversation to continue.

* Serve tea when:
    - Your friends need a good chat.
    - you need to pamper yourself.
    - you need to cheer up.
    - to calm down after a difficult neighbour.
    - you've had a hard day.

* Do not drink tea in the middle of the night. If you cannot sleep, take a swig of strong whiskey.

<u>Emily's tips about tea (continued)</u>

* Have several tea strainers –
  They are not all created equal.

* Always let the water come to a
  rolling boil for at least 30 seconds.

* Except green tea which you steep
  after water has cooled a bit.

* Do not drink tea when it's too hot.
  you can burn your vocal chords.
  and you cannot appreciate
  the true taste.

* Add milk to orange pekoe and
  black tea to avoid canker sores,
  or serve tea with cookies
  (especially to Pete.)

* To avoid stiffness in your muscles,
  limit your green and black tea
  consumption to one cup a day.
  (Even less if arthritis sets in.

* A decent (although inadequate) substitute
  is red tea or rooibus

**Emily's Tips: How to Make Tea**

# *Chapter Eleven*

Johnny Aimer's house stood at the top of a rise overlooking Champlain Creek. The design was typical of farmhouses built by United Empire Loyalists in the early eighteen hundreds in Upper Canada.

As a historian, Emily was quite familiar with the traditions of early Canadian settlers. They built their homes to last for centuries with granite fieldstone walls three to five feet thick, timbers from ancient pine forests for roofs and floors and expansive fireplaces on each floor. Broad verandas with formal entranceways protected the houses from prevailing northern winter winds. Wood sheds, carriage houses and granaries clustered around the main farmhouse usually situated with a dominating view.

Johnny Aimer's house perched regally on top of a hill. Emily surmised that a gun dealer might well benefit from such a well-placed establishment. He could see who was coming up the driveway well before his visitors arrived on his doorstep.

"I've actually never been here before," Colleen admitted as they drove up the steep laneway. "We got the listing, and my boss was kind enough to give me this house as my first consignment. I'm quite excited to see the property. Mr. Dynamo says this place is a sure sell."

Emily had her doubts, but she kept them to herself.

As they neared the top of the hill, the gravel laneway opened out into a broad parking area.

A Honda Civic and an SUV were in the garage. A white cube van, with Quebec plates and a bilingual company logo of Bella Vista Transport was parked near a storage shed across the yard. A fourth vehicle, a rusted and abandoned jalopy covered with vines, looked like someone's attempt to create a rustic lawn ornament in the middle of the yard.

In Eastern Ontario, ruts and puddles were a sure sign of mud season on the brink of spring. The earth was bursting with moisture oozing from its pores. Melting frost turned into water on the surface and slippery ice underneath. Saturated ground looked solid but gave way under the slightest pressure. Before the grass grew, mud prevailed. Solid surfaces in country driveways were deceptive.

Johnny's yard was no exception. The approach up the driveway was rutted and slippery.

"Be a bit careful where you park your car, dear," Emily said. "We wouldn't want to get stuck up here."

"I think we're safe to park near the house."

Front doors in the old houses were rarely intended to be used. Only formal visitors approached from the veranda. Most people entered by the back door, often through a shed. One removed one's shoes at the doorstep.

Emily considered Colleen's white suit and high heels highly impractical for a visit to a country property. Perhaps the costume was the sign of a successful real estate agent.

*I'm not sure exactly who she's trying to impress,* she thought, *but who am I to know what a young person would be expected to wear to show houses to clients?*

Still, when she saw the mud in the driveway, Emily was glad she had worn practical footwear. She opened the car door and immediately confronted a puddle, which she carefully circumvented without getting her feet wet. Colleen, on the other hand, confronted what appeared to be solid ground leading to flagstones approaching the house. Emily rounded the back fender of the white vehicle just as Colleen's long legs and pink high heels emerged from the driver's side. The tight skirt and short white jacket seemed oddly incongruent with the setting.

Colleen led the way toward the back entrance, a jaunty stride accentuating swinging hips and enhanced by the wobbling of high heels on uneven stones.

Johnny Aimer and his wife were waiting in the kitchen. They looked surprisingly ordinary. Emily had expected them to appear more dramatic, perhaps even a bit outlandish.

Johnny was not a tall man. His generous paunch overhung a large belt buckle, presenting more an image of Humpty Dumpty than Darth Vader. Sagging cheeks sported three days of whiskers. Bloodshot eyes drooped at the corners. His eyebrows grew like wild bushes beneath an imposing forehead. His greying hair flew in all directions. He wore a faded denim farmer's shirt and baggy blue jeans.

Mrs. Aimer was tidier in appearance but rather mousey in demeanour. She stood in her husband's shadow, even when he wasn't nearby. Short, wavy hair framed a tired and wrinkled face. Her eyes were timid. Their steely colour faded into the grey pallor of her skin. The only brightness around Mrs. Aimer was her cherry-red lipstick smeared beyond the lines of delicate lips, producing the impression of someone wishing to be anyone other than herself.

Colleen entered the kitchen with bravado, towering over the others and attracting attention with a hearty handshake. "I'm so glad to meet you both in person," she said with glittering smile. "I'd like to introduce you to my client, Mrs. Emily Blossom. I'm sure your house is exactly what she's looking for."

Emily was eager to get on with her inspection of the premises. She knew exactly what she was looking for but did not know what she would do if she found it.

The kitchen and living room were neatly furnished, not too cluttered. A person might feel comfortable without fear of disturbing the décor. Exposed hand-hewn beams ran the length of the house. The floor was carpeted throughout. Wide windowsills in pine accentuated the depth of the stone walls of the house. Upstairs, three tiny bedrooms huddled under a slanted roof, and one bathroom on the second floor had been added in the 1950s. However, interior decorating and room layout were the least of Emily's interest. She wanted to know if there were closets.

"I just love the country look you've created in the kitchen, Mrs. Aimer," Colleen said, fairly gushing with compliments. "The living room is so cozy with that airtight fireplace in the corner. Don't you love the deep windows, Mrs. Blossom?"

"It is a lovely old house," Emily agreed, "but I'm concerned about closets. I have so many clothes; I'm a person who needs lots of storage space."

Before the Aimers could object, Emily was giving herself a guided tour of each closet behind every closed door in every room. Sure enough, in the hallway beneath the stairs she found what she was looking for: a cupboard full of guns, neatly stacked on their stocks, barrels pointing at the ceiling. Each gun had a tag of identification hanging from the trigger. Without flinching, Emily gently closed the door and continued her investigation of the premises. In fact, every closet she investigated was full of guns, different models, lengths and sizes—hundreds of guns.

*Thousands, and thousands,* she thought. *As Pete would say, "Hunnerts even."*

"Would you mind if I go into the basement?" she asked. "I'm curious to see if there's any dry rot in the beams from underneath. Sometimes in these old houses, a wet basement is the worst culprit."

Colleen's smile faded into uncertainty. "I'll just wait for you here. I'm not really very fond of dark, damp spaces. Spiders, you know."

Emily happily descended the rickety stairs unaccompanied and found plenty of proof that the rumours about Guns 'R Us were accurate. Gun parts, barrels, sights, triggers and paraphernalia were scattered throughout a makeshift workshop in the room opposite the hot water heater.

"Someone spends lots of time down here building weapons," Emily whispered to herself, to calm her nerves. "I wish Pete were here as a reality check. I wonder where they test all this artillery."

When she emerged from the depths of the cellar, she said. "This is a wonderful house. I'm just in love with everything I've seen so far."

Mr. and Mrs. Aimer seemed to breathe a collective sigh of relief. Of course Emily was not about to disclose her real purpose in visiting their home. Colleen, as the selling agent, might have been more aggressive in showing the property, but Mrs. Blossom preferred to investigate without interference. She was perfectly capable of evaluating the essentials of the property on her own.

"May I have a look around the property?" Emily asked, addressing her question directly at Johnny. "Perhaps you would show me the grounds? Colleen, would you like to come or would you prefer to stay?"

Colleen's shrug indicated that she felt obliged, at this point, to accompany her client on the tour outside. Mr. Aimer donned rubber boots and grabbed a walking stick from the mud room. Emily retrieved her shoes from the door mat and neatly tied the laces in place. Colleen managed to slip the high heels on by wiggling her feet into the shoes without bending.

Johnny Aimer led the way down the garden path; Emily followed, and Colleen brought up the rear of the little brigade. They proceeded across the soggy lawn, leaving footprints in the yard as they went.

Unexpectedly, Emily heard a yelp behind her, and then a splash. When she looked around, all she saw were long scrambling legs attached to a floundering figure struggling to escape from a mud puddle. Apparently the high heels had sunk into the earth, catching Colleen off balance and sending her face-first to the ground. Needless to say, the white suit was now covered with brown splotches, and Colleen's pretty blonde hair straggled over cheeks streaked with mud. Emily and Johnny rushed to her assistance and lifted her, dripping, out of the quagmire.

When she looked down at herself, Colleen burst out wailing. "Oh my God!" she cried. "How can this possibly have happened to me? What a mess!"

"Come back into the house," Johnny said. "My wife will help you get cleaned up."

"Oh dear, oh dear," Emily said, "what a terrible predicament!"

They escorted the bedraggled Colleen into the mudroom and left her in Mrs. Aimer's capable hands.

Emily and Johnny resumed their tour of the property. He walked ahead, waving his arms, indicating the expanse of rolling hills that stretched out beyond the house. "This is one of the prettiest spots in the whole area," he said. "Just look at that view."

The road stretched into the distance below them, over a bridge at the creek, and toward the purple mountains of Quebec in the distance. Pine forests surrounded the base of the hill. The red hue of dogwood bushes and budding pussy willows followed the valley along the creek bed. Red-winged blackbirds trilled from invisible perches in the swamp; crows cawed from treetops and chickadees and English sparrows twittered and chattered in the eaves of the old shed behind the house.

"How lovely this setting is," Emily said, quite enjoying herself. "Is that a pond I see over there, in the glade of those maples?"

"Oh, you don't want to go over there. It's definitely too muddy. Come this direction! I'll show you the spruce forest we planted twenty years ago. The trees are so tall there; you can hardly see the sky."

However, the more he protested, the more Emily was determined to see what it was Johnny wanted to avoid. Chattering like an excited child on an adventure, she hurried across the driveway toward the pond. "This would be a perfect swimming hole in the summer," she said cheerily. "You must love to come here on hot, sweaty days."

Johnny waddled after her scurrying figure. He caught up with her and grabbed her elbow just as she approached the edge of the water.

"Well, actually, you can't swim here," said Johnny. "It was an old quarry. There are blood suckers."

Emily peered into the depths of the pool and was surprised she could not see past the surface. She refused to be dissuaded. She sensed Mr. Aimer was hiding something. "Is the water contaminated? It looks awfully murky for a quarry pond."

Her persistence paid off. Johnny gave in. "It's toxic. We unload waste here from the sewage plant in the city. They need a place to empty the lagoons if they get too full, before they overflow into the Ottawa River. The dumping fees pay the mortgage . . . very lucrative."

Emily nodded and controlled her impulse to recoil in disgust. *A perfect place to hide dead bodies, actually.* Emily Blossom, Ace Detective, was thrilled with her investigation so far. "May we see that building over there? It looks like a large warehouse or hay storage."

Aimer obliged, gladly guiding her away from the sewage pit toward a long, low storage shed.

They walked past an old car covered with ivy. Emily opened her mouth to comment on the clever lawn ornament when she was startled to see something move inside. Upon closer scrutiny, Emily saw a pair of golden eyes staring at her. Then she saw a set of gleaming white fangs. A black panther sat on the front seat of the jalopy, growling a low guttural warning. Its lips twitched like a cat on the hunt for hot meat dinner.

Johnny spoke as if to his dog. "Easy, Samba, it's okay. We're just passing through."

Emily stepped to the other side of her escort as they walked past the jalopy. "Is that a pet panther?"

"Actually, Samba is a very effective guard animal," Aimer replied. "Nobody tangles with her for long."

"I don't imagine so," Emily said, feigning indifference.

"She prefers live prey," Johnny continued. "She eats the bones and all."

Emily gulped. "Are you suggesting someone in particular, Mr. Aimer?" she asked with a disarming smile.

"Oh, no—but you get my drift."

"I'm not sure I do." Emily refused to back away from his veiled threats.

"Let's just say she's been well fed and leave it at that," he said, turning his back and leading the way through the undergrowth.

They approached a building overgrown with weeds and wild grapevines and entered a long open hall with a padded wall at one end.

"This is where we do our target shooting, testing the guns," Johnny said in a conversational tone as if he were bragging.

Emily was startled by his candour. "You test guns?"

"Yes, Mrs. Blossom. That's our business. I thought you knew. We manufacture and refurbish weapons."

"Oh." For once, Emily was speechless.

The tone of his voice changed abruptly, and he stared into her eyes in steely confrontation. "Now that we've gotten that detail out of the way," he said, "tell me why you really came up here, Mrs. Blossom. I suspect you're not really interested in buying this property at all."

"Why do you say that?" Emily asked with an unsuccessful effort to manage a smile and a twinkle. Her fingers inadvertently brushed the stray lock of hair from her eyes and tucked it behind her ear.

His voice was hard and sharp, like a knife cutting metal. "What would a frail old lady like you want with a property like this?" the gun dealer asked. "You hardly look capable of doing the housework, much less keeping up the gardens and grounds." He had stopped pretending to be nice. "Now why don't you tell me what you're really looking for."

Emily straightened her clothes and considered her options. She had two choices. She could continue her guise and never admit to her real intentions, or she could get to the point. "I'm not old, and I'm not as fragile as you think," she said, poking her chin in the air, standing as straight and tall as four-foot-eight could be. "I'm investigating a murder."

"Oh ho!" Johnny exclaimed, "Forgive me for underestimating you!" He cocked his head and looked down at her out of the corner of his eye. He could not suppress the laughter that rose from the depths of his large belly. "Surely you're joking!"

"Mr. Aimer, one does not joke about murder. There's been a dead body found down at Blossoms' Corners. I thought you might know something about it."

"Mrs. Blossom, let me explain the facts of life to you. You don't honestly think I would have anything to do with dead bodies. I'm a gun dealer, not a murderer. Besides, I'd be a damn fool to dump a body so close to home—that is, if I had a body. People in my line of business cannot afford to be mixed up with the police."

"How can you sell guns and not take responsibility for what people do with them?" This was a question Emily had wanted to ask ever since she learned from Pete about Guns 'R Us.

"Mrs. Blossom, you confuse guns with crime. They are not the same. I sell guns to revolutionaries, people who want change, who want freedom. Selling guns is not illegal."

"It's what people do with them that's against the law," she said.

"I'm not responsible for the actions of others. I sell guns to make a living; that's it; that's all. What they do with them is none of my business."

"Guns are used to wage war, aren't they? Surely you don't condone the killing of innocent people?"

"The guns we're talking about, Miss Blossom, are so outdated compared to today's weapons of war that we're talking about antiques here, not modern artillery."

"Oh, that must mean they're only good for killing old people."

"Sarcasm does not become you," Aimer said, his lips twitching at the corners of his mouth. "I'm not sure whether to treat you like a joke or to take you seriously."

"Oh, Mr. Aimer, I'm quite serious."

"I'd prefer to avoid you altogether, but you're like a bull dog. You don't know when to let go."

"Guns murder people," Emily said, throwing caution to the wind.

"People murder people."

"There's no purpose to guns other than to kill."

"People kill each other no matter what weapon they use. It's the nature of humanity."

Johnny was no longer amused, but Emily refused to back down. "No other species in the world murders its own kind."

"I'm not responsible for the future of the human race, Mrs. Blossom. I make a living, that's all. Now, if you'll excuse me," he said, dismissing her in no uncertain terms, "I have other things to do besides justify my lifestyle to the likes of you."

"The likes of me," she said, "can be dangerous, Mr. Aimer, to the likes of you."

"Are you threatening me?"

"I'm merely pointing out that many women have managed to change the policies of men in power. We may not fight with guns, but we have our ways of influence."

"Mrs. Blossom, I would mind my own business, if I were you. You don't scare me." He roughly took Emily's arm and firmly guided her toward the car.

Colleen sheepishly joined them. She was a bit cleaner, but her face was as flushed as the pink of her purse.

"Shall we agree to disagree?" Emily asked, reaching her hand out to Johnny.

He accepted the gesture, but the hand he proffered was limp and inconclusive.

"Thank you so much for your hospitality, Mr. Aimer," Colleen said. "I'll get back to you when Mrs. Blossom and I have had a chance to discuss a possible offer."

Emily could see the gun dealer's profile against the late afternoon sky as he watched them drive away. He looked like a hawk sitting on the highest branch of a tree, waiting for its prey to skitter out from under shelter to look for food.

**Johnny Aimer's House**

# *Chapter Twelve*

"I am so mortified," Colleen said as they drove back to the village, toward the rosy sky and setting sun. "I don't think I'll ever recover. I've never felt like such a fool in my life."

"Now dear, don't you worry," Emily said. "Ten years from now you'll look back on this afternoon, and you'll say, 'You won't believe what happened to me on my very first sales call!' and you'll laugh when you tell the story."

"Oh, Mrs. Blossom, I hope you're right. I can't imagine ever getting to that point."

When they pulled up next to the curb in front of Emily's house, both were relieved the afternoon was over.

"Thank you, dear, for your help," Emily said. "I'm actually not sure that Aimers' will be the right property for me to buy. Now that I see how much work is involved with keeping up a property like that, I realize I have too many other important things to attend to. I just won't have time for all that gardening and lawn mowing."

"I hear where you're coming from," Colleen said, "but a person with your energy could do anything you decide to do. I have that feeling about you. I'll keep your request on file. I'll let you know if something comes up that would be more suitable."

*

Emily turned the key in the latch and opened the door to her cozy house. Her cat greeted her with loud purring, winding his furry body around her legs. "I'm so glad to be home, Charlie. I'm sure you are too. Let me get you your treats."

She hung her coat on the hook beside the door. Slipping off her practical shoes, she wiggled her toes into more comfortable slippers.

"What a good thing I never had any intention of moving from here. It's a wonder that young Colleen woman never became suspicious of my motives. Poor thing. Way out of her league, I'm afraid."

She made her way to the kitchen, where Charlie knew his treats were stored. She carried on a lively conversation while she prepared herself a cup of tea.

"What are we going to have for supper? I must admit, even tea seems like a bit of a chore at this point. Maybe I'll just sit here for a moment and have a little snooze before I worry about dinner."

Charlie settled into her lap, purring loudly as she stroked his soft fur. Soon they were both snoring peacefully. The grandfather clock ticked gently in the hallway, and the house creaked and settled. Daylight in the room faded, gradually replaced by beams from the streetlight on the corner. Emily and her cat slept soundly until they were awakened by the rude ringing of the telephone. Emily started at the sound. Charlie jumped to the floor. He showed his disapproval of intrusions by glaring at her from underneath the couch.

"Hello. Yes, Daisy, it's me, Emily. Whom did you call?"

"I called you," the voice at the other end of the line said.

"Well, that's a good thing, Daisy, because it's me you're speaking to. For dinner? Pete's coming by for dinner? But I don't have anything ready . . . Oh, I see, he's coming to pick me up and we're coming to your place for dinner. That would be lovely, dear. I'm too tired to cook for myself. Is there anything I can bring? Fine, lavender tea it is . . . fine choice for the evening. We'll see you in a little while then."

She hung up and sighed. "You know what, Charlie? I'm too tired to change for dinner."

She continued to sit for a moment but fidgeted restlessly. "That's the lazy way out, isn't it? I'll just go freshen up and change into something more comfortable. I'll feel much better if I do."

With that, she navigated the stairs, refusing to let complaints from her weary bones impede her progress. By the time the doorbell rang, Emily was transformed. She wore a bright red shirt and chequered wool pants to match. Her down-filled jacket had a red lining as well. She fluffed up her hair in an attempt at carefree curls.

"Don't I look bright and cheery?" she asked Charlie. "Looks can fool even an old fool."

The cat appeared singularly unimpressed.

"Apparently, you're not an old fool of a cat though," she said, picking him up and scratching him behind the ears. "Don't act as if your dinner ticket is walking out the door. You're not about to starve to death. I promise I won't be long."

She carried the limp, furry feline under her arm into the kitchen and selected lavender tea from her tea collection. Then she filled Charlie's dish with fresh, moist cat food. She put him on his stool and stroked him to soothe his sulkiness. He looked at her with disdain.

"Ordinary cat food is not what you prefer? I know you take issue with anything that deigns to label itself 'finicky cat'. I know . . . 'gourmet' cat food is just a ploy. Please don't starve yourself while I'm out enjoying myself, just this once. I'll make you some good dinner tomorrow night, if you don't fade away into a former shadow of your sweet self, in the meantime."

The cat would have looked down his nose at her if it wasn't so flattened into his furry face. So he turned his back on the food dish, tipped his fluffy tail and left the room.

"Okay then . . . resign yourself to your tragic fate of deprivation."

*

When she opened the door, Pete was leaning on the doorframe. His cowboy boots were actually shiny. One foot crossed over the other. He even wore clean jeans. With his pipe in his mouth and his leather hat dipped over one eye, he presented an air of dapper elegance. He stared down the street at some unspecified object. He appeared so concentrated on whatever was in the distance, Emily was inclined to look in the same direction to see what he focused on, but there was nothing of particular interest. She realized Pete was just being himself.

He offered his arm and escorted her to the passenger side of his truck. He helped her climb into the seat, waiting until she was properly settled in and buckled up before he slammed the door. The heavy truck shuddered. Emily took a deep, happy breath as she surveyed her surroundings.

*Nothing is quite like riding in a big pickup truck loaded with fine antiques to make a person feel perfectly smug,* she thought. Then she said, "How nice of Daisy to have us over. I've had quite a day. It will be so nice to have someone else prepare a meal. Daisy's always such a good cook. How long has it been since you've been to her place for dinner?"

"Too long," he said vaguely.

"I'm not sure why she's inviting us out to the farm. She's not been particularly friendly these past few years. Ever since her boyfriend, Michel, died, really. I know she's my sister-in-law, but we've never been all that close. My husband and I would visit once in a while, but I don't think she really approved of him all that much, even if he was her brother. She was never all that welcoming, even when we were first married. I think she knew he was a no-good son of a b. She just never let on until I found out the truth. Then at least things were out in the open. She didn't need to pretend she didn't know what was going on anymore. I guess, like a lot of wives, I was the last one to find out what he was up to."

Pete kept his eyes firmly on the road. Pipe smoke swirled around his head. His hands intently gripped the steering wheel.

No comment was necessary to encourage Emily's rant. He'd heard it all before, one way or another. Still, she needed to tell her side over and again.

"I just have to get it out of my chest."

"Don't you mean 'off your chest'?"

"Yes, I knew you'd understand. It's important to get those things off one's chest. Otherwise it eats away at a person. Hate kills, you know. You get consumed by evil thoughts. Before you know it, you become just like the person you're angry at. He was not good enough for that. He just wasn't worth all the grief. I learned long ago not to carry around heavy garbage."

"Baggage . . . get rid of your baggage."

"Yes, yes."

"Emily, I've wanted to ask you this for a long time," Pete said, changing the subject. "Why is it that you always mix up your words? You're intelligent. You know what you want to say. How come you use the wrong words all the time?"

"Oh, I don't have time to worry about that. Time is too precious. I just want to get on with saying what it is I have to say. I hate it when old people are constantly searching for words and names. There's this long dead silence in a conversation. Everyone stares blankly into space trying not to be impatient while some old fogey tries to find the word she's looking for. I haven't got the time for all that."

If Pete suspected there may have been more to it than Emily's explanation, he decided not to go there.

"I hate the term 'old heimers' disease," Emily went on. "That makes me want to throw up."

"You mean woof your cookies."

"Positively vomit."

"I get it."

At that point they were rounding the corner to Daisy's. There was no more need for discussion.

# Emily's List of Teas

BREAKFAST TEA ←→ ORANGE PEKOE

HEARTY MORNING TEA ←→ ASSAM BLACK

ENERGIZER ←→ JASMINE GREEN

AFTERNOON ←→ BUCKINGHAM PALACE GARDEN TEA

STOMACH FLU ←→ CAMOMILE TEA

TRANQUILIZER ←→ ARTICHOKE TEA

CHEERING UP FROM SADNESS ←→ ROSE TEA

COZY AFTERNOON FOR LONG TALK WITH BEST FRIEND ←→ BLOSSOM TEA (SERVED IN GLASS TEA POT) ((REFILL 3 OR 4 TIMES))

MID AFTERNOON BOOST ←→ CHAI TEA WITH MILK & HONEY

LIGHT REFRESHER ←→ MINT TEA

EVENING BEFORE BED ←→ LICORICE

NO CAFFEINE BUT SUFFICIENT EDGE ←→ YERBA MATE OR ROOIBUS

LEAF TEA
IS ALWAYS
BETTER THAN
TEA BAGS

**Emily's Tips: The Best Time for Tea**

# Chapter Thirteen

Friday emerged from the woodshed. He greeted the truck with excessive wagging of his white-tipped tail and two large dog prints on the driver's side of the truck.

"Get down, you old mutt," Pete said in an affectionate tone that Emily had rarely heard him use before.

"Don't you dare come near me with those muddy paws," she said, far less amicably than Pete.

Pete held the dog's collar so Emily could navigate the path to Daisy's door without interference. He patted the huge head gently, and the dog replied with a long, soggy lick.

"Come in, come in," Daisy sang, tending to the cooking of dinner from her place by the stove. "Take off your coats and make yourselves at home. I'm so glad you could make it. We're having lamb stew with the last of my potatoes wintered over from the garden and lots of onions."

"One of my favourites," Pete said.

"Daisy never forgets what people like. Here's the lavender tea. I'll bet you've even got a gooey-in-the-middle dessert for the boy."

"I'll get some wood." Pete volunteered without asking. From the woodshed he collected an armful of split maple and deposited it into the wood bin in the kitchen. Then he returned for another armful for the living room, where a bright fire crackled in the stone fireplace. His efforts were accompanied by loud grunts, doors slamming, logs clattering to the floor and squeaking stove doors opened for wood loaded into the firebox. The house smelled of wood smoke and succulent dinner.

Daisy stirred the stew, boiling in a heavy cast iron pot on the cook stove, which chucked a warm, cozy heat into the kitchen. The white cat watched the proceedings with golden eyes. The little chick scratched at its own supper in its box. The ring-necked turtledove slept above the door sill with its head tucked under one wing.

Pete helped himself to the newspaper hanging on the back of the chair. "Spring training's well underway in Florida. I need to catch up on the scores. I don't even know who's playing for the Jays this year."

He hung his hat on the chair and plunked himself down at the head of the table to analyze the scores and games while he waited for dinner. He disappeared behind the sports section at every opportunity to catch up on the latest statistics. Pete was renowned around town for his ability to win bets on playoff matches.

Rarely was Pete without a hat to contain the unruly crop of curls he had not cut in years. To an outsider, he appeared rather neglected around the edges. His hair escaped from hats with little regard for style. His clothes were worn: cuffs ragged and in need of a good washing. The boots that he never removed when entering someone's house were scuffed and muddy. He distracted superficiality with the obvious and hid his inner character for those more willing to look beneath the surface.

"The boy keeps track of the seasons according to sports playoffs. In spring, hockey ends with the Stanley Cup, and baseball begins with spring training," Emily said, as if Daisy did not know Pete very well.

"I'm so glad you invited us for dinner. I'm famished, and I just didn't have the energy to cook tonight. I've been too busy investigating."

Daisy was eager and jumped in to the conversation.

"Did you hear any news from the police? I'm so upset about that girl; I just couldn't stand my own company anymore. I needed some visitors for distraction. I can't stop thinking about her body, all cut up like that. What a terrible thing to happen to anybody. I can't get the vision of her hand out of my mind: those delicate fingers and that tattoo of the snake on her ring finger."

"Daisy, you're too sensitive. You take things too much to heart."

"I can't help thinking about the young girls around here. What if one of them was murdered? It could have been anyone, you know. I'm sure that young woman never thought, when she woke up that morning, that it would be her last day on Earth. So young, so much promise. She had so much to live for. I just can't imagine why anyone would want to do that to a person," Daisy said.

"A reasonable young woman would not put herself in that situation. She wouldn't hang around with those kinds of people."

"Yes, but what kind of people are they?"

Pete emerged from under his paper. "You don't want to know."

"Who would do such a thing?"

"You don't want to know."

"Let's change the subject, shall we?" Emily asked. "Pete, tell us about your antique hunting. That house call you made—did you find anything interesting?"

Pete reluctantly put down the sports section and allowed himself to be drawn into the conversation. He was usually quite willing to narrate a good story to a receptive audience.

"Well, I recognized the place right off the bat. Nick Sauvé described to me where the motorcycle guy lived, on the outskirts of Hamilton Mills. When I drove up the driveway, I remembered I'd been there before. A few years ago I made a house call there and talked to a little old lady who looked a lot like Gramma Moses. I remembered the place. When I was there the first time, she had an old pickup truck in the driveway for sale. I lost interest as soon as she told me it had no motor. I've always had a weakness for old pickup trucks 'cause I remember my dad's old truck."

His voice faded into a faraway wistfulness invoking reminiscences forgotten or ignored.

"One time I drove it across the yard when I was eight years old, and I got the shit kicked out of me for it."

"Oh, really?"

"Yeah, I remember that truck. It was an orange Mercury."

"It was your dad's truck?"

"Actually, I don't remember whose truck it was. I can't imagine my dad ever had a truck, but I do remember driving it across the yard. How the hell I knew how to put it in gear and how to stop it, I don't know."

He paused. The only sounds in the room were the dove preening her feathers, the ticking of the clock and Daisy's spoon stirring the stew. He rarely spoke about himself or his past.

"I loved that truck. I was standing on the floor boards with my ass on the seat, driving across the yard, looking through the steering wheel."

The two women laughed, Daisy in a low chuckle that rippled throughout her whole body, and Emily's titter slightly hysterical and giddy.

Daisy said, "I can imagine you as a mischievous, curly haired redhead driving an orange 1940s pickup truck across a poverty stricken farmyard. I can practically see the chickens scattering out of the way."

Emily piped in. "I see the laundry on the line about to be mowed down by a careening truck."

Emily picked up the story, prodding Pete to resume where he'd left off. "So you knew the place this morning. You'd been there before?"

"As soon as I drove up the driveway, I got a sense that things were not the same as the last time I'd been there. For starters, there was a rope across the end of the driveway. The yard was full of junk. I was pretty sure the old lady was long gone."

"What kind of stuff was lying around?" Emily asked.

"There was a tempo in front of the garage with a Harley in it, so I knew I was at the right place. Then there was this dog, this pit bull, on a chain attached to the side of the house. The dog was extremely agitated."

"How long was his chain? Long enough to reach across the doorway?"

"I went the long way round to the front door. I don't like pit bulls to start with. I knocked on the front door, and that's when this guy appeared. When he opened the door, three things struck me right away: first the smell; secondly, the total chaos in the hallway behind him, and third, the guy himself."

"What was the smell like?"

"Musty, as if the house hadn't had a window open in years. It smelled of rotten food garbage, and dog shit."

"Dope?"

"Probably."

"So what did this fellow look like?"

"He was about five ten and slim. He had a muscle shirt and three or four days' growth of beard. He had a drawn face, like the guys you see in an action movie, hollow cheeks and staring eyes, with lots and lots and lots of lines in his face—scars."

"What kind of scars?"

"I couldn't tell if they were marks from a knife or from some sort of accident. Let's just say he wouldn't win any beauty contests.

"Just as I opened my mouth to ask him a question, another dog, a Doberman, came around the corner. The guy started screaming. He began beating on the dog. While he was yelling at the dog to get out, he was punching and kicking it. When the dog started to retreat, he chased him into the kitchen."

Pete recounted the incident as if he had been mesmerized, watching an absurd insanity play out in front of his eyes. Words and impressions tumbled out of his mouth, hardly making sense of the actions he witnessed.

"The Doberman was on a chain attached to something in the other room. The guy was kickin' the dog out the door. For some reason I followed him into the kitchen. I was just standing there watching him beating up on this dog and cursing. 'I'll kill you, you son of a bitch!' He said that more than once. The dog would slink out the door and then come back for more. The guy kicked him again and again. It was as if they were playing some sort of sick game of abuse."

"That's so sad," said Daisy. "The fellow should be reported for animal abuse."

"The place was filthy, just absolutely filthy with dog shit. The whole time the television was on . . . a big ol' 1950s television. This smarmy talk show host was interviewing some woman about her fashion statements. The whole scene was totally bizarre."

"Were there any antiques?"

"Yeah, there were some. He takes me out through the back door, where the other dog is tied. We walk into a garage, and the floor's covered with junk: lumber, and shit and corruption—and the best antique I've seen so far."

"What was it?"

"A sideboard, raised panel doors and ornately carved backsplash. In the meantime, I'm making a list of the stuff I've seen so far. A few pieces were interesting, but I was getting more and more nervous about being in that place."

"People like that are downright dangerous," said Emily. "Did he tell you anything about himself? Where he came from? What he was doing there?"

"I couldn't help thinking, 'This crackhead's off his rocker'," said Pete. "He talked about working for the Hell's Angels for years, running dope for them and collecting money. He said there was a gang war starting up in this area. Some newcomers set up shop down in the valley with a grow-op, dealing drugs from the city. He said they were trying to intimidate all the other dealers around and that they meant business. Most of what he told me didn't make much sense. I couldn't tell the truth from what he was making up.

"The guy was just totally out of control. "I'm tryin' to be cool, but deep down inside I don't want to have anything to do with this guy. How do I know that even if we can make a deal I'm gonna to be able to walk out of here with this stuff after I buy it?

"Finally I said, 'Okay, I'll get back to ya. I'll figure out my list, and I'll get back to ya?'

"I'm supposed to make an offer, but I'm not goin' back, just too scary, not worth the aggravation. How do I know that even if I buy something from him, he isn't going to come and steal it back?"

"Do you think he's capable of murder?" Detective Emily was fully engaged by this point. "Do you suppose there's a link between the gangsters and the frozen pieces of cadaver?"

"I wouldn't put it past him. What really scared me was the way he was beating up on those dogs. Not only beating on them and kicking, but he was screaming at them at the top of his lungs."

"A man who treats his animals badly is probably quite capable of doing worse with humans," said Emily.

"Those poor, helpless creatures, especially when they're chained and can't get away," said Daisy, shaking her head, wiping her hands with a dish towel.

"On the other hand, he's not calculating enough," Emily said. "He may be too crazy to premeditate murder. He certainly doesn't sound capable of plotting an elaborate cover-up. I wonder who he's referring to when he talks about the new gang down in the valley. I wonder if our severed body was a victim caught in the middle of a gang war."

"Well, I'm not easily put off the scent of good antiques," Pete said, "but I'm not goin' back to that place again to find out."

"How about if we get down to eating?" Daisy suggested. "I think we're all ready for a good feed. Emily, would you prefer red or white wine? Pete, the beer's in the fridge. Help yourself."

The kitchen table was set with a red-checked tablecloth and matching cloth napkins. Daisy generously filled soup bowls to the brim with piping hot lamb stew. Chunks of unpeeled potatoes, carrots and succulent lamb cubes swam in thick, brown gravy spiced with dried herbs. Homemade bread with a hefty crust was still warm from the oven, and butter melted into the thick, doughy slices. Soon all three were blowing on their spoons full of delicious meat and vegetables. The room settled into sounds of slurping and chewing while the tea kettle whistled and the fire crackled in the stove. They ate in silence, savouring the delicious variety of tastes from homegrown produce and country cooking. Dessert was a lemon pie piled high with swirls of toasty meringue.

"That was a meal fit for loyalty," Emily pronounced as she delicately dabbed at the corners of her lips.

"Royalty. You make us feel like royalty, Daisy. Em's right: everything was not good."

"Not good? What didn't you like?" Daisy asked, taken aback.

"Not good—great," Pete said.

"I knew that's what he was going to say," Emily said. "He always uses that line on Ilsa and Maria at the Country Kitchen. Gets 'em every time."

"Well I hope it was good."

"Good? Good? That's not the word for it."

"Great?"

"Yes, of course great."

"Shall we adjourn into the living room? Methinks the fire beckons," Pete said.

"If I settle down into that couch in front of the fire, I'll be asleep in no time," Emily said. "Can we help with the dishes, Daisy? I know Pete likes to dry."

She tossed Pete a dish towel and was rewarded with a reluctant scowl.

"I'm not exactly used to helping with the dishes," he said. "It hurts my driving fingers."

"Yes, we know," Emily said, "but once in a while a fellow has to exercise his right to contribute to a good meal in a proper way."

"I do contribute. I eat the food and enjoy the company, and I always compliment the chef."

Their banter was interrupted by the telephone ringing. Pete picked up the phone and held the receiver, while Daisy wiped her hands on his dish towel. As soon as she answered, he slipped into the living room while Emily eavesdropped.

"Hello, Roger. I didn't know you had a dog. Yes, I can help you fix up a dog house for him . . . I'm free tomorrow . . . in the morning, after chores . . . yes, that would be fine . . . Where are you living now? Spring Valley Road . . . the farm on the left, up on the ridge, where Mrs. Beaulieu used to live. I'll see you tomorrow morning then. Good night."

"Roger Major?"

"Big or small? *Le gros Majeur? Ou le mineur Major?*" Pete asked from the other room.

"Roger, you know. Roger Major."

Pete spoke Franglais, a mixture of both French and English but with an English accent. He teased them with his wordplay. "Roger, with an accent aigue, or Roger, with an rrrr?"

"Pete!"

"Go on, Daisy. Don't listen to him."

"Le majeur Major? Or the major Major?"

"Pete! Quit!"

"Le Major Roger, ou Le Majeur Roger Major?"

"Get on with your story, Daisy. He'll get tired of interrupting eventually."

Emily shut the door between the kitchen and the living room.

"Yes, well, anyway, someone's given Roger a dog. He wants to fix up a good spot for it, so it'll be comfortable and won't run away."

"Anyone would run away from that man," Emily said.

"Roger's heart's in the right place. Someone gave him the dog. He needs a friend, and a dog would be the best thing for him."

"Open the door," Pete's voice said from the other room. "I can't hear what you're saying."

Daisy and Emily ignored his pleading. Daisy continued in a low voice designed to provoke his curiosity. Her ploy worked. Pete got up to open the door but returned to his sports section on the couch.

Daisy raised her voice sufficiently for him to overhear. "Roger must lead a rather miserable life, as crippled as he is with cerebral palsy. He never had too many breaks in life. I admire his courage and determination. A lot of people would have given up long before this, but he just keeps on going. He gets work here and there and keeps that old tractor running somehow so he can get around. I don't mind helping him if I can."

"I'd feel more comfortable if you didn't go up there by yourself, Daisy," said Emily.

"The man's harmless. He may be disadvantaged, but he's certainly not dangerous."

"After Pete's story about motorcycles and drugs, I'm feeling a bit spooked. Roger's place is in the middle of nowhere. How about if we go together? You can pick me up on your way. Two is always better than one."

"Really, Emily, that won't be necessary."

"Take her along, Daisy," Pete said from the other room. "She needs the fresh air."

"Pick me up on your way through town. I'll be ready."

"I know better than to argue with you, Emily Blossom. If I say no, you'll only push harder. Better to give in and avoid unpleasantness. Besides, I wouldn't mind the company. You always do have an intriguing interpretation of reality."

"Daisy, why do you always have to make things so complicated? It's a simple offer. Take it or leave it."

"Suit yourself. You're the one who's squeamish."

If Emily were to reconsider, it was too late now. She'd already committed to another adventure.

"Who knows? Maybe a visit to Spring Valley will further my investigation."

"You always have such a clever way of justifying being a snoop."

"Snoop? Look who's talking."

"I'm not the one who spreads gossip around town."

"Gossip? Now look here, Daisy, you're going too far."

"Now, now, ladies," Pete said from his comfortable seat on the couch in front of the fire. "Don't let's go getting into an argument. After such a nice dinner, can't we all get along for just one evening without quibbling over who's talking about whom about what?"

"She's the one who started it," Emily said, throwing the dishtowel onto the dripping dishes in the rack. She left the kitchen and took a seat on the couch beside Pete in front of the fire.

Daisy drained the water from the sink, dried her hands and arranged the wet towels on a rack hanging from the ceiling above the stove. Then she joined the others and relaxed into her favourite rocker by the fireplace. A cozy silence settled over the three of them. They stared into the flames of the crackling fire. Soon all three were dozing in the warmth of the evening.

# Chapter Fourteen

Emily woke to a winter wonderland. Freezing rain overnight had laced the countryside in ice. As the sun rose, the tree branches began dripping and sparkling.

"Spring is so fickle," she said to Charlie when she saw the weather outside her window. "Just when you think it's here for good, winter comes back and spoils everything."

The last thing Emily wanted to do was leave her cozy nest of warmth and comfort to venture into a stark, soaking cold. Nevertheless, not only had she cajoled Daisy into taking her along to Spring Valley, she promised to be ready when Daisy's truck pulled up in front of her doorway. To make matters worse, she had slept in. There was not even time to luxuriate in dreamy reveries, much less take a hot shower and brew a cup of tea.

Charlie was his usual unimpressed cat-self. Her need to rise and dress was none of his concern; his need to eat and enjoy was most important.

"I know you're getting impatient with my gallivanting around the countryside, but it simply can't be helped. I have a big mouth, and last night I put my foot in it once again. So now I have to pay for my expressions, and you will have to miss breakfast. "How can I ever make it up to you?" she asked him.

Charlie observed her preparations for leaving through green, calculating eyes.

"I know, I know, I'll pay with blood and tears. You're going to ignore me mercilessly when I get back. No purring and cuddles for at least a day. Then I'll have to feed you oodles and oodles of your favourite treats and cuddle for days on end before you'll deign to forgive me. How could I possibly think anything was more important than treats and petting? I know you'll make me pay dearly for neglecting you."

A brief blast of a truck horn told them both that Daisy had arrived on time. Emily hustled on with her winter overcoat and rubber boots. She even resorted to gloves and a toque in spite of risking a bad hair day for the remainder of the afternoon.

*One must never underdress in blustery weather. Be prepared for every emergency. Layers can be removed if one gets too hot, but once the cold penetrates under the skin, it takes hours to warm up again. I need to look after myself because no one else will be here to pick up the dirty laundry.*

As she locked the door behind her, she could see the drapes at the window shift aside. The shadow of a fluffy cat hovered behind the curtain, a reminder of her promises to be fulfilled upon her return.

Daisy's truck was not nearly as impressive as Pete's. Emily had to yank on the handle of the door of the passenger's side. The door sank on its hinges when opened; then, once she managed to climb onto the slippery seat, Emily couldn't heave it shut.

With a deep breath of resignation, Daisy reluctantly descended onto the sidewalk. She steadied her weight, leaning on the hood, to keep from slipping on the ice, as she navigated around the front of the truck to slam the door closed. Emily crossed her hands in her lap. She posed her chin cocked at the appropriate angle to indicate she was properly settled and ready to depart.

Reinstalled in the driver's seat, Daisy hunkered with her arms draped over the steering wheel like a hug. Her long, pearly hair straggled over her forehead and shoulders; somewhere, halfway down her slouched back, a ponytail gathered. She wore a farmer's shirt, plaid, insulated and predictably torn at the bottom and tattered at the sleeves. Steel-toed boots with laces knotted in several place miraculously managed the gas and brake pedals without interfering with each other. Her jeans were baggy and stained.

Emily had little patience with the way Daisy dressed. She always looked so sloppy.

*Her only redeeming feature is her skin*, she thought. *But there's no reason to pay her a compliment so early on in the day.*

The colour of Daisy's cheeks was iridescent. Emily didn't like to ask what cosmetic ingredient could produce such a vivacious effect. She knew she wouldn't like the answer. After all, Emily considered herself the expert on personal care and appearance. Once, in a moment of weakness, Emily did ask what brand of soap Daisy had in her bathroom. Daisy had the nerve to claim she never washed her face with soap and the pleasant aroma was actually wild strawberry incense from the Dollar Store.

Resolving to be as pleasant as possible, Emily resorted to her safe topic of conversation—the weather.

"I see you're dressed to suit the weather. You're both drab and dreary."

"Good morning to you too. You rather closely resemble the Michelin Man yourself."

With the truck windows closed, the odours of cat pee, sheep manure and rotten banana mingled to create an intense aroma, which Emily feared would indefinitely cling to her clothes. Two empty Tim Horton's cups, rims rolled and printed with a "Please Play Again" message littered the floor along with an oily rag, a used air filter from the tractor and a half-solved crossword puzzle. Daylight showed along the base of the door through rusted panels. Seat covers, once intended to hide the rips and foam beneath worn upholstery, crumpled into the cracks behind the seatback. As a result, springs and stuffing escaped from the confines of the cushions and poked the truck's passengers in the most uncomfortable places. Coffee stains made the plastic linings sticky. The web of a dream catcher, adorned with feathers, dangled from the rear view mirror. Wipers slapped and banged, angrily splashing the rain away from the windshield with an elaborate crack meandering across the driver's view of the road.

*I'm not particularly impressed with the nature of my adventure so far this morning,* Emily thought. *However, nobody said the job of a detective was supposed to be comfortable. To my own credit, I'll refrain from commenting on the mess and be polite. After all, it was my idea to come along.*

Daisy drove in two speeds: she slowed for stop signs to a crawl, without making a full stop, or she drove at sixty kilometres an hour, regardless of the posted speed limit on the highway. Impatient drivers appeared in the mirrors, tailgating until they could pull around in a passing zone and disappear over the horizon ahead. Emily was glad they weren't going far from town.

"This is waiting weather," Emily said above the roar and rattle of the truck. "It's as if all the trees and bulbs are holding their breath waiting for the frost to disappear. They stick out their little noses to test the air. If it smells like snow, they tuck themselves back into hiding until the sunshine tickles them out again."

"Yes, you can barely see the tinge of colour on the trees. They've been like that for days. If the sun comes out after this rain, the buds will burst and everything will turn bright green all of a sudden."

"Then we'll forget how it looks with snow on the ground."

"Funny how quickly we adjust to the new seasons."

"I don't know if I could live without winter."

"This year was long and cold. Then, once spring arrives, we take off the long johns and complain that it's too hot."

"That's Canada for you."

As they drove down the highway, ploughed fields lay in wait for sunshine before planting season. The trees were still skeletal, waiting for the heat to explode into leafy brilliance.

The old truck shook and shuddered along the rough road broken by cracks and frost heaves. A motorcycle roared up behind them, and, barely hesitating, pulled out to pass in a no-passing lane.

"Some people are in such a hurry."

"Motorcycles on the road are a sure sign of spring, though."

The motorcycle disappeared over the next hill as they approached the intersection with Spring Valley Road. The gravel road caused the truck to vibrate and bounce like a jig gone wild, as they drove past a field with Canada geese feeding on corn stalks, rimmed by swampy lowlands teeming with ducks scouting for nesting sites. The farmhouse they sought was perched on top of a steep sloping ridge, rising sharply above the meandering valley.

"Well, here we are. Roger wasn't kidding when he said it was a long laneway. I hope we don't slip off into that muddy ditch."

"Or get hung up on a pothole. Looks almost abandoned."

"Roger probably can't afford to live in a better place. I hope the rent's low."

"I hope so. The house looks like a wreck."

The rattling truck swayed its way up the driveway. The closer they got, the more rundown the old farmstead appeared. The house had once been quite elegant, commanding a view of the rolling valley below, but now it was neglected and dilapidated. The wraparound porch had broken posts and rotting floorboards. Paint peeled from the weathered walls. The shingles on the roof lifted and curled toward the peak. Garbage was strewn throughout the driveway. Several out-buildings were in varying states of disrepair. A door to the garage hung askew from its roller. The roof of the chicken shed was completely rotted and falling in. A dairy barn, built at the turn of the century, seemed in better shape than the other buildings, but daylight could be seen between the wallboards. An exterior wood furnace and tin housing seemed the newest addition to the crop of ramshackled buildings, scattered across the brow of the hill like afterthoughts.

A beat-up Ford truck had been abandoned in the middle of the yard, parked as if its owner had intentions several years ago to leave in a hurry but never succeeded in escaping. A newer compact with a dented fender appeared to be the current vehicle used to drive to town on errands. In a woodshed next to the house, Harley Davidson motorcycles were parked almost out of sight just inside a door on rusting hinges. The brazen machines with shiny chrome and black leather seats looked out of place in such neglected surroundings. A cube van, similar to the one Emily had seen at Johnny Aimer's, was parked between the woodshed and the barn.

Several old tractors in various states of disrepair were parked next to a machinery shed. Roger Major's primary means of transportation, an old Fordson tractor, lopsided, with a crooked cab and bush hog attached was parked in the driveway. When Roger was on the road, the old tractor could be heard for miles, clanking and clacking down the highway at twenty kilometres per hour. Roger perched beneath the canopy, crooked like the tractor, with a lopsided farmer's hat and permanent toothy smile. He never returned waves from passersby because he needed a firm grip on the steering wheel to prevent the tractor from straying onto the shoulder. Even the tires appeared to roll in different directions.

"It's a wonder that tractor stays on the road."

"It's a wonder Roger can keep it from rattling to pieces."

An entrance to the house was not obvious.

"He said he lived upstairs, but I don't see a door, do you?"

"It looks like you might go in through the back shed."

"I'll go," Emily volunteered, eager for an escapade. She heaved open the truck door and descended onto the running board. Then she stepped directly into a puddle, soaking her pants cuffs. Usually Mrs. Blossom would be annoyed, but today she was on an adventure.

*A detective never lets the discomforts of nature get in her way.*

Making her way through the dark hall of the back porch, past scattered boots and shelves stacked with indefinable objects, Emily found a door. She knocked, gently at first, and then, when she heard a murmur of voices inside, she rapped more loudly and called out in her most friendly and cheerful warble. "Yoo hoo! Anybody home?"

Before she could knock again, the door slid open as if by remote control. The room was hazy with smoke. Inside, several men sat hunched around a table cluttered with coffee cups, beer cans and ashtrays. They looked like a collection of freaks escaped from a bankrupt circus. Each of them was disguised in whiskers, straggling hair, fleshy cheeks and bizarre ornamentation. They behaved as if they had been caught engaging in either a mischievous prank or something illegal. They were obviously not expecting the likes of her. Emily was very careful not to speak to anyone in particular and not to stare.

Emily's first impulse was to run for safety. However, her resolve remained unshaken. *Stay calm no matter what danger one encounters.*

"I'm so sorry to disturb you. We're looking for Roger Major. We can't find the way up to his apartment."

One of the men wore a bandana on his head. His T-shirt depicted a skull in the shadows of a hooded robe. His gestures were so innocuous that words emerged from his direction, as if spoken by the skull. "Go out around to the front of the house. The door's on the far side. Just open and go up. He'll meet you at the top."

"Thank you so very much."

She closed the door gently behind her and made her way from the dark to the daylight, to find Daisy sitting in the truck with the motor running. Emily walked to the driver's side, and Daisy rolled down the window. She was listening to the CBC traffic report but clicked off the radio to hear what Emily had to say.

"It's okay. The entrance is around the front, upstairs. They said to go on up. Roger's there."

\*

The door to a stairway creaked open when they knocked.

A strong male voice shouted from above, "C'mon up. The door's open."

Roger waited at the top of the stairs. His legs were twisted, like old stumps; his knees buckled in the middle and rested against each other while his boots balanced his torso precariously from a tripod stance. He kept himself upright with a hand braced on the wall. As he spoke, his head swayed from side to side, and he talked from the side of his mouth. His eyes rolled, unable to focus on a fixed object. Thick glasses magnified the size of his eyeballs, as if he surveyed his surroundings, like a caterpillar on the hunt for a juicy leaf. He had a thatch of black hair growing in all directions. Beautiful, straight white teeth were incongruous with the wild ruggedness of Roger Major's general appearance. He spoke in loud, clipped English, grammatically correct, but almost too perfect—an indication that he was perfectly bilingual and probably spoke colloquial French Canadian with a nasal twang.

"C'mon in and meet Poochie. I wasn't really expecting visitors. The place is a bit of a mess, but it's home."

The one-room apartment was strewn with clothes and bedding. A torn curtain welcoming the damp grey day into the dinginess of the room hung across the window. Roger apparently slept on the couch. Blankets and a worn sleeping bag lay in a pile on the floor. Remnants of several meals were stacked in plates on the edge of a coffee table. On one wall, a crucifix depicted the pained figure of Christ hanging in midair from nails piercing his bleeding palms and feet. A small television flickered silently; soap opera figures mouthed daily dramas unfolding in kitchens throughout the country.

In the corner behind the sofa shivered a small, brown, speckled dog. His whole body was enveloped in violent trembling. His eyes were sad and hopeful at the same time.

"Here's my problem," Roger said to Daisy as if Emily were not present. "My friend gave me this dog after a fire in his house. He needed to find him a home, but the mutt is afraid of everybody. Nobody would want a dog that's afraid of his own shadow. The dogcatcher will just put him down without giving him a chance. I can't keep him upstairs because I can't take him out for walks. He always runs away if I let him go loose. I need to tie him up, but he keeps breaking the collars I have. The guys downstairs ran over their own dog one night. They say they'll kill Poochie if they catch him loose. I know you're good with animals, and you're the only one I could get hold of who might help me."

Daisy crouched down and spoke in a soothing tone, which set the dog at ease. "Hey, fella. There's a good little dog. Nobody's going hurt you. It's okay. We're here to help."

Slowly the little mutt gathered up his courage and wiggled his way out of the corner, leaving a trail of pee behind him. Daisy let him sniff her fingers. Eventually the pup allowed her to pet him under the chin. His little tail began to wag, slowly at first, and then with more confidence.

After a few moments of sizing up the situation, Daisy said to Roger, "I'll help you. Let's put him on a leash. We'll take him out for a walk around. We'll figure out where would be the best place to keep him."

"I've got just the spot," Roger said, relieved to find a sympathetic collaborator. "I've even got a dog house with a blanket and a pillow."

Daisy picked up little Poochie and headed downstairs. Emily followed. At the bottom she turned to watch Roger clunk down the stairs behind her. Each step was a feat of balance and negotiation of his uncooperative legs. He could easily pitch head first from the top step to the landing below.

While Daisy and Roger were busy, in spite of the rain, cleaning and arranging a spot for the dog, Emily took the opportunity to look around the property and poke into some of the sheds and the barn. She used the excuse that she was always on the lookout for old furniture or artwork.

*You never know what you're going to find in a place like this. Keep an open mind, and who knows what might turn up. A good detective never makes uncalculated guesses.*

Mostly the sheds were full of junk, old wood, cobwebs and rotting manure from animals long since dead and forgotten. In the old barn, cow stanchions were still hanging open, waiting for the cows to return for milking. A horse-drawn cart stood in the back of a loafing barn, and a wheelbarrow with a broken handle lay on its side in the shadows. The only sign of recent activity was in the dairy, where someone had set up a woodworking project. Wrenches and screwdrivers lay where they had been discarded for other tools. An electric table saw looked as if it had recently functioned. It was the only piece of equipment not covered with a layer of dust.

*Detectives need to look beyond the obvious*, Emily reminded herself.

Upon closer inspection she discovered the project for which the saw had been used: a new plywood wall closed the far end of the barn, with one small door in the corner. Emily navigated past the feeding stanchions to investigate the recent construction more closely. A large padlock prevented her from opening the door, but bright lights in the room behind the barrier filtered through cracks around the rough concrete floor. Emily also noticed a new heavy electrical cable running into the room from the panel at the dairy.

*A person doesn't have to be a genius to recognize a dope-growing operation when one sees one. Better not to be noticed snooping around here.*

Emily began to wonder whether there was a connection between this farm on Spring Valley with the place which the motorcycle man had spoken to Pete about. Hadn't he mentioned a new gang creating friction in the area?

Satisfied there was little of interest to her in the out buildings, Emily decided to take her investigation right to the source. While Daisy and Roger were chatting happily and the little dog surveyed their progress, Mrs. Blossom retraced her steps. She returned to the back woodshed leading to the house. This time she noticed an old freezer beneath the winter coats, gloves and hats piled on top. She knocked firmly on the door and opened it before she heard a response.

"Hello there," she said in her most chattering tone, as if speaking to newly met friends. "I'm terribly sorry to disturb you again."

The men were still sitting around the kitchen table in a haze of blue smoke. Although cigarettes burned in the ashtrays, Emily noticed that the chubby man held a joint under the lip of the table, cradled in the palm of his hand in his lap. The wafting smell was sweet and clinging.

The four gang members were remarkably different from one another.

One was merely a boy, with short hair and smooth cheeks. He had clear blue eyes, and pimples. He had a small, silver, hooped earring in his left ear and a matching earring in his left nostril. The kid practiced drum rhythms with his hands on the edge of the table. A Coke can bounced and jiggled, adding to the beat. He had the oblivious look of youth: self-absorbed and unaware of the consequences of his actions.

Opposite him was the man who had spoken to Emily earlier. Wearing the T-shirt with the hooded skull staring out from dark shadows, he was the apparent gang leader, donning an air of careless authority. His hair, streaked with grey, was long and straggled over his shoulders, tied back with a bandana perched on the brim of his skull. Emily guessed he was probably self-conscious about his balding spot, afraid any obvious weakness might threaten his influence over the others. He appeared older than the others by about ten years. He wore gold earrings and a chain with a simple cross at his throat. His dark eyes held secrets; he had a look of wisdom beyond his years, incongruous with his surroundings. He was strangely out of place, as if he had been born to inherit comfort and luxury instead of spending time in this dismal setting.

The chubby man with the joint had the expression of a child caught with his hand in the cookie jar; a smile pasted crooked on his face; eyes bloodshot and just a little too wide open. Upon closer scrutiny, Emily realized the man's lips had been scarred into a permanent grin, revealing teeth filed into canine fangs. His whole face was covered in tattoos so his skin was entirely blue and red, with designs so complex they were difficult to decipher. His cheeks were flabby and carried the menace of a sumo wrestler. His round head sat between broad shoulders. Corpulent upper arms braced on knobby elbows made the table sag under his weight. His body was so large it overflowed the seat.

The fourth of the group was tall, slim and snake-like. A handlebar moustache draped itself around his fine, pinched lips. His eyes darted around the room like an adder on the hunt. His ears were rimmed in a series of nuts and bolts. His eyebrows, nose and lips were pierced with a variety of metallic objects. In front of him, was a dish that he pretended was not there. Fine, white powder was laid out in four thin lines on the plate. He wore a black sleeveless shirt revealing his arms covered with tattoos.

"I'm so embarrassed," Emily began to chatter, as if uncontrollably. "I have to go to the bathroom."

She giggled, and her hand strayed to cover her mouth while her eyes twinkled. She had read somewhere that wrinkles around the eyes were enchanting on the elderly. She practiced in front of the mirror to perfect the effect. She could make her wrinkles grow by broadening her smile so that her cheeks pinched upward, causing gloriously enchanting crow's feet to grow from the corners of her eyes.

"My friends are so pokey out there, and I just had three cups of tea before leaving home. The cold rain makes it worse. Would you mind terribly if I asked to use your ladies room? I forgot to wear my Depends today, of all days. Usually I'm very careful not to stray too far from a bathroom, but I just got caught off guard. I hope you don't mind."

The bandana man signalled with a nod that the bathroom was around the corner. "Help yourself."

While scanning the room Emily scurried in the direction indicated, taking note of any detail that might prove interesting. She noticed a pen and ink drawing on the wall above the TV. At first glance the design looked like an intricate Celtic knot, but there was something familiar about the sketch that made her uncomfortable. She couldn't quite put her finger on what bothered her about the details.

Afraid of looking suspicious, she hurried to the bathroom. She studied her smile in the mirror. *Not bad . . . not bad at all. I never imagined that wrinkles would really have any practical advantage. Just goes to show . . . you never know . . . Never jump to assumptions.*

She waited long enough to produce the proper impression of having done her business, and then she flushed the toilet and let the water run in the sink. Then she emerged from the bathroom, smoothing down her clothes and rubbing her hands dry.

"There, that's much better. Thank you so much. You've saved an old lady a good deal of embarrassment."

In the living room a sectional couch was torn and faded. A couple of crumpled blankets on the floor indicated that someone occasionally slept there. Flimsy curtains hung from unhooked rods, with dust accenting the lace patterns. The plaster walls were cracked, showing lath and batten where chunks had fallen to the floor. Two rifles in a gun rack on the wall were the only items in the room not covered with a thick layer of dust. A bookcase with torn paperback books on the shelves and a fifties-style sideboard were the only other pieces of furniture in the room except for an antique upright parlour piano that commanded one corner of the room. The lid was open, and the ivory keys were chipped and worn from use.

"I never expected to see a piano in a house like this," Emily said. "Does one of you play?"

Bandana Man's expression flickered, and Emily realized she had hit a nerve. She fingered the pages of sheet music propped on the rack above the keyboard.

"Someone here must be a pretty good musician. *The Moonlight Sonata* by Beethoven?"

A faint smile trembled on the gang leader's lips.

"Would you play it for me?" She flirted, a tickle of her eyebrows and crow's feet fully engaged. "That's my favourite piece."

B. Man took a deep breath and scraped his chair back from where he sat. He wiped his hands on tattered blue jeans and approached the piano with deference. The skull on the T-shirt stared down at the keys. The pianist's hands brushed the polished surface of the instrument like a tender caress. When he sat at the bench, his stature changed. Raising his arms and crackling his fingers into a backward stretch, he hunched forward and merged with the keyboard.

His fingertips glided effortlessly over the keys, producing a magical sound. Music filled the dingy room and transformed the bleak atmosphere into harmony, invoking images of moonlight on a glassy lake. At first the notes were flat and out of tune, but the master musician was able to create such fluidity in tone and synchronization that soon the piece wove

111

its own melody. He transported the listeners beyond the limitations of the ancient instrument. The room was cast in a trance until the last note faded into silence. Then they all breathed at once; silence filled the space where music had cast its spell. Only then did the drab reality of pervasive negativity reappear.

"Oh, that was simply marvellous," Emily whispered, genuinely overwhelmed. "Thank you so very, very much. What a wonderful gift you have."

B. Man made no comment. He simply lifted himself from the piano bench and returned to his place at the table. He took a sip of cold coffee, as if he had never moved.

"How did you learn to play like that?" Emily asked while glancing around the room, buying time so she could snoop more thoroughly.

B. Man shrugged. "Been playing since I was a kid."

"I bet you was a snot-nosed son-uv-a-b when you was a lad," the fat man said with a twinge of a British accent. "I wouldn' a wanted to be your ol' lady."'

B. Man stood up quickly, knocking his chair backward onto the floor. He grabbed Fat Man by the collar, his face close enough to spit on his surprised victim. "Watch what you're sayin', Fatso!"

The tattoos and wolf teeth apparently did not mean the large man underneath the surface was as brave and evil as he appeared. His scarred lips trembled in spite of his artificial grin, and he begged for mercy.

"I didn't mean it, man! Cool it! I didn't mean nothin'!"

"Don't you ever mention my old lady again!"

"I didn't mean nothin'!" Fatso exclaimed. His eyes were bloodshot, and his flabby cheeks shivered in fear.

"Lay off, man," said the Snake. "Cool it. He's just stupid."

The Kid reminded them they were not alone. "Not in front of the lady."

"Now, now, boys, never mind me," Emily said. "Don't spoil the peaceful mood created by such lovely music. I didn't mean to cause a commotion."

B. Man released his hold on his challenger's shirt and shoved him back onto his chair. Fatso readjusted his collar; the Kid took a sip of his Coke; and the Snake hissed under his moustache. B. Man lit a cigarette and blew smoke into the air while contemplating the ceiling.

Emily casually glanced around the room. She pretended to notice the sketch on the wall by accident. "What an interesting drawing."

Upon closer examination she recognized what had bothered her at first. Instead of a Celtic design, the image was actually intertwining, writhing serpents, each one eating the other's tail. The drawing was crude and hand drawn with a marker on lined note paper, but the artist's intention was quite clear: a vipers' nest. The artist's name, Rosie, was written in miniscule letters in the shadow of a snake's rattle.

Emily shivered as a chill ran up her spine. She thought she recognized a similarity between the snakes in the drawing and the tattoo she had seen on the finger of the severed hand in Daisy's kitchen. She tried to hide her discomfort behind a wide smile of wrinkles. "Do you know the artist? This is a very interesting drawing."

"I think it's time you were leaving," the Snake said. He menacingly approached Emily as if to escort her to the door.

Emily realized she had gone too far. The Snake's darting eyes glared at her, hatred dissecting her as surely as a well sharpened knife. She had no idea what she might have done to offend him, but she didn't wait to find out.

"Thank you again so much. I'll be going along now. It's been very nice meeting you all and have a lovely day."

With that, Emily shuffled out the door. When she emerged, she welcomed the rain pelting her face, washing away the dust and tension she left behind her. She was relieved to see Daisy sitting in her truck with the engine running. This time she had no difficulty slamming the door once she had scrambled into the passenger seat.

**Spring Valley Farm**

# *Chapter Fifteen*

"Well, that was a wonderful adventure," Emily said over the rattle of the truck. "I never expected to have such an interesting experience."

"Yes, I feel much better about the little dog now," Daisy said.

"Did you see how rough that place was? There were some pretty shady things going on around there, I think," Emily said.

"I don't think Roger really has many choices. He told me most people won't rent to him because of his disability and because of his tractor. He can't get a driver's license, so the tractor is his only means of getting around."

"Do you know the people living downstairs? Has he ever mentioned who lives there?"

"No, I really never asked him any personal questions. I don't want to be too nosy." As usual, she tended to see the world from a very different perspective from her sister-in-law. "I thought I was doing some good . . . now I'm not so sure."

"Do you think Roger is in trouble?"

"Oh no, not Roger . . . I was quite worried about Poochie. I'm torn when I see an animal like that little creature at the mercy of whoever takes charge of its life," Daisy said. "Animals are so vulnerable to the whims of humans."

"Don't you trust Roger to take care of him?" Emily asked, glad for a topic that didn't require an explanation of her discoveries on the farm.

"Roger will do his best, but no dog should spend its life chained up."

"I'm sure it's the fate of some inferior beasts to accept whatever happens to them. I got the impression Poochie has suffered a lot worse things, before Roger got hold of him. Besides, Roger needs a mutt. I don't imagine he has all that many friends who care about him the way a dog would. Man's best pal and all that."

"I worry that he won't get fed properly. I worry that he won't have enough water. I worry that he'll be too hot in the summer and too cold in the winter."

"Didn't you tell Roger how to care for him?"

"Oh, yes . . . yes, several times."

"I'm sure you were quite clear about the importance of treating an animal properly."

"Yes I was."

"Well, then, you've done your best. Now let it go. Don't keep dwelling on things you can't control. Worry is a bother. A person should make decisions and move on in life."

"Still, I'm worried."

"Daisy, you're a worry worm."

"Worm? You mean 'wart.' A worry wart? No, I'm not."

"Yes, you're a worry wart. You let things get to you, and then you stew on them for years."

"No I don't. But animals are so innocent. I don't worry so much about people."

"Yes you do. You're a softie through and through."

"No, I'm not. Don't start, Emily. I know how you are. Everyone thinks you're so prim and proper but you're different in private. You always pretend to be so superior, as if you're responsible for telling me about all the things I've done wrong in my life."

"I'm just looking out for your welfare." Emily would not let go this time. She was building up to a discussion that had been brewing for a long time. She had to get it off her chest. "Take Michel for example. You'd have been a lot better off if you just accepted what happened to him and got over it. Like I did with your brother."

"Let's not go there, okay? Michel and my brother—your husband, whom, I might point out, you willingly chose to marry—were not the same and you know it. The situations were entirely different."

"I don't mean to drag up bad memories," Emily said, determined not to let the subject drop without a resolution as it had so many times before. "Michel died under very unfortunate circumstances, I agree, but Daisy, that was 40 years ago. You could have moved on, fallen in love with somebody else. There's lots of other fish. Even Pete was interested at one point, wasn't he? Didn't he hang around your place for a while? Surely you could have done worse than him."

"Pete's not a bad sort," Daisy admitted, "but some people just can't move on. Once you've really had the perfect love, you always compare that person to the new one. Nobody else is ever as good. You can't forget."

"Pshaw." Emily could not help herself. She had always been impatient with indulgent sentimentalism. "Michel wasn't all that great. You've just forgotten. He drank too much. He smoked too much . . . and he was mixed up with the wrong crowd. That's what got him killed. Don't go pretending he was all that perfect. He was flawed, like all men."

"Not with me he wasn't." Daisy gripped the steering wheel so tightly her knuckles were white. Strands of her wispy hair strayed over her cheeks. She brushed the stragglers away, pretending tears had not found an outlet along the wrinkles leading to her mouth.

"You don't need to go getting upset about this. I just think you're missing a great opportunity. Pete won't wait around forever, you know."

"Emily, if you like Pete Picken so much, why don't you take up with him? We discussed marriage long ago, and—"

"You? You discussed marriage with Pete Picken?"

"That was ages ago, and we both realized it wouldn't work out. He's not my type. Besides, I would never really satisfy his needs."

"I'm still trying to get over the fact that you had a relationship with Pete—"

"It wasn't a relationship. It never got to that point. We were just friends."

"—and I never knew about it."

"Emily, there are a lot of things you don't know about." Daisy tried not to sound arrogant. "You just don't know what you don't know."

"You and Pete Picken?"

"Besides, he wouldn't be the easiest person to live with either."

"Yes, perhaps you're right. Let's change the subject. Do you remember the tattoo on that girl's hand?

"Tattoo? What girl?"

"You know, the evidence, the murder victim—she had a tattoo on her hand. Do you remember what it looked like?"

"No, no," Daisy said after some effort to recall the incidents leading up to her grisly discovery. "Everything that day seems a bit of a blur. I can't say I remember a lot of details. I remember we thought she was a nail biter. And remember? We thought she must have been a nervous sort, and not too old. It was almost a child's hand, so soft skinned, so delicate, but I don't remember what the tattoo looked like."

"Well, then, here we are, back on the Hill. I feel safer already. Could you drop me off at the Country Kitchen?"

Daisy pulled close up to the curb so Emily didn't have to step down too far. The clouds opened a window of blue, and sunshine beamed onto shining pavement. An aroma of fresh bread and sweet pastries wafted on spring air from the bakery. Gentle breezes puffed and swirled through the alleys, tickling tulips into sprightly dance.

"Just like Canada," Emily commented, as she descended from the truck. "One moment you're freezing and the next you're basking in sunlight."

Daisy smiled, turning her face to feel the radiating warmth. Rain clouds had completely dispersed, leaving a clear blue sky.

"Would you like to come in? I'll buy you a cup of tea." Emily did not usually offer to buy tea.

"Are you feeling bad for saying such awful things about me?" Daisy quipped. "Perhaps you're apologizing for your bad manners."

"No, Daisy, I have nothing to apologize for. I'm feeling generous. Nothing like a cup of tea to smooth the waves."

"It's too late to smooth the waters, Emily. Really, I have to go back to the farm and finish my chores. Some other time."

"Some other time may be too late." Emily's eyes twinkled as if she kept secrets in her pocket, ready to dole out when the moment presented itself.

"I still have to feed the sheep their second feeding, and the chickens will be needing a bucket of water. I have to get back before Friday eats all the eggs."

"You should do something about that dog," Emily said. "He's useless, and he's a pest."

"Bye, Emily." Daisy gladly put the old truck into gear and drove away, even while Emily still had her hand on the door handle.

# Chapter Sixteen

Emily was just about to enter the café when she spotted Marie Cartier approaching at full throttle. Her hips swung like a pendulum, side to side. Her waddle was accentuated by poor balance over flat Chinese slippers, which barely contained the chubby feet stuffed inside them. She wore a turquoise jacket embroidered with red flowered beads, and her neck was draped with several heavy beaded necklaces. Her flimsy hair was dyed red, but the roots were pepper-grey and thinning. She wore heavy makeup: bright red lipstick and turquoise eye shadow, which matched the jacket. Her dark eyes sparkled.

Emily pretended she was not going into the restaurant, hoping to divert Marie onto a side-track. She redirected her plan, as if to do errands at the other end of town.

"Bonjour! Bonjour! Emilie," Marie sang gaily. "How lovely to meet you on such a beautiful morning. You are like sunshine on a rainy day."

Emily cringed. "Hello, Marie. I'm just headed for the post office to check my mail."

Marie fell into step alongside, her hips and little feet shuffling to keep up.

Emily considerably quickened her stride to test Marie's stamina. The two women, chatting breathlessly, fairly jogged up the street as if they always hurried to get wherever they were going.

Marie asked, "Isn't it terrible? All the junk mail they put in the boxes?"

"Such a waste of trees. All I ever get is fliers and bills."

"I do love to shop by mail, though," Marie said. "It's wonderful all the catalogues you can get, all the most recent fashion trends and products. I love shopping, and today I'm looking for garden furniture."

"Have a good day then. Hope you find what you're looking for." Emily navigated the steps to the post office two at a time.

Luckily, Marie continued toward the hardware store. Emily knew her mailbox would be empty since she'd checked it the day before. She waited until Marie's swinging hips disappeared into Home Hardware and then sauntered back down the street to the Country Kitchen. Emily chose a seat at a small table in the corner.

The Country Kitchen provided shelter for customers in any kind of weather. During the long Canadian winters, Maria's ovens provided a welcome respite from snow and storms. On rainy days, the dining room was warm and dry. On hot days, a cool breeze floated in from the shade of an alleyway next door. Today, a fresh breeze wafted through the dining room, fluffing the curtains and tickling the tablecloths.

The menu was plentiful, but privacy was not one of the amenities offered. There was room for only seven tables. Customers sat beside each other, brushing shoulders and elbows. Conversations flew between tables, and comments from all parties were freely offered, regardless of the topics. Gossip was especially fertile; everyone provided their bits of information, and everyone else spread the news around town. The accuracy of details was not essential—merely an approximation of the facts would do. The townsfolk enjoyed good stories, made all the better with embellishments and dramatic license.

Several customers turned eyes to survey the latest arrivals. Suzanne Duval and her mother were settled into their usual corner table. Old Mrs. Duval was wrapped in her self-absorbed daze, and Suzanne barely glanced up from the book she was reading over muffins and tea. Mrs. Seguin, the would-be mayor, and her mousey friend Dora occupied the table next to the window. They could survey the passersby outside and eavesdrop on conversations inside at the same time. There would be no escape from their prying.

As usual, the Country Kitchen on the Hill was buzzing. All seven tables were full, and the diners were talking at once. Ilsa was busy serving customers, and Maria prepared breakfast in the kitchen. Conversations were animated, varied and equally intense.

Ilsa approached Emily's table for her order.

"So, are they all talking about the murder investigation?" Emily could not help but inquire. "Is the gossip flying?"

"Actually, everything seems to have gone back to normal," said Ilsa. "People have short memories. They don't seem very concerned since nobody seems to know the victim, and no one they know has gone missing."

"That's a small town for you . . . fairly short-sighted if you ask me," said Emily. "I'll have hot tea with a butter tart, please, Ilsa. That'll lift my spirits nicely."

Ilsa gathered up plates and cups and disappeared into the kitchen to prepare her orders. Emily listened in on the various conversations at the other tables.

"I went into the clothing store yesterday, and Marie Cartier was there." Dora was in mid-gossip with the would-be mayor. "She actually had the nerve to say, 'Dora, how long has your hair been so grey? You look so old'. I was so embarrassed; I couldn't do anything but giggle."

"Why didn't you hit her with your purse?"

"I just didn't know what to say. How dare she?"

"That woman should learn to think before she speaks."

"Thinking would be a good start, but I don't think she's actually capable of that."

"Does she consider herself the expert on makeup? She's one of those people who plucks out all her eyebrows."

"Have you seen some of the young girls who actually take off all their eyebrows and then tattoo them back on?"

"What happens if theirs grow back in again? Then they'd have two sets of eyebrows."

"How about the ones who glue on new eyelashes? They add them on to the ones they have."

"It's very expensive."

"What keeps the eyelashes from falling into their eyes?"

At the next table, the ministers of the community were having their weekly get-together: the Presbyterian minister was seated so that he had ample room for his large stomach. Grace, a lay member of what Pete called the "disunited church" sat primly opposite him. Charity Simons, the minister of the United Churches, wore a harried expression due to the disparities between her five congregations all requesting equal attention for half the salary. Reverend Halloway, the Anglican, appeared only vaguely interested in the conversation. Baptists and Catholics were absent, as usual.

"I hear we're offering an ecumenical service at the fairgrounds next month," said Peter the Presbyterian, who had the habit of singing about himself to his parishioners during turkey dinners. "Who is actually going to perform the service?"

"I thought we could choose a passage from the Bible, and all of us would take turns interpreting the meaning," Grace, wide-eyed and enthusiastic, said.

"I'm not sure our minister would be able to attend," Charity Simons said. "We have only one minister, and we are already overcommitted."

"Isn't that the idea?" Grace asked. "We could do one ceremony to bring everyone together."

"Not the Catholics; I doubt they'd come," the singing minister said. "Unless we offered the service in French."

"Even then, the priest probably won't allow his flock to take communion anywhere except in his cathedral."

"What happens if we get Muslims and Jews who are participating? They won't be able to take communion."

"They're not really invited. Ecumenical means Christian."

"Does that include the Baptists?"

"They probably won't come anyway. They do their own thing."

At another table, Serena, a well-respected yoga teacher in the area, tittered with her friends. Ladies who specialized in alternative health therapies were labelled by Pete as "the ologists." They were expounding on the benefits of feng shui.

Constant Black, a retired accountant who frequented the Country Kitchen when he was not glued to the Internet, sat at the table by the window telling Burton Barton, Cecelia Allen's boyfriend, about the impending earthquake that would wipe out all of Eastern Ontario.

"The fault zone runs right through Emerald Hill. These brick houses are not built to withstand earthquakes of that magnitude. We haven't seen anything like it in 5,000 years, so it's only a matter of time."

Franny Appleton was discussing the Women's Institute meeting with her elderly friends Betty Biddy and Ethel North. All three ladies were white-haired. They spoke with expressive hands, fingers adeptly manipulating tea cups and conversational gestures with equal enthusiasm. Their bright eyes twinkled as if they had a lot of experience smiling in spite of many years of sadness.

"There are not that many of us left. Starbrook group is down to two members. Sarah Smiley doesn't go out anymore and can't attend the meetings. Fenahvale is down to three members, and since Wilamena's passing, we're down to five."

"The young people just don't have time anymore. Most of them are working on the farms, raising children and driving to after-school activities every day."

"Not to mention cooking meals and doing housework."

"The WI ladies don't really like changes. They use the same recipe for turkey dressing, the same mashed potatoes and gravy. Don't try to alter the table layout—and heaven forbid anyone should suggest a new décor for the place settings. They've done things the same way time after time. The young women of today get tired of the same old ways of doing things year after year."

"Why fix something that's not broken?" Betty asked. She had never redecorated her kitchen since the day she was married. Her furniture in the brick farmhouse at Happy Valley was arranged exactly as it had been when she moved in 50 years ago.

"We're outdated, plain and simple," Franny said. "It's time we tried something new."

A warning glance passed between Betty and Ethel, but Franny had long since learned to ignore their scepticism.

"I think we should learn belly dancing. The women were talking about it at church. The dancing group is going to do a demonstration at the St. Patrick's Day Parade."

"Pete Picken is announcing the parade again this year. I'm sure he'll have something to say about the belly dancers."

"He always does."

"I'd like to try belly dancing. If they can do it, why shouldn't we?" Fanny asked with a wiggle and a flourish. "I think it would be good for us. Who knows—maybe we'd get some new members to join us!"

"I doubt that," Betty said.

"We could take photos and sell calendars," Ethel said, surprising everyone, even herself, with the idea.

"Really, Ethel!" Betty said. "Don't get carried away."

To dodge the blush on their cheeks, the WI ladies all reached for their tea cups at the same time.

Emily's solitude at her table in the corner did not last long.

"How is Daisy coping with that terrible experience?" Mrs. Seguin asked from across the room. "What an awful dog. Why would anyone keep a dog like that? The neighbour down the road says she can't walk past the place, that the dog comes running out to bark at her."

"Friday is a very good dog." Even though Emily claimed the right to criticize Daisy's dog in Daisy's presence, she would never permit the nosy townsfolk to do so. "He's very obedient. He looks after Daisy and protects her property. People who live in the country need guard dogs."

"Daisy lives alone, way out there all by herself," the would-be mayor said. "I don't know how she does it."

"I'd be afraid to live in the country alone like that," Dora, who usually supported Mrs. Seguin's opinions even if she didn't agree with them, said.

"Who says she's always alone?" Mrs. Seguin said with a suggestive wink designed to elicit gossip. "If I were her, I'd make sure I had someone to drop in to check on me, just in case."

"Daisy Blossom is very independent, and she's quite capable of looking after herself," Emily said.

At this point the bell rang again, and Marie Cartier's large frame blocked out the sunlight as she stood in the doorway. Her grin and sparkling eyes homed in on Emily's table. Too late, Emily realized there was an empty seat at her table.

"I thought I might find you here again. Would you mind if I joined you?" Marie asked with a polite familiarity that was impossible to avoid. "I'm so glad I caught you. I have a question I've been meaning to ask. I hope you don't mind."

Marie had a unique way of grinning sideways and cocking her eyebrows. A slight tip of her head encouraged a lock of hair to fall over one eye, as if she were hiding behind a coy gesture of intimacy. Everyone else's business was her favourite topic of conversation. She whispered at Emily from across the table, "It's about Daisy."

"Why is it that everyone's so interested in Daisy Blossom all of a sudden?" Emily asked for everyone to hear. She considered whispers in secret as dangerous as outright lying. "Nobody ever really cared all that much before."

"Now, now, Emily," the would-be mayor said. "Don't go getting huffy. We're just concerned for Daisy's welfare. She might be in danger, you know. Somebody might think she knows something she shouldn't."

"Actually, I'm more worried about Pete," Marie said.

"Pete?" Emily asked. "What does Pete have to do with Daisy?"

"Pete and Daisy?" Mrs. Seguin repeated, eager for more details she could repeat later.

"Pete loves Daisy?" Suzanne's mother, holding her hand to her ear to try to decipher the conversation, asked.

"That's what I want to know," Marie said. "I heard that maybe Pete got arrested because Daisy put him up to something no good."

"Daisy did not put Pete up to anything," Emily said, "and he wasn't arrested."

"I thought he found the body," Suzanne said, emerging from her book when the discussion became more interesting than fiction.

"The police took him to the station for questioning because he spotted the body in the ditch on the Boundary Road," Emily said. "There's nothing between Pete and Daisy."

"That's what I was hoping," said Marie Cartier. "Daisy's really no match for Pete Picken. He could do a lot better than her."

"You're not suggesting anyone in particular, are you?" Mrs. Seguin asked, winking obviously at her confidante Dora.

"No, no," Marie said. "I just think a lot of people take Pete Picken for granted. I think he deserves better than that."

"Anyone with her eyes on Pete better know how to cook something gooey-in-the-middle," Ilsa said, emerging from the kitchen to take Marie's order. "That boy has quite a sweet tooth."

The bell on the door jingled, and all heads turned.

A police officer entered. The room melted into silence. The black uniform accentuated his ample paunch, decorated with gun holster and belt paraphernalia. His hair was closely clipped. He had dark eyebrows and fleshy lips. His shiny boots clicked on the floor tiles as he made his way to the counter. "Do you have those fabulous butter tarts today?" he asked when Ilsa appeared from the kitchen.

"Yes, they're hot out of the oven," she said. "You came at the right time."

"Great, I'll take half a dozen, and one cup of black coffee to go, please."

Emily tried not to stare, but the sight of the officer reminded her of the next stage of her investigation. She finished her tea and approached the cash register so she could pay her bill before the constable received his order. "Bye, Marie," she said, gathering her coat from the back of her chair. "I'm late for a very important date."

"A date? You have a date?" Marie's face lit up with delight.

The would-be mayor practically fell off her chair.

125

"Emily has a date?" old Mrs. Duval shouted.

Suzanne pretended not to listen.

"It's a figure of speech," Emily said.

Marie's disappointment was so obvious, Emily almost felt guilty. But not quite.

# Chapter Seventeen

Donning her detective's demeanour, Mrs. Emily Blossom left the Country Kitchen just ahead of the constable. She fell into step beside him as he approached his patrol car.

"Officer, may I speak with you just a moment?" she asked in her sweetest, most grandmotherly approach. "I wonder if you're on your way to headquarters in Hamilton Mills. I really need to talk with Inspector Allard. He's expecting me. Would you take me with you?"

"No, ma'am, I'm sorry. It's against the regulations. No civilians in the vehicles."

Emily read the name tag just above his shirt pocket. "Constable Wilson, I'm sorry! Of course you didn't recognize me. I'm not really a civilian. Let me introduce myself: Mrs. Emily Blossom—*the* Mrs. Emily Blossom, also known as Detective Emily Blossom. I'm the one who helped solve Emerald Hill's only murder. Inspector Allard and I are working on another case together."

Emily did not miss the raised eyebrows and sceptical expression the officer cast down on her from his officious height. Emily was quite accustomed to strangers assuming she was tiny and frail. She made it a point to rectify their mistake by drawing herself to her full four foot, ten-and-a-half inch height. She lifted her chin to emphasize her authority and lowered her voice to a commanding alto.

"Perhaps you should either confirm with Inspector Allard by cellular communication or take my word as an order, young man, because if your superiors were to find out—not from me, you understand, Wilson; I would never rat on a poor unfortunate officer—that wouldn't be very considerate, now would it? If your superiors were to find out that you refused to convey me to headquarters, I would not want to be in your shoes, trying to explain how you did not recognize the importance of my request, and why you did not immediately comply."

She could see him wavering.

"Your grandmother must be so proud of you, young man. You're so handsome in that uniform. She must tell all her friends how pleased she is that you have become so successful."

His cheek muscles flickered. She thought she saw his resolve wavering, so she continued in the most convincing manner she could muster.

"How would you ever explain your dismissal, if you refused an undercover detective her most urgent request?"

"Have you got any identification on you, ma'am? I'm not aware of any undercover detectives operating in this area."

"I operate in an unofficial capacity . . . quite successfully, I might add . . . I suggest you phone Inspector Allard; he'll give you the assurances you need."

Without taking his eyes off Emily, Constable Wilson reached through the open window of his vehicle and retrieved the receiver.

"Allo, Station Hamilton Mills. Ici, Wilson. *J'ai quelqu'un devant moi qui s'appelle* Madame Emily Blossom. *Elle me demande que je l'amène au bureau central. Elle veut voir Inspecteur Allard. Est ce que j'ai la permission de l'apporter la bas?* There's a Mrs. Emily Blossom here who's asking me to bring her to the station to see Inspector Allard. Do I have permission to do so? Please advise."

"*Un moment, s'il vous plaît.*" The receptionist's voice crackled over the air and went silent. Wilson peered down at Emily as he waited for a response.

"You're doing the right thing." Emily reassured Constable Wilson with a gentle pat on the shoulder. "You'll see."

The young constable was obviously dubious. He regarded her with a mixture of curiosity and fear. If she really were an undercover agent, she certainly wore a good disguise; if she were just a crazy old broad, he would have been embarrassed to have been taken in by her manipulation. Permission came in over the walkie-talkie.

"*Oui, tu peux la ramener au bureau.* You can bring her into the station. Inspecteur Allard wants to talk with her."

Emily gently pried the box of butter tarts out of his hands and approached the passenger's side of the vehicle. Holding the pastry box with two hands like a treasure chest, she indicated with a nod and a wink that he should open the door for her. A quick glance back at the Country Kitchen reassured her that her manoeuvre had not gone unnoticed by the clients of the diner.

"That's a good boy," she said as he helped her into the seat. "I knew you'd recognize the face of reason when you heard it. Inspector Allard is an intelligent man. He knows I'll have some very interesting information to help him with his investigation."

# Chapter Eighteen

Emily watched as the young constable struggled to fit himself behind the wheel. The bulletproof vest and bulky gun belt of his uniform were difficult to manipulate into the small space of the driver's seat.

"You hardly look old enough to be driving," said Emily. "Your grandmother must be so proud that you turned out so well."

"Yes, ma'am."

He turned the key and navigated the back streets of the village to the highway, leading to Hamilton Mills.

"While we're on our way, catch me up on the investigation, young man. What have the police been doing? Has anyone conducted tests on the hand? What about the body parts in the bag? Did they fit together like a jigsaw puzzle? Do they know the identity of the deceased yet? I'm dying to know what's been happening on your end."

"I'm sorry, ma'am, I'm not permitted to discuss the details of any case with a civilian. Even if I knew what progress Inspector Allard has made . . . which I don't."

"I'm hardly your ordinary civilian, Constable Wilson." Emily puffed herself up and sniffed loudly. "I have my own investigation underway, I can assure you. I was just wondering whether the police were making any progress on their end."

"I haven't spoken to Inspector Allard, and I'm not assigned to that investigation at this point."

"Well, young man, I'm sure you'll work your way up the ranks to a position of responsibility eventually. In the meantime, I do appreciate your very kind offer to drive me to my meeting with the inspector. I'll put in a good word for you with him when I see him."

"Yes, ma'am."

Constable Wilson escorted her to the reception area, where he indicated she should take a seat until Inspector Allard was ready to see her. Emily reluctantly released her grip on the precious cargo of pastry into his care.

A receptionist sat behind a partition, out of Emily's view. Her desk was well below the level of the window with a hole, through which visitors had to speak.

As Wilson disappeared into the inner offices, pastry box in hand, Emily heard him say, "Hey, lovely lady, feast your girlish figure on these here tarts—the best butter tarts in the world, from the loveliest town in the province."

Emily's curiosity was piqued; she tried to imagine what a lovely lady with a girlish figure feasting on tarts would look like. As soon as the door closed behind the constable, she stood up and wandered, as if aimlessly, around the room. The walls were bare: no notices, bulletin board or paintings. The décor was designed as if to say, "This is a serious place of business. No distractions allowed." She casually approached the window behind which the receptionist was hidden. She raised herself onto tiptoes to look down over the partition, through the bulletproof window.

She was surprised to see an elderly woman, with glasses that magnified her eyes to look like marbles, and hair the colour of late autumn straw. The secretary had a trace of crumbs around the corners of her lips, which fell into her lap when she spoke with her mouth full. "May I help you?"

"Oh, yes, I was just wondering . . . have you ever had better butter tarts?"

"They're very good, absolutely, but I shouldn't eat them too often. Not good for my sugar levels."

"You know what they say, 'There's no calories in Country Kitchen cooking'."

"Is that right?"

"Oh yes. Maria the cook uses special ingredients—only real butter and maple syrup. So no calories at all. In fact, they're very healthy."

"Thank you for telling me that, Mrs. Blossom. You've made my day."

Emily smiled and returned to her seat.

*I'm certainly glad to know that girlish figures are not restricted to a person's age,* she thought.

In the waiting room, a large clock dominated the room. The second hand steadily clicked off the minutes into hours.

*Time is strange,* Emily thought. *Ticking away the seconds into minutes; circular, not linear; cyclical and repetitious, always returning to where it began, yet never the same concurrence. People's lives run much the same way: each on one's own path from birth to death; some ending almost before beginning, like what happened to our young murder victim . . . and mine at the other end of the pendulum. I am at a stage where the roulette wheel is losing options. My chances of survival become slimmer with every breath I take.*

*Funny how the youth are not afraid of dying. They live every day to the fullest. As for us old timers, we worry all the time about the future. We've already enjoyed years of hours and 60 times more minutes of experience, yet we're more afraid of dying than the young people who have more to lose. The older I get, the more I marvel at how life takes twists and turns we never expect. Yet time is so predictable: running through 24 hour days, with the sun rising every day, and the stars in their constellations, always the same . . . until infinity.*

Emily's meditations on time lulled her into a comfortable snooze.

"Mrs. Blossom?"

She had no idea how long she had been waiting when Allard's greeting startled her awake. She pretended she was alert, even though she had difficulty at first remembering where she was and why she had come to the police station. "Oh, allo, Inspector Allard, *comment ça va*? I have so much to tell you. My investigations are proceeding quite nicely. I'm so glad you had the time to see me."

*

Inspector Allard was a tall man. He was used to looking down at his suspects, but the little woman who chattered beside him was almost out of sight. All he could see was the top of her head and the tip of her nose as she trotted down the hall to his office. He was relieved when he could offer her a seat so they were looking at each other eye to eye. Then he could see her vivacious enthusiasm, highlighted by sparkling grey eyes and an enchanting map of wrinkles that animated each word she said.

"That nice young constable who brought me here should receive a special citation. He immediately recognized I was an important resource in your investigation into the murder at Blossoms' Corners. I commend him for his insight and assistance. Please tell him I said so."

Allard, to this point, had not spoken. He didn't need to. Emily was perfectly capable of carrying on a conversation for two.

She went on unabated. "I've been doing my homework, Inspector Allard, and I have three plausible suspects in the case. First, the gun dealer, Johnny Aimer: I visited his place recently and am convinced he is a criminal—selling guns should be illegal—but I don't think he's our murderer.

"Second, there's a member of the Hell's Angels living just on the outskirts of Hamilton Mills who offered to sell Pete Picken some antiques. He actually seems rather off his rocker. He would be perfectly capable of committing such a crime, but I'm not sure he's got a motive.

"Third, but not least: I came across a rather seedy group of men up on Spring Valley Road who could be our suspects. I think we should definitely follow up on them."

With his elbows on a pile of papers on his cluttered desk, Allard fingered a pen, tossing it between his fingers like a majorette practicing with a baton. The faster Emily talked, the faster the pen twirled, until it went flying across the room and conveniently interrupted her flow of information.

Allard retrieved the pen and his side of the conversation. "Mrs. Blossom, I do appreciate your enthusiasm, but your lack of experience as a detective is hindering your objectivity."

Emily sniffed and wiggled in her chair. *Detectives are born, not made . . . or is it the other way around? I can't quite remember this one.*

Allard persisted. "I appreciate your efforts, but perhaps you might listen to a few words of caution from a seasoned policeman.

"You need to know some details about the criminal element. Gangsters are not the same as weapons dealers, and petty thieves are hardly going to commit murder. You have to be able to tell the difference before you go looking for suspects in such a heinous crime as the one committed in this case."

"Yes, yes, that's what I'm saying. Johnny Aimer needs to be brought to trial; a person should be accountable for selling guns to dictators to put down idealistic protestors. However, I did realize he's not going to get mixed up in chopping up young women. He lets other people do the killing and pretends he is merely providing a service to those defending freedom. We all know it's the innocent ones who get caught in collateral garbage."

"Garbage? Don't you mean damage?"

"Yes, yes, that's what I said, collateral damage."

"Mrs. Blossom, you should be more careful about what you say in public. Men in Aimer's position don't take kindly to public criticism. He works very hard to maintain a low profile in this community."

"As well he should," Emily said, ruffling her feathers and obviously settling in for a frank discussion. "Inspector Allard, let's understand each other. I'm an old woman. I've lived a long life. I have nothing to lose and everything to gain by saying what I think. I've spent too much of my life being quiet and proper. If I have regrets, it's that I didn't speak up when I had a reason to. I always deferred to others. Now it's time for me to act."

"I understand, but we're not playing games here, Mrs. Blossom."

"Won't you call me Emily, Inspector? I appreciate respect for the elderly, but I'd rather you, of all people, use my given name. It's more informal."

"Whoever committed this murder really won't care all that much whether you're elderly or not. They've proven they're perfectly capable of brutal violence. I don't want another homicide on my desk. I don't want to be picking up your body parts in the ditch, Mrs. Blossom. If you get in the way of these guys, they might very well decide to wipe you out too."

"Inspector Allard, I'm quite capable of talking my way out of difficult situations. Besides, no one suspects me. They think I'm a stupid, little old lady. No one takes me seriously."

"That's the point, Mrs. Blossom. I take you very seriously, and I'm telling you to stay out of danger."

"Don't you worry, Allard. I'll look after myself. Now, back to my suspects."

"Mrs. Blossom, we already have a prime suspect. In fact, we have two suspects. We're just waiting to complete the paperwork in order to make the arrests. That's what I wanted to talk with you about."

Emily puffed herself to her fullest size with pride. "You want to consult me, Detective Emily Blossom, for advice? Finally. This is very exciting. How can I help you?"

"I believe Daisy Blossom is your sister-in-law. Is that correct?"

Allard's tone of voice changed so subtly, Emily almost missed the innuendo. He was now interrogating a collaborator; however, she apparently was no longer on his side; she was a participant in the scene of the crime.

She suddenly became aware of a hush in the room, as if sound was stifled by an ominous cloud. The furniture was drab, and the décor purely functional. Even the walls were cold as grey steel.

"Daisy Blossom? Yes, she is—was—my husband's sister. I mean, he's dead, and she was his sister. I guess that still makes us sisters-in-law. She's not dead. I've known her since before I was married. Why?"

"Are you aware she was once involved with a man who was known to police as a member of the Mafia in Montréal? Michel . . . Michel . . . ?"

"Yes, Michel Mercure. He was murdered years ago. Daisy's heart was broken. I don't think she ever really recovered. We were talking about that just this morning. But what does that have to do with the present murder?"

"Really, Mrs. Blossom!" Allard could hardly disguise his disdain for her lack of insight. "You don't honestly believe Mrs. Blossom is not involved, that it's just a coincidence the body was found near her property? That Pete Picken came across the remains of a murder victim just by accident!"

"Pete Picken?" Emily's head was reeling. "Daisy Blossom?" She could not comprehend what Allard was getting at. "Murder?"

"Yes, we have fingerprints on the evidence. We're just confirming identification."

"Inspector Allard, you couldn't be more mistaken. Daisy Blossom can't even kill a fly in her own kitchen. She saves every stray and wayward animal for miles around and nurses them back to health, when most people would give them up for dead. Daisy's just not capable of murder. And Pete? Well, we all know Pete. He's as gentle as a lamb underneath that gruff exterior. No, no, no, it's not possible. I can't believe you really . . . you'd actually consider . . . no, no. You're totally wrong, barking up the tree in the wrong direction."

"My experience is that the victim is usually known to the perpetrators," he said.

"You know who the young lady is—was—then?"

"No, we haven't found a match to the fingerprints yet."

"What about motive?" Emily could hardly maintain a level tone to her voice, but she knew she had to present a professional appearance. *A detective's analytical skills are only credible if she appears to be objective.*

"We suspect they're hiding something. We found all the remains of the body in Pete's truck, except the head. Their motive is still under investigation."

"Inspector Albert Allard, I have great respect for your integrity and ability as a detective, but you've gone astray on this one. Perhaps you've forgotten to consider your suspect's history and lifestyle. There's no way

Daisy Blossom has ever had any involvement with the criminal element, aside from choosing the wrong guy to fall in love with in her foolish youth. She lives down on that farm by herself and hardly even goes to town for groceries. The only people who visit are locals; mostly they drop in on her to check to make sure she's okay. And Pete Picken may be lots of things, but he's no criminal. I'll vouch for that."

Allard quizzically lifted one eyebrow and looked askance. "You're hardly an objective witness when it comes to Pete Picken, Mrs. Blossom. Isn't that right?"

"Objective?"

"You do spend a good deal of time with the man, isn't that correct?" he said. "You've been seen in his truck."

"Sometimes we go antiquing together, and we did collaborate on solving that murder in town. I mean, I did ask for his assistance when I needed transportation. As you know, I don't drive. But I wouldn't say we're seeing each other. He'd be totally horrified to hear anyone suggest such thing."

"I see," he said, obviously not seeing at all.

"He prides himself on his independence—especially from women."

"Is that so?"

"He likes to keep us all guessing." The explanation seemed quite plausible to Emily, but did not appear to sway Allard from his suspicions.

"That's how he gets so many home-cooked meals."

"Oh?"

"For free."

"Um." Emily was beginning to feel trapped in a way she never anticipated.

*Distract the opponent,* she thought. *Change the subject.*

"Inspector Allard, what about the tattoo?"

"Tattoo? Whose tattoo?"

"The one on the victim's hand. I believe there was a tattoo, but I didn't get a clear look at it."

Before he could answer, the inspector's cell phone rang. A break in the interrogation was very welcome.

"Yes, thank you," he said to the caller, "I'll be right there." He closed the phone and stood up, towering above Emily, who sat in a chair with her feet barely touching the floor. "If you'll excuse me, Mrs. Blossom, I'll be right back."

Emily could not decide whether the call had been planned or had been excellent timing. In any case, she folded her hands in her lap and scanned the room while she waited for his return.

As soon as Allard shut the door, leaving her alone, Emily looked around the room for some indication of interrogations that had taken place here previously. The walls were painted beige. There were no distractions: one door . . . that was all; no windows, no decorations; a table, two chairs with hard seats and straight backs. The room was designed for strict utility, nothing more. There was no indication of previous occupants. There were very few scuff marks on the wall; no cigarette burns; no dents where a person might have slammed the wall with a fist in anger; no visible drama anywhere.

# Chapter Nineteen

There was nothing else to do. Emily soon tired of sitting, so she decided to make use of her time.

She followed Allard down the hall, looking for a door she assumed would be closed. The "Evidence Room, Authorized Personnel Only" sign showed her where to go. She hoped someone had left without locking.

*You can always count on people, even the police, to be sloppy once in a while, when their guard is down.*

She pushed down on the handle. The knob was firmly locked.

*No such luck.*

Emily put her ear to the door. She heard someone shuffling papers inside. Then she heard footsteps approaching from inside the room.

*Quick thinking will save the day.*

Glancing around, she spied a vending machine at the end of the hallway. A small space behind it was just large enough for her to tuck herself into the shadows. The butter tart–eating receptionist emerged and trotted down the hallway. Emily quickly tiptoed to the door before it closed and sneaked into the room.

The cupboards were neatly labelled. Packages of green leafy marijuana lined shelves beside plastic bags of white powder, all locked behind wire cages. Each item was like a speechless witness to crimes committed in the underbelly of Eastern Ontario.

Emily was looking for a refrigerator or freezer, and she was not disappointed. The fridge was almost empty. Without hesitation, she opened the freezer compartment.

She recognized the small severed hand lying, palm up, in a freezer bag marked "For DNA Sampling." The gesture was frozen in time: fingers slightly raised and open; thumb cupped; dirty cracks in the skin and bitten fingernails. The open palm was like a supplication from someone begging for a pittance.

*A small life, but the only one she had. Daisy's right: the young have so much to lose. She would have had so much more to learn.*

Emily picked up the package and examined the hand more closely. The tattoo quite clearly depicted a frightening image: a snake with an evil eye wound around the ring finger of her left hand, with its own tail in its teeth.

*Just like the drawing I saw at the Spring Valley house this morning.*

Emily was startled by a sharp scolding.

"Mrs. Blossom, I must ask you to leave immediately!"

Allard's voice startled her so badly she dropped the evidence on the floor. The sound of ice hitting tile cracked the silence of the room.

"I was looking for the ladies' room," she protested. "You made me so nervous, I just had to—"

"The door is clearly marked."

Emily could not stifle the tickle of a contrite smile on her lips.

"I took the liberty of including myself in the category of authorized person, considering my skills as an accomplished detective, you understand."

"I see you found what you were looking for," Allard said.

The two bent at the same time to retrieve the bag, and Emily knocked Allard's reading glasses off his head when she stood up. They attempted to retrieve the glasses, and this time, their hands brushed one another's. The physical contact between them broke the tension, as if releasing static electricity. They laughed, and he put his hand on her shoulder to escort her back to the interrogation room.

"You're quite the ticket," he said. "Whoever made you must have broken the mould when they were finished."

"Luckily for the world," she agreed. "I don't think there would be room for two of us."

When he had closed the door behind them, Emily resumed discussion on a more serious note.

"I think that's a very good idea about the DNA sampling of the evidence. Perhaps you'll find some foreign DNA from the people who handled the body . . . in addition, of course, to dog DNA from Friday."

She smiled, obviously pleased at her own cleverness.

"I gather you have not identified the victim," she said. "What about a portrait shot? Do you know what she looked like? I'm assuming the person is a female. The hand looked so petite and delicate."

"Yes, we've confirmed the female gender of the victim from the remains found in Picken's truck," said the inspector.

"The head is missing. That's the one part of the body not accounted for."

"Strange that the head would be missing . . . but then, that would be the primary means of identifying the body quickly, I suppose. The murderers would probably prefer to delay positive identification if they're buying time to make a getaway."

"That would rule out our current suspects," admitted Allard. "Neither Miss Blossom nor Mr. Picken seem to be in a hurry to hide."

Emily was quick to deflect the suspicions against her friends. "Precisely, Inspector; there's very little motive for them to commit such a crime. However, I believe the tattoo on the ring finger of this young woman is significant. I have some important information to follow up on."

"We have no time, Mrs. Blossom. We need to make an arrest."

"Please, delay the request for arresting your suspects, just a day. I believe I can deliver your real murderers, with undeniable proof, if you just give me some time. If you arrest Daisy and Pete, you will be very embarrassed when they prove to be innocent, and the real criminals will have a chance to get away."

"The real criminals?"

"Your superior officer would not appreciate a false arrest, but he would be very impressed if you were able to solve this terrible crime within days of finding the body."

"My superior officer?"

"No community likes the idea of having a serial killer on the loose, not the least, sleepy little Emerald Hill. The national media would love to get their hands on this story."

"The national media?" Inspector Albert Allard finally began to get the picture. "Tell me what you're up to then," he said.

Inspector Allard did not really understand why he listened to this mite of a woman, except that he had been very well trained—by his mother. How Emily could convince him to take her seriously had a lot to do with his own mother. She was small and feisty too. All his life she had dictated to him how to run his life: what to study in university; whom to marry; which house to buy. She even bought his shirts for him; she knew better than he did what colour best matched his blue eyes. He went every Friday to her house for dinner, without his wife, who was never invited. He called her every day. In fact, it was she who had just interrupted his discussion with Mrs. Blossom to tell him to bring his laundry to the cleaners. There was a striking resemblance between Mrs. Allard and Mrs. Blossom, and the detective inspector had a healthy respect for both of them.

"I don't have too many details at this point," Detective Blossom said. "Let's just put it this way: you would be hard-pressed to get a search warrant based on the evidence at hand—if you'll excuse the pun. But I believe I can get you plenty of proof very shortly, to support a judge's order for a raid. For example, are you aware of a grow-op on Spring Valley Road?"

"Spring Valley?"

"I didn't think so."

She hesitated. He rose to her bait.

"There's a grow-op on Spring Valley Road?"

"Yes," she said with finality. "There's also a sawmill, where someone might cut up a body, and a large freezer, where such a body could be stored. There's more too: an exterior furnace where one could burn bodies—or parts thereof—quite easily. But the real clue is a drawing on the wall in the house, which could be directly linked to the tattoo on our dead woman's finger."

"Really?"

"Yes, but I can't prove it yet."

"Mrs. Blossom, are you leading me on just to protect your friends?"

"Inspector, you know me better than that."

"Yes, I do; that's why I'm asking."

"Discretion is the better part of value. That's why I need more time. Just give me a few days."

"A few days? I thought you said one day."

"I need a bit of leeway, in case I hit a snag."

"Snag?"

"You know what I mean. Now, could you ask that lovely Constable Wilson to drive me back to Emerald Hill? I'll get on the case right away, as soon as I can put my plan into action."

"Mrs. Blossom, with all due respect, you have no business snooping around pretending to solve crimes that you know nothing about. Give me the information you have collected, and I'll conduct this investigation . . . not you. If you do not comply, I'll have to arrest you for obstruction of justice."

Emily stood up and collected her purse.

"Now, now, Inspector, that won't be necessary. I promise I'll cooperate in every way possible. Just give me a little more time. I'll be in touch."

She gently closed the door as she left the interrogation room.

He felt as if a weight had been lifted from his shoulders. He wasn't sure if it was because she was gone from sight or whether he actually had confidence she would be able to follow through on her leads and her intuition. He knew he would be hearing from her soon. He just hoped she would bring good news and not disaster. In the meantime, his mother was expecting him to return her call and confirm that he would be at her bridge party next week, to meet her friends and to serve them tea.

# *Chapter Twenty*

By the time Emily and Daisy were on their way to Spring Valley, Pete Picken had already put in almost a full day's work. On Tuesday mornings, Pete rose before dawn. He and his truck were on the road heading east by the time daylight brightened the horizon, a thin line of rose and turquoise beyond dark hills. His destination was the flea market on the Quebec side, a gathering place for antique dealers from Eastern Canada and the United States. Strong Tim Horton's coffee and the thrill of the chase quickened his heartbeat.

On the way to the flea market, Pete gave himself a pep talk. One of the hazards of the antique business was buying too much and selling too little. There was a thin line between antiques and junk. A growing inventory of items he couldn't sell tied up money which could be spent to make a profit on something more marketable. He also had a tendency to buy tools and clothes which he did not really need. He had developed an imaginary conversation in his head to help keep himself from buying unnecessarily.

He called his imaginary characters Sales and Purchasing. On his way to the market they usually had the same discussion.

Sales: We've been doing pretty well lately, selling what you've been buying, but don't mess up today by contributing to dead stock.

Purchasing: It all depends on what's out there. If we get there in time, we won't miss the bargains, but you never can tell who gets in ahead of you.

Sales: Don't get greedy. Look more carefully before you buy. Last week you were lucky to get rid of that table you bought with the broken leg, but you got stuck with the box with the bad paint job. It was made to look old but it was new as the dawning day.

Purchasing: If you don't take chances, you might miss something special.

Sales: We've got a whole shed full of something specials that we couldn't sell.

Purchasing: That's inventory.

Sales: We don't need inventory. What we need is income.

Purchasing: Right!

Sales: Right!

Pete grinned. He was happy with his pep talk to himself. He felt optimistic about his prospects of making money. Seldom was he more content than when he was driving in his truck in pursuit of a good deal.

This was his favourite time of the day, when the line on the pavement led directly to the base of the sunrise and the sun burned the ribbon of road to an orange glow. The rhythm of the tires pulsed on hardtop. The cool air was brisk and invigorating, but the heater in the cab kept him warm and cozy.

The countryside slept: inhabitants lay in their beds; frites stands stood with empty parking lots; church bells remained silent; and houses' windows were dark and cars were parked in the driveways.

However, as he approached the market grounds, activity was well underway. Trucks laden with odd shapes and curiosities pulled into the lot. Shadows of vendors arranged tables and unloaded boxes of items wrapped in newspaper. Furniture balanced precariously on the grass. Occasionally the tinkle of breaking glass meant someone lost a potential sale. Buyers with flashlights wandered the field, shining beams into truck cabs and trunks to find hidden treasures. Dark figures rushed to and fro, poking and prodding, trying to get the dealers' attention to make an offer before their competitors saw what was for sale.

Purchasers and vendors alike observed an unspoken etiquette: once a potential buyer asked for a price on an item, no one else was permitted to make an offer unless the first client turned down the deal. If the buyer bought an item, he was permitted to flip the purchase for a profit to anyone willing to pay more.

As the sun brightened the field, more buyers and sellers appeared. The market became a colourful hive of activity: items changed hands, vehicles were loaded and unloaded and bills rolled off in wads and were counted out loud. Offers, haggling and bargains were conducted in English and French. Jokes bounced around the field interspersed with laughter and exclamations of French slang swear words like "tabernac" and "colin de bin."

Anything and everything was for sale, from clothing to vegetables to household wares to animals. Whatever the human race discarded might eventually turn up at the flea market: outdated computers, sinks with taps, beds, barrels (old and new), vintage and vinyl, shining or broken. Wonders of the human imagination were represented here at some time in some form. Money kept score, but the art of the deal was usually far beyond the actual price of settlement.

In the skill of bargaining, few could match Pete Picken.

At one point, he spotted a homemade pedal car. The toy was wooden, painted red, with chrome headlights and a handmade steering wheel—it even had a little grille on the front.

"*Combien pour ça?*" he asked the dealer. "How much?"

"*Cent pieces.* A hundred dollars. "

"*Cinquante?*"

"Ah, monsieur, Monsieur Pete, I'm not going to take $50 for that piece. It's worth much more. *Donnes moi quatrevingt.* Give me 80, and it's yours."

"*Je te donnerai soixante.* How about 60? That's enough. *Ça c'est suffisant.*"

"*Oh, monsieur, pas capable, pas capable.*"

Then Pete got to use his favourite line: "*Pas capable est mort, son frere s'appelle essayer.* 'Can't' is dead; his brother's called 'Try'."

"*Ah, monsieur, je peux pas . . . soixante quinze, ça suffit.*"

"*Soixante quinze.* Okay."

Pete peeled off $75 and handed it to the dealer. Together they hoisted the little red car into the back of the pickup truck.

As the day grew brighter, the hype dimmed. The antique dealers started to fade away. They took their purchases, loaded their trucks and headed for home to begin work. Pete had seen pretty well everything there was of interest, as far as he could tell. He bought what he could. He missed some things. He was sorry about that old cupboard somebody else had gotten to ahead of him, but in the long run he was probably better off without it. There was no backing, the crown moulding was missing and the door was cracked. Too many repairs would raise the cost beyond profit, and he had too much unsold, dead stock in the shed.

*That's just about all I'm gonna buy,* he thought.

By full daylight, Pete was feeling satisfied. He had sold one of the tables he carried on the rack of his truck and was able to purchase two good lamps and a dish cupboard, which he was confident he would sell at a good profit. He had even bought some ladies' hats. Fashion was always in style among vintage clothing enthusiasts. Most of the good deals were gone, but he was still poking around, browsing.

As he was leaving, one of the vendors approached his truck.

"Pete," he said in perfect English. "I got something just for you. Come on over to my truck before you leave. I'll show it to you."

Just then the toy car salesman knocked on the hood of his truck. He had a toy gun in his hand, made of wood and painted brown, with a fake trigger.

Pete said, "*Non, monsieur. J'achete pas ça.*"

"But it's the same vintage as the car. *Faite par le même gars.* Made by the same guy. Folk art, you know."

"No, I don't buy guns. They give me the willies. Not even the fake ones. I don't buy anything that even looks like a weapon. Thanks anyway." Pete wandered over to the end stall, where his friend Shorty had told him he had something of interest.

"Look in my truck over there," Shorty said. The truck was an old beaten up pickup with Ontario license plates.

When Pete glanced inside, there was a box of old milk bottles and a dented, oily chainsaw in the back. "What you got here?" He reached into the box and took out one of the bottles. "Emerald Hill Dairy, Emerald Hill, Ontario. Whoa, these are kinda cool. How many of them are there?"

"Three. You don't see those anymore, you know. It's been a long time since there was a dairy in Emerald Hill."

"I'll say. I never even heard of it before."

"Oh yeah, there was an old farmer, MacDonald, who had a dairy. They used to fill those bottles and deliver them around town. When the train stopped at the station, they would pick up the milk and deliver it to Montréal."

The bottles had a picture of a rather fat cow, with a large udder, big ears and soft eyes, looking backward.

"They're pretty cool. How much you want for them?"

"Gimme ten bucks apiece."

"Ten bucks!"

"They're rare. You don't see too many bottles like that anymore. It's worth it. There'll be somebody on Emerald Hill give you good money for those."

"You know I'm a sucker for anything that says Emerald Hill on it."

"Yes, I know."

"What's this chainsaw you got here?"

"Oh, that's just a hunk a junk. I got the bottles and the chainsaw from the same guy. I doubt it runs. He certainly wasn't a woodcutter."

Pete took a closer look. He had a weakness for tools. He owned several chainsaws, but none worked. One would break, and he'd get it fixed and use another one until it broke. He cut his own wood for the winter. To keep the house warm, he kept the stove stoked.

He lifted the chainsaw out of the truck for closer scrutiny. When he realized what he was looking at, he felt sick to his stomach. Close to the base of the chain he realized the saw blade wasn't covered with grease, as he had at first assumed. It was covered with blood. Between the links was skin, and some hair—human hair—stuck between the teeth of the chain.

"Where'd you get this?" he asked.

"Some guy whose name I don't know. I never saw him before. He said he lived on Spring Valley Road south of Emerald Hill. He came up to my place last week. He said he had some tools and milk bottles and a couple of other things he wanted to sell."

"What'd he look like?"

"He was tall and thin and kind of gawky. He wasn't a man to use a chainsaw, that's for sure. He had tattoos all over his arms, snakes and devils—nasty lookin' things—metal in his ears, a long ponytail and shifty eyes. I just bought the stuff to get rid of him. I didn't want to know anything about him. I didn't pay him much money. He was pretty quick to want to get rid of the stuff. In fact, he sold me the milk bottles and threw the chainsaw in for free.

"I don't want anything for that piece of junk. Give me $30 for those bottles and take the chainsaw too."

Pete stored the bottles safely in his cab and put the chainsaw in the back, along with all the other things he bought that day. He handed Shorty $30. "Well, that's enough for me for today."

"Did you get some good things?"

"Yeah, I didn't do too bad."

"Times are tough. I don't know. It's not looking too promising this year. There's not many buyers."

"It'll pick up once the weather gets warmer. June, July, things'll get a lot busier. During the construction holidays end of July, there's always lots of people."

"Well I hope so. You gotta live on somethin'."

"Thanks a lot. Let me know if you get anything interesting," Pete said.

# *Chapter Twenty-One*

Pete climbed into his truck and headed down the highway. He didn't feel all that great about having that chainsaw in the back of his truck. However, he thought his friend Emily would be very interested in it.

Around about this time of the morning, he started to feel a little bit dozy. He'd already put in a full day's work buying and selling, and the warmth of the sunshine on the windshield lulled him into daydreaming about butter tarts and beer. The truck practically knew its way back home across the bridge into Ontario. He wasn't paying much attention when he got to the foot of the bridge.

Before he knew better, he saw police lights and heard a siren. He looked around to see who was getting caught. He couldn't believe it was him. His truck was being pulled over. He drove onto the shoulder. The cop obviously wanted to talk to him. He got out of the truck before the constable had a chance to approach the driver's seat.

The cop said, "That your truck, Pete Picken?"

"Yeah. That's me."

There wasn't much point in denying the obvious. The sign on the furniture rack read, "Picken in His Truck," and then in smaller letters along the bottom: "'Picken's the name, Antiques the game."

"Well, I'm afraid we're going to have to take it in."

"Take my truck?" Pete asked, repeating the words as if to better understand their meaning. "I can't . . . you can't take my truck! But why?"

"They want it for evidence. That murder down at Blossoms' Corners . . . apparently they think you had something to do with it."

"I didn't have anything to do with the murder. All I did was pick up garbage by the side of the road. It just so happened that garbage was full of body parts. I didn't have anything to do with it."

"Yeah, yeah, maybe so, but it's not up to me. They have an order out to impound the truck. There's a tow truck standing by to take it to the impound yard."

"Well, I . . ." Pete didn't know what to say. He was lost. The mere idea of not having his truck was beyond comprehension. He could not actually fathom the concept of being without his truck.

The cop called a tow truck that was on standby. The driver arrived and loaded the truck onto the ramp with a clanking of chains and squeal of hydraulic pumps. Seeing his prized vehicle chained and helpless was like torture for Pete.

He rode with the tow truck driver to the yard to see where his precious cargo was going. The impound yard was surrounded by an eight-foot-high chain-link fence. There were two other trucks, a few cars and some bicycles stored inside.

"What are all these vehicles stored here for?" Pete asked.

"I don't know," the truck driver said, "I don't ask no questions. I don't need no answers. I just drive 'em here, and I leave 'em here."

Pete was at a loss for words. He didn't dare take anything out of the truck. The constable who had impounded the truck had followed.

He said to Pete, "Come on over to the station. You can get the information you need about how long the truck will be here and how to get it back. Give us the keys. We'll look after them for you."

Just as Pete and the constable were pulling into the parking lot of the police station, he thought he saw Emily Blossom getting into a cruiser.

*Emily? What's Emily doing here?* he wondered.

The constable parked beside the other cruiser. Pete jumped out and ran over to talk to Emily.

"Emily, what's going on? What are you doing here?"

He couldn't believe how relieved he was to see her. As for Emily, her face lit into a brilliant smile.

"I could ask you the same question," she said. "You're truly a sore sight for eyes."

He looked more ragged than usual. She was used to his torn jeans and stained T-shirts, and his moustache often carried signs of pipe juice and crumbs from previous meals. This morning, however, his steel blue eyes were sagging. His face drooped with the look of a lost boy.

"I'm here because they impounded my truck," he said with a flush through three days' growth of beard. Getting the better of himself, he added, "Thanks to you."

"Thanks to me? I didn't know they were going to impound your truck. Did they arrest you?"

"Emily, they have nothing to arrest me for. You know as well as I do I didn't do anything wrong."

"I know that," she said, "and you know that. But maybe they don't know that."

She cocked her eyebrows and nodded toward the constables, who were chatting beside the police cars.

"Stop fooling," Pete said, visibly shaken.

Emily had pity on him. "I'm sorry. I was just teasing. I don't like seeing you in a weakened state. It makes me nervous."

"I'm not weakened. I'm mad and upset about my truck."

"I think I can arrange for a ride back to Emerald Hill," she said, changing the subject.

"Wait for me. You can take me back at the same time. I have to go in and give them the keys. I'll be right with you."

"I hope so," she said, as he disappeared into the police station.

He went in and explained to the receptionist about his truck.

"We'll call you, Mr. Picken. We have the information we need from your driver's license. What's your phone number?"

"Well, I'm kind of hard to get hold of," Pete explained. "Call Emily Blossom. She'll give me the message. She's easier to get hold of than I am. She's got a message machine and all that."

"Okay, Mr. Picken, we'll let you know when your truck is available. We have to examine it for evidence."

"Well, what am I going to do without the antiques in it?"

"You have to call Inspector Allard about that, and he's gone out."

"Oh, okay. When will he be back?"

"Sometime this afternoon. He'll be back later this afternoon. You can call him before five. Something important has called him away from his desk."

\*

Pete returned to the cruisers, where Emily was talking to Constable Wilson.

"Wouldn't you love to have another butter tart?" Emily was saying. "When you drive us back to the Country Kitchen, me and Pete Picken, I'll buy you butter tarts."

151

"No, ma'am, we're not allowed to take anything like that. We're not allowed."

"That's fine," she said, patting his shoulder. "You don't have to decide right away. It's a little secret between you and me."

"We're not allowed to accept gifts from clients."

"Constable Wilson," Mrs. Blossom said, barely disguising the patience required for her to maintain her composure. "I am not a client, I am a cohort . . . a coworker. Don't you know? I am a detective—an undercover detective—so you could accept butter tarts from me if you wanted to, but"—she smiled sweetly, willing the crow's feet wrinkles to spread out from the corners of her sparkling eyes—"we won't say anything about this now, will we?"

She convinced herself that her enchantment could almost sprinkle fairy dust on his soft brown hair, but when he actually agreed, she was quite surprised when her ploy actually worked.

"Hop in the car then."

Emily got in the front seat of the cruiser, and Pete sat in the back. Emily carried on her usual banter as they drove from Hamilton Mills to Emerald Hill.

"I think I'll have to talk to Ilsa about having fresh muffins ready for breakfast. I'm famished. She and Maria are so busy making lunch in the morning that she doesn't get around to having hot pastries for breakfast. Have you ever eaten their cinnamon buns, Constable Wilson? They almost rival the butter tarts."

"I prefer gooey-in-the-middle," Pete said from the backseat.

"You can't have gooey-in-the-middle for breakfast, Pete. Nobody has dessert for breakfast."

"Who says?"

By the time they pulled in front of the Country Kitchen on the Hill, mouths were watering in anticipation. Pete and Emily climbed out of the cruiser. Pete headed for the restaurant, while Emily spoke to the constable.

"Now you wait right here, Constable Wilson," she said, leaning in the window with her hands braced on the edge.

"But, but," he protested, though weakly.

"Right here," she said. She fairly skipped into the little restaurant, demanding of Ilsa in a loud voice, "Ilsa, Ilsa, quick! I need six butter tarts real quick, and one black coffee to go."

152

"What's your hurry?" Ilsa asked.

"Ilsa, don't argue. Six butter tarts, as fast as you can."

"Okay, okay," Ilsa said, carefully filling the box. She meticulously arranged the tarts into neat rows without damaging a crumb of the crust.

Emily grabbed the tarts and coffee off the counter. Ilsa winced when Emily crushed the box against her chest as she heaved the door open with one hand and balanced the coffee with the other.

"That'll be $6," Ilsa shouted at Emily's disappearing back.

"I'm coming right back, Ilsa, don't worry."

Emily tossed her words over her shoulder as she raced to the street with her treasured tarts. She sidled up to the cruiser backward, pretending she was just walking by. She handed the butter tarts to the young constable through the window from behind her back, as if she was just turning around and happened to drop them in his lap. The coffee was presented as an afterthought. She was hoping no one would notice.

He was hoping so even more.

"Thank you very much, young man. You've been absolutely beyond the pale."

"The pale?"

"An asset to the community, a true representative of the way a police force is a servant of its citizens. I commend you heartily."

The tires of the cruiser squealed as Constable Wilson pulled away from the curb. He ran the light turning from yellow to red and vanished in the direction of Hamilton Mills.

**Main Street, Emerald Hill**

# *Chapter Twenty-Two*

When Emily returned to the Country Kitchen, Pete was already heavily involved in an intense discussion with Constant Black, the retired accountant. They were hunched over a small round table, heads close together.

Pete had not removed his leather hat, so the brim covered his eyes as he listened intently with head cocked. His curly hair straggled over his collar, and he leaned on his elbows as if the weight of the world were on his shoulders.

Constant Black was rather like an ancient ship navigating rough waters. His eyes were the same colour as his wavy grey hair. He had bushy eyebrows, which twitched and rolled, punctuating the drama of his sentences. His lavish lips spewed like cresting waves when he spoke. "What is isn't, and what isn't is."

Emily approached the table. "Sounds like a discussion that should be going on at the next table," she said, nodding toward the funeral director, Mr. Underhill, who sat with Jack English. Emily assumed they were making arrangements for the memorial service for Jack's late wife, Janet.

She didn't need to hear what Pete and Constant were saying to know what their conversation was about. Whenever Mr. Black was involved, everyone knew the discussion was about impending disaster.

"Are you sure?" Pete repeated. "What isn't is, and what is isn't?"

"That's right. And when the end of the world comes, everything will be revealed. Those who are the chosen ones will be saved, and those who aren't stay behind."

"What I am is hungry," Emily said.

Ilsa approached the table, wiping her hands dusted with flour on her apron. "Are you people going to order before the world ends?"

"Ilsa, I want to talk to you about muffins."

"Banana pecan or raspberry?"

"Are they fresh?"

"No, they're from last week," Ilsa answered with a straight face.

Pete and Constant actually looked up from their conversation to assess her statement. The restaurant was silent for a spark of an instant, waiting.

"You must be kidding."

"Of course I am," Ilsa said with her hands now firmly planted on her hips. "When have you ever known Maria not to have fresh muffins in the morning? It's the first thing she does when she comes in."

Pete looked at Emily, who shrugged and glanced at the ceiling.

"What about cinnamon buns?" Pete asked.

"A cinnamon bun and a coffee?" Ilsa said.

"Are they gooey in the middle?"

"A cinnamon bun and a coffee?" Ilsa repeated, with one cocked eyebrow and a scowl.

"I thought you'd never ask," Pete replied.

"I'll have the same only raspberry pecan," Emily said.

"Banana pecan or raspberry—that's your choice. With coffee or tea?"

"Raspberry, with coffee, please."

"Cinnamon bun with gooey in the middle and lots of icing."

Ilsa returned to the kitchen. Pete, Black and Emily returned to their conversation.

Emily began. "So what's new?"

"I know," Pete said.

"You do?"

"Ilsa's got fresh muffins."

"Yes, we got that far," Black said.

Then Pete resumed where they had left off. "So what's happening with the conspiracies on Emerald Hill this morning?"

"Do you mean the Satanists or the Illuminati?

"The Illiterati," Pete said with a smirk.

"When the world ends, you're either one of the chosen few or you get left behind. Some people are volunteering to stay behind and look after the animals—for a fee."

"No, I'm talking about the ones buying up large tracts of land."

"Where?" Emily asked.

"When the oil runs out, and people are dying of mass starvation, the really rich people have a plan. They're buying up big portions of land:

restoring farmland and old orchards, planting crop and setting up security fences to protect their food sources."

"Haven't people always done this in times of uncertainty? During the Second World War, it was Victory Gardens. The wealthy have always bought country properties for refuge in times of famine, plague or other disasters that happen to the common riffraff."

"This time it's different," Black said.

"I'm sure everyone always thinks this time is different."

"They know something we don't. They have so much money; they don't worry about what to spend it on. They've got more money than you can imagine."

"I thought country living was just a hobby for them," Pete said. "They're dabbling in the game of farming a bit of land and raising cows?"

"They might have more money than they know what to do with, but they're not just spending it for fun. There's a larger plan out there. They're expecting a worldwide disaster."

Emily narrowed the subject down to the news she heard on the radio. "You mean like the floods, wildfire and earthquakes? Thousands of people are killed because of climate warming."

"Climate change or global warming?"

"Either one; the result is the same."

Black's theories were well worked out. His explanations rolled off his tongue with a tinge of dread and a healthy dose of conviction. "That's not a lot of people compared with mass famine. You're talking about tens of millions of people starving to death because of a lack of food. The present economy isn't sustainable. When the oil runs out, there won't be enough resources to produce enough food to feed all the people on Earth. You have to cut back on the population one way or another."

"You mean wars?"

"Or starvation. They'll have to go one way or another."

"Are the rich people buying up land all around the world? Not just in Canada?"

"It's all over the world. The rich people are preparing for an economy when there will be no oil. No oil, no transportation, no food leads to world famine. Don't kid yourself. There are no human rights—it all has to do with force. If you can get it, you have to keep it. To keep it you have to have the power, military or weapons."

"They say the security systems in the United States are out of control."

"Nobody knows exactly what the CIA is up to. There are a lot of other security systems operating under the Homeland Security Act."

"Is it all about oil then?"

"Oil, yes, but it goes further than that. The countries where the wars happen are all places where there is no central bank. It's interesting that where the revolutions happen, somehow the rebels are able to set up a central bank almost immediately."

"It's about money then?"

"Someone is controlling the money flow."

"The Rothschilds, the Bloomburgers, the big guys?"

"That'll do for a start."

Emily wanted to bring the discussion closer to home. "What about the gangsters? Aren't they buying up land as well?"

"Well, gangsters are a different story. If you cross the mob, they just kill you."

"The whole thing is . . . the whole thing," said Black, "once you understand that, you just buy some popcorn, sit back and watch the show."

Constant Black scraped his chair back from the table, punctuating his message of finality. He stood up, and like a ship on the crest of a wave, he hovered as if in midair before crashing into a trough of despair. "All I'm saying is prepare yourself. There's disaster coming."

Emily followed Mr. Black to the door. She had a hunch she needed to follow up on.

"Mr. Black," she said, with her hand on his sleeve, "you're a man who has spent a lot of time researching the trends, isn't that right?"

"Yes, you could say that. I study the conspiracy issues carefully."

"Have you noticed any changes in this area? Are there any goings on around here that would make you believe that your theories might just be coming true?"

"How about the fact that agricultural land has increased in value more than ten times over in the past few years? You can't even buy tracts of land around here anymore. How about the fact that farmers are finding marijuana plantations in their cornfields? I heard of a farmer who had five tractors ruined with sugar in the tanks just because he reported marijuana growing on his land. Used to be that you knew everyone in the area . . .

Now there are properties out in the country with big fences and locked gates. Who are these people and what are they doing here?"

"You know this for a fact?" Emily said.

"Things are changing faster than we know," said Black. "Keep your eyes open and you'll see for yourself. We might be out of the way here in this small town, but the world is creeping up on us from the outside. We're no safer than anybody else."

When she returned to the table, Ilsa was serving Pete's breakfast. "We had our own excitement yesterday," she said as she served the pastries and poured coffee. "A pop can exploded."

"What happened?"

"A can of Pepsi rolled under the fridge, next to the compressor. It heated up, and all of a sudden we heard this bang and a fizzing sound."

"Did you run for cover?"

"It was a mess to clean up," Ilsa said.

"Better than in Montréal," Pete said. "With the gang wars going on there, they're throwing fire bombs into the pizza parlours. Those are explosions!"

"I wonder if Malarkey would feature a pop can explosion in the *Hill News*," Emily mused.

"Maloney. Mr. Maloney."

"That's what I said. I can see it now in big letters on the front page: Pop Can Explodes at the Country Kitchen on the Hill."

"A sure sign of the apocalypse," said Emily.

"Speaking of the apocalypse," Pete said to Mr. Underhill, interrupting Jack mid-sentence from across the room. "You're on the town council. Are you aware that the Township of Scottsdale is the major sponsor of our St. Patrick's Day Parade? How does that look for our own Village of Emerald Hill, eh? The local councillors look rather silly, don't you think? They don't even bother to enter a float in the parade. Is that any way to show pride in their community?"

"They say they don't have any money to support an Irish parade."

"Irish? Everyone in town is Irish on St. Patrick's Day. What does that have to do with it?" Pete asked, eyes flashing and cheeks rosy. "How does it look to the people who vote for council? They want to see their village represented, especially if the next town over thinks it's worth their while to solicit our customers to go down there to do business."

"Pete, we have a very limited budget."

Obviously annoyed, Underhill neatly summed up the funeral arrangements with Jack. They scraped their chairs back from the table and gathered their coats.

As the bell announced the door opening, Pete could not resist a parting shot. "Don't say I didn't warn you."

# Chapter Twenty-Three

After Daisy had dropped Emily off at the restaurant in town, she gladly returned to her farm, animals and familiar surroundings. Daisy was not a person who liked to stray too far from home.

Emily often chided her for not being more adventurous. "Why don't you travel? Take a break from the farm once in a while. Robin could look after things while you're gone. It would be good for you to get away and change your perspective. You'd come home refreshed. You'd appreciate what you have more after seeing how other people live."

Daisy's response was always the same. "I have a whole world all around me. Why do I need to leave? I love it here. Every moment of every day is precious."

To that, Emily would say, "You're just hiding your head in the dirt. People like you have no imagination."

Imagination or not, Daisy treasured time to ponder the realities of her life. The best place for thinking was in the barn. "Cleaning stalls represents the epitome of life," she would say to Robin. "We all have to shovel manure in one form or another."

Daisy would never use the s-word and expected the same from others in her presence. Except Pete Picken. He could say anything he pleased and get away with it.

Today, after her visit to Roger Major's home, and after being with Emily for more than an hour, Daisy was in need of a good think. She had the impression that lost threads were dangling in her world, like cobwebs cluttering the corners. The automatic repetition of physical labour was always therapeutic for her. She could work away cleaning corners, literally and figuratively.

Work was like music. The rhythmic scraping of shovel on concrete reminded her of drumming. Sweeping was a brush on symbols. The chickens sang clucking songs with the rooster singing soprano. Sheep munching their cuds provided the bass line. Even the peacock, whose name was Percival McGuinty the Third, might be billed as an impresario, according to Daisy.

"Who needs Muzak?" she mused, and then settled herself into a routine of cleaning stalls. She let her mind wander.

First was the task of figuring out what was bothering her. Where were the unfinished thoughts niggling at her peace of mind? Most obviously she was terribly sad for the girl. Even though she had no connection to the unidentified murder victim, Daisy could not help but empathize. She was a nurturer. Every living creature, regardless of how small or helpless, deserved a chance to survive: a chick rejected by a broody hen; an orphaned lamb, whose mother had no milk; even a tree with slashed bark, or a flowering weed threatening her garden, or a butterfly trapped in the house and flailing against a window pane searching for escape . . . all were worthy of equal care. Daisy could not remain neutral to loss or abandonment. She would feed a baby chipmunk by hand; warm a fallen fledgling sparrow beneath her shirt; massage and cuddle a cumbersome, downed cow with affection. She was convinced that by paying attention to one's existence, through affection and love, a person could ignite an injured creature's will to live and to heal. She had brought baby peacocks back from the depths of fear and despair, just by holding them under her shirt next to her beating heart.

Daisy was convinced the girl with the tattoo was a wayward waif gone astray, a victim of circumstances beyond her control. She did not need to know more details. The child had been murdered and sawn to pieces through no fault of her own. Innocent miscalculations had led to her terrifying death. Daisy's biggest regret was that she had never met the poor person in time to redirect her fate.

Still, living on a farm taught Daisy the limits of her abilities as well. The cold truth of mortality was inevitable. There were always casualties. Weak babies lost the will to live; animals died of unknown causes.

Mr. Jones, an old-time farmer from Britain, used to say, "You can't have livestock without dead stock."

Seasons came and went. For every spring and celebration of birth, autumn would bring the cycle round to demise and regret; winter was a time of waiting and ice was inexorably suffocating. Daisy learned patience and acceptance over the years. Some answers became clearer from a perspective of age.

The unexpected appearance of Luigi Rocco revived feelings Daisy had chosen to bury in the past long ago. Her unfulfilled longing for a warm body and tender love left her with scars as deep as her very being. Entirely grounded as she was to her presence and to her surroundings, Daisy could not separate herself from her desire to be with the man of her dreams, the one and only man who would ever have been worthy, Michel Mercure. She was not deluded. Daisy knew he had been a loser. Every choice he had made in his life led him to disappointment. He was a drug abuser, an alcoholic and a gangster. However, she was certain she could have saved him. She could have shared with him her life of peace and harmony. She would have loved him enough to rescue him from himself, if only they had not taken him so soon—if only he had had one more chance.

Rocco's intrusion into her life sewed seeds of questions. For the first time since Michel left that last night they were together, Daisy wondered why he had not returned. She had been so sure . . .

The scraping of the shovel on the concrete floor soothed her trembling. She allowed the tears to flow, unimpeded, along the wrinkles of her cheeks. They rolled down her neck, underneath the flannel collar of her farmer's shirt. Friday's muzzle crept underneath her hand resting on the handle of the shovel. With persistent nudges he insisted she pet him. He leaned all his weight against her leg. Sweetie, the white cat, sat on the ledge of a stall door and watched her with a steady gaze.

To soothe her injured spirit, Daisy listened to the animals, content in their security of a good home. The chickens were clucking to each other. The roosters crowed and boasted to the world about their conquests over the hens. The sounds of sheep munching hay and chewing their cuds punctuated straw rustling and bodies shifting. A fragrance of last summer's hay wafted on this spring's promising breezes. The old beams of the barn hovered over her in a protective arch of security. This barn had sheltered life for more than a century. Daisy comforted herself with the thought that many tears had no doubt fallen here and had been whisked away with the dust of time passing.

Presently she became aware that a hush had descended over the animals. All the beasts shifted their gaze toward the door. Friday's bark galvanized their awareness to the presence of a visitor. His wagging tail meant the intruder was a friend he recognized.

A lanky silhouette paused in the doorway. Then the familiar shuffling gait of a gangling teenager proceeded down the aisle. Daisy sighed and wiped her cheeks with the back of her hand. She brushed her straying hair back from her forehead before Robin rounded the corner. She was relieved to be distracted from her heavy thoughts. She leaned on her shovel and pretended to be resting from exertion.

"I figured you were in the barn. Friday's never far from where you're working. I just finished cleaning down at Mrs. Steel's and thought I'd drop by to see if you needed a hand with chores. It's been a while since I've ridden Bella. She could use the exercise, and so could I."

The horse in the end stall nickered in response to the familiar voice of her owner. Robin approached the stall. First she stroked the horse's soft nose and then scratched underneath her forelock, along her soft ears and under her chin. Robin performed this ritual practically every day of the mare's life, since she first boarded Bella at Daisy's farm.

"Funny how horses never get tired of a routine," she said. "I could be here all day scratching her favourite itching spots. She'd never budge. We all love loving, don't we?"

"Have you made any progress with your resolution?" Daisy asked.

The girl's hand paused in its petting, and the mare nudged, asking for more. "Well, I did see Andrew McDonald in the post office this morning when I was picking up Mrs. Steel's mail."

"And?"

"And? He smiled; I pretended not to see him and he left."

"You didn't say anything?"

"No, I couldn't think of anything to say without sounding like a fool."

"How about, 'It's a nice day, isn't it?' That might do the trick."

"Oh, Daisy, he wouldn't fall for that. He'd think I was after him. Nobody says that these days. It sounds stupid."

"Really?" Daisy could not disguise the genuine surprise in her tone. "I never knew it was stupid to comment on the weather. Everybody talks about the weather in the post office. What else is there to talk about—except maybe gossip? You have to start somewhere."

"People my age don't talk about the weather, Daisy," Robin said with a touch of exasperation in her voice. "In fact, most of them are so busy texting each other they don't bother talking at all."

Daisy furrowed her brow. She was genuinely puzzled. "I always wonder what they're saying when they're texting. I see those fingers flying around on the keyboard so fast. What are they talking about?"

"Usually it's about where they are and what they're doing. That's about it."

"Do they talk about ideas or the news or anything important?"

"Not really. Sometimes it's about how drunk they got the night before, and who made a fool of themselves."

"What do they say when they're at parties? Politics? Shopping? Plans and dreams?"

"Mostly drunk talk."

"Drunk talk?"

"I don't actually go out much. I'd rather spend time with Bella. She's much more understanding, and I don't have to pretend."

"I know what you mean."

"Were you ever in love, Daisy? I often wondered. You never talk about yourself much."

Daisy picked up her shovel and resumed cleaning. The wheelbarrow filled quickly. A smelly, sweet odour of manure mingled with dust and cobwebs formed a cloud around her.

"Love is a state of mind," she said over the sound of scraping and dumping.

Robin leaned against the wall with her hands in her pockets, watching Daisy work.

"I saw a young couple walking down the street yesterday holding hands, and I wondered what it must be like to feel that way. They both had silly grins on their faces, like they had a secret just between them that nobody else could imagine."

"It can be beautiful," Daisy admitted, "but it can also be like a disease."

"I wonder what it must be to feel that way about someone."

"It gets hold of you, and it won't let go."

The wheelbarrow was full to overflowing. Usually Daisy preferred not to push such a heavy load to the manure pile, but Robin had failed to catch the hint. Usually the girl was very good about offering to help and recognized, without being told, what needed to be done. Today her head was elsewhere.

When she returned from her trip across the yard, Robin was petting Bella's nose and gazing fondly into the horse's soft brown eyes. "Imagine gazing into someone's eyes, feeling his lips on your lips, melting into his arms . . . I wouldn't be able to breathe."

"You get over it." Daisy moved to the next box stall and began shovelling furiously.

Robin continued mercilessly. "Imagine waking up in bed with an irresistibly handsome guy lying next to you."

"My sister-in-law says, 'The best thing about falling in love is falling out of love'."

Robin conveniently ignored Daisy's input. "I can't get rid of that little demon in the back of my head telling me how stupid I am to think anyone would think I'm beautiful."

"The beginning is the best part, but the passion eventually wears off," Daisy said, picking up a broom and sweeping cobwebs from the ceiling. "Then you have to look at yourself in the mirror every morning."

Robin began to stir uncomfortably as her reality settled in. "I just can't get past the 'hello' part," she said with frustration.

Daisy continued talking to the ceiling. "I know so many intelligent young women whose brains seem to disappear whenever a guy comes around. They become giggling fools."

"Well, at this rate, you don't have to worry about me," Robin responded, throwing her arms in the air and wandering aimlessly down the aisle. "It's not gonna happen anytime soon."

"Life happens when you least expect it," Daisy said, putting away her broom and shovel and settling the wheelbarrow into its corner out of the way. "Now let's get on with the day."

As they proceeded down the barn, the sheep were lazing on fresh bedding, stomachs full, contently chewing their cud. A multicoloured rooster charged across the pen and grabbed a hen's neck in his beak. He jumped on her back, furiously wiggling his feathers as she squawked in mock protest. When finished, he flew onto a beam and began to crow loudly. The hen resumed her scratching for seeds in the dust.

"Roosters are pretty brutal, aren't they?" Robin asked.

"They're not called cocks for nothing," Daisy answered as she closed the barn door.

The two meandered across the yard toward the house, accompanied by Friday and the white cat.

"Well, I'll be on my way," Robin said. "Just stopped by to report on my lack of progress."

"Keep up the good work," Daisy said, always willing to encourage even the smallest of efforts toward self-improvement. "You'll never get there if you don't take the first step."

A restlessness overwhelmed Daisy as soon as she entered her kitchen. Usually she felt comforted by her familiar surroundings. She appreciated her cozy nest of possessions and preferred the unchanging security of living alone. But today she couldn't sit still. She was unsettled with a yearning she could not identify and could not ignore. She needed someone to talk to who would listen . . . not necessarily someone who would understand, but a person who would not judge or jump to conclusions. Try as she might to perform routine housework, she could not accomplish the simplest tasks: the dishes remained on the counter, the floor needed sweeping, winter's residue still spattered the windows.

She sat at the table, drumming her fingers on the place mat, staring out the window without seeing the greening of spring in the sunshine. Glancing down, she noticed that business card next to the salt shaker. Absently, she picked it up and resumed her drumming with the edge of the card until she became aware of the printed message:

Luigi Rocco
La Bella Vista
235 Boulevard St. Laurent
Montréal, Quebec

She stared at the card, blankly at first, until she remembered that Mr. Rocco had handed her the card before leaving so unceremoniously after Sunday's visit. His unexpected appearance had stirred up those unfinished memories and vague questions, which she had conveniently managed to suppress for 40 years. She felt as if she had the dregs of the coffee pot stuck in her teeth.

Finally, after a few moments of aimless futility, Daisy changed out of her chore clothes. She put on a clean pair of jeans, which she had recently bought at the secondhand store. They had beaded pockets and fit her more tightly than her usual farm clothes. She brushed her hair and formed a tidy ponytail to contain the straggles. A glance in the mirror told her the beige shirt she wore highlighted the twinkle in her deep brown eyes. She chose her favourite warm, cozy sweater to put over her shoulders. It was a bit sloppy, but it made her feel comfortable and safe. After a long, blustery winter, she was used to being cold. She needed the sweater as a security blanket. She grabbed her purse and got in her truck.

"Look after things for a while, Friday," she said to the dog, who studied her uncharacteristic behaviour with curiosity. "I've got some business to attend to. I'd better go before I change my mind."

# *Chapter Twenty-Four*

When Daisy entered the Country Kitchen, Emily was cleaning the muffin crumbs from her plate. Pete had removed his hat in honour of Emily's company. His hair scattered in all directions around his bald spot. He still had some icing dripping from his moustache.

Emily gestured in an attempt to tell him to use his napkin. Failing to take notice of her subtlety, he answered in a loud voice, "I'm saving it for later."

Daisy approached their table. Her eyes betrayed a mixture of anxious expectation and relief. "Hey there, I'm glad I found you. Pete, where's your truck? When I didn't see it parked outside, I figured you weren't back from the flea market yet."

"It's a bit of a long story," he mumbled, lapping his coffee and the icing with his tongue from the tips of his moustache.

"Did you finish your chores already?" Emily asked.

"Were you missing me?" Daisy asked. "We haven't seen each other in such a long time."

Emily ignored her sarcasm.

"Daisy, how are you feeling today? Are you over the shock?" Ilsa asked. "Can I get you a cup of tea? Maybe a piece of strawberry pie? I know you like Maria's pie."

"You didn't offer us any pie," Pete complained.

Ilsa's hands flew to her hips and she quipped, "You didn't ask. And besides, it wasn't out of the oven yet. Daisy's timing is better than yours."

Pete lifted his eyebrows and pouted. "How about another cup of coffee then? Is that too much to ask?"

"Not if you say 'please'."

Around midmorning in the diner, there was often a lull in customer traffic. Clients who had come in for breakfast went to work, but it was still too early for lunch.

On the way up to the Hill, Daisy had been practicing how she would pose her questions. She knew Pete would listen, and even if he didn't understand, he would have a worthwhile opinion. She also knew she would not be able to have Pete to herself, so she would simply have to put up with Emily's arrogance.

After the coffee arrived and pie was finished, Daisy formulated her quandary. "Suppose something happened to you a long time ago, and suppose someone hurt you pretty badly, but you never understood why. Then suppose you decided to let it go, and you never found out what the real story was. You got on with your life and tried to forget about it." She paused to collect her thoughts.

Emily opened her mouth to make a comment, but Pete's sombre silence made her think better of speaking. She resisted the urge to interrupt.

Daisy continued. "Suppose many years later somebody comes into your life, out of the blue. That person reminds you of what happened way back when. All of a sudden, all those questions come rushing back into your head. You realize you never really did let it go after all.

"Do you try to find that person and ask him what really happened, or do you put it all back on the shelf and try to forget again? Since it's been so long ago, it doesn't really matter anymore, does it?"

Pete fingered his coffee mug and continued to stare at the tablecloth.

"I assume you're not asking me," Emily said in an unusual display of sensitivity to the obvious.

Daisy did not glance in Emily's direction at all but continued to address Pete as if Emily were not there.

"You don't really know whether this person knows what happened, or if he does, whether he'll tell you what he knows."

Ilsa cleared the plates, filled their cups and disappeared into the kitchen without a word. Emily stirred restlessly. Her lips were pursed into a pout, but she did manage to remain silent.

When he was satisfied Daisy had finished, Pete spoke in a low, husky manner that he used only for very serious conversations. "Seems to me you don't have a choice. You didn't forget then, and you can't forget now."

Daisy's eyes watered. She blinked, pretending she had something in her eye. The quaver in her voice gave her emotions away. "I can try."

"Look, Daisy," Pete said. His steel-blue eyes stared into the depths of her gentle grey ones. "Try is all a steer can do."

Daisy smiled through her tears. Emily snickered, rolling her eyes.

"You want to die always wondering 'what if'? What if I had asked, what would he have told me? What if I knew the truth, would it really have made a difference?"

He paused, waited, and then continued. "You really don't have a choice."

Daisy looked at the wall for what seemed a long time. She knew what the next question had to be, but she was afraid of the answer. She needed time to summon her courage. "Would you go with me?"

This time, Pete didn't hesitate. "I don't have a truck . . . nowhere else to go . . . nothing else to do . . . sure."

"I'm coming too," Emily said. "Where to?"

"Montréal. Here's the address."

Daisy reached in her purse and pulled out Rocco's card.

"Do you know where this is?" Pete asked.

"St. Laurent? I've been there before. So has Emily. Remember, Em? St. Laurent Boulevard, also known as the Main . . . not hard to find. I'm up for it."

Pete stood up and headed for the door, expecting the two women to follow his lead. Daisy carefully replaced Rocco's business card in a special pocket of her purse and scurried after him. Ilsa was just emerging from the kitchen when she saw her customers leaving.

"What about the bill? Who's paying today? There are also the butter tarts, Emily. Who's paying for them?"

Looking around the empty room, Emily shrugged. "How is it that it's always my turn to foot the bill, Ilsa?"

Ilsa rang up the total. The cash register drawer slid open. "Funny how that is," she said, as if to the wall. "You have a nice day now."

**Daisy's Truck**

# *Chapter Twenty-Five*

When Emily emerged from the restaurant, Pete was leaning against the truck with one boot perched on the running board. Daisy clutched her purse with two hands, self-consciously glancing up and down the street. They all understood that Pete would be driving Daisy's truck to the city.

Pete escorted the two women around to the passenger side. He helped Emily into the seat in the middle, where she had to nestle her legs beside the stick shift on the floor. She tucked in her elbows to make room for Daisy, who settled into the passenger seat, resting her elbow on the open window.

Pete sauntered around the front of the truck, stood on the running board and hoisted himself into the seat behind the wheel. The engine roared. The truck shook and rattled as it pulled onto Main Street, eastbound.

"We're off like a herd of turtles," Pete said, peering out from under his hat through the cracked windshield, his two large hands on the steering wheel.

"I do believe we're heading out on an adventure." Emily chuckled. "What fun!"

"I can't remember when I've been so far from the farm," Daisy said. "I just don't take the time to get out very much."

Pete extracted his pipe and tobacco from his pocket and deftly filled the pipe and lit it, all while he steered the truck from the wrists. His fingers were shaped perfectly for tamping the tobacco into the bowl of the meerschaum pipe. His moustache curled around the pipe stem, which fit neatly between the spaces of his missing teeth. The cab quickly filled with smoke. Both Daisy and Emily turned their heads toward the open window to breathe fresh air.

They were engulfed with the smell of pipe smoke mixed with exhaust escaping from the muffler through the floorboards. The truck vibrated, and the doors shook with every bump in the road. Emily could see the pavement passing beneath them through the rusted holes in the doors. The seats were broad and covered with several layers of farm dirt. Since Daisy seldom had fellow travellers, the driver's side was discernibly lower than the passenger's. As a result, Pete looked quite a bit shorter than he already was.

The highway followed a vast valley known by the Algonquin natives as the Outaouais. Just over the border between Ontario and La Belle Province, the Ottawa River joined the St. Lawrence. The meeting of the two great rivers formed around the island of Montréal. The St Lawrence Seaway then continued hundreds of kilometres eastward, past Quebec City, before pouring its waters into the Atlantic Ocean beyond the Gaspé Peninsula.

The route linking Ottawa and Montréal ran along the shores of the great rivers. Not far from Emerald Hill was the border between Ontario and Quebec. However, differences in the countryside between the two provinces were subtle. Most noticeable was the language of the road signs. In Quebec, French predominated.

"Let's take the back roads to the city. It's almost as fast as the highway, and we don't have to worry about traffic and speeding," Daisy said.

Pete settled into driving mode: elbow on the open window, pipe perched in the corner of his mouth. He slouched against the door with one hand on the steering wheel.

Emily sat upright, her hands in her lap, knees together and pants carefully pleated so they wouldn't wrinkle in transit.

Daisy balanced her body with shoulders hunched and neck outstretched. Her clothes fit her like a tent, comfortable and cozy, with no effort to contain her ample figure.

Both women had wayward locks of hair that refused to stay put. Pete's hair made no attempt at control, and curls stuck out from under his hat in all directions.

When they drove out of town, the commentary began, tossed back and forth like a ping-pong ball. They talked about the people who lived in the houses they passed along the way. They commented on the fields, ploughed or seeded; about the weather; about the history of the area.

"We have always been considered newcomers, even though we've been here almost 50 years."

"Unless you can count your ancestors back seven generations and have a deed from a land grant, you'll always be a foreigner here," Pete said.

"How long have you lived here, Pete?"

"Long enough to know better and too long to care."

"What does that mean?"

"It's a long story."

"You mean you didn't fit in? Was it religion?"

"If you're not Protestant or Catholic—or white—you're different. Even these days you don't see all that many immigrants."

"Why didn't you ever move on then?"

"Nowhere else I'd rather be. Besides, I couldn't make a living anywhere else. Picking's still good around here, even though it's harder and harder to find good stuff to buy."

"Why didn't you ever leave, Daisy?" Emily asked. "You could have done something with your life. You could have gotten an education, found a well-paying job, married a professional. You could have done better than stay out here in the boonies."

"I looked after my parents." Daisy's tone was flat and sharp at the same time. "You know that."

"Yes, but afterward," Emily said, blithely pursuing a subject that she knew was a sore spot.

"We've been over this before. Let's not get into it."

"You must have been good in school, the way you read books and think so much. You were pretty once. You probably had lots of boyfriends at one time. You could even have gone to university. I never really understood what kept you here."

"Emily, you never did understand. You never approved of what I did, what I wore or who I spent time with."

"Well, Daisy, you would have been so much better off. If you dressed nicely, some pleasant man would marry you. If you looked after yourself better, someone would be attracted to you. Isn't that right, Pete?"

"Daisy's okay the way she is. She knows what she wants."

"You don't get fancied up to go to the barn."

"You're only as good as you feel."

"Of course, that goes without saying."

"No, I mean, you only look as good as you feel."

"Really?"

"Or feel as good as you look? I'm not sure," Emily said.

"Whatever. Does it really matter?"

"Now I'm confused," Pete said.

"What I mean is," Emily said, refusing to let the subject drop before she had her say, "a person needs to dress to make herself feel good about herself. Going around in dirty old rags all the time is not good for one's self pristine."

"Esteem, Emily. One's self-esteem."

"That's what I said. Daisy's self-esteem could be better."

"Well, look who's talking. You were married to a jerk and a drunk for how many years? And you're talking about self-esteem."

"That's a whole different story," Emily said, straightening her pants and cocking her head at an appropriate angle. "Don was not like that when I married him. Besides, most people were unaware of his drinking problem. You only know because he was your brother."

"What kind of a woman stays with a guy who cheats on her for years, eh, Pete?"

"Well it's better than falling in love with a jerk who walks out on you and then gets himself killed."

"Now, come on, you two! Haven't you said enough? Why don't we change the subject?"

"So why did you move to Emerald Hill then, Emily?" Daisy asked. "Don was no longer in the picture. It wasn't because you got on all that well with us, after all. You never really seemed to like the country, and you certainly never wanted to live on a farm."

"A farm would have been the last place I'd live. You're right there," Emily conceded. "But I do like the village of Emerald Hill. It's perfectly charming. I like the small town atmosphere. You know where you stand with the townsfolk, even if you don't belong."

"Could it be because you think you're so much better than everyone else?" Daisy asked. "Kind of like being a big fish in a little pond?"

"No, no, I'm not like that."

"Really?"

"Now, girls, cut it out! I've just about had enough of your bickering."

The three fell silent. The old Chevy bumped and rattled along the back roads, running parallel to the major highway between Ottawa and Montréal. The countryside changed gradually as they approached the city. New developments, condos and big-box stores sprawled where ploughed fields used to be. Soon, the spring tinge of the countryside began to change as they neared the outskirts of the city.

"Tulips already."

"We've barely got crocuses even in town."

Pavement broadened, and the temperature rose perceptibly as they drove over the bridge spanning the Lake of Two Mountains. Montréal Island appeared on the far side, as if the shoreline marked a tangible boundary between the country and the city. Suburbs gave way to factories and industrial buildings. The traffic on the highway thickened. Transport trucks bullied their way along the outside lanes. SUV drivers leaned on their horns before speeding past in the passing lanes, only to brake further along for slow vehicles blocking their progress.

"Everyone's in such a hurry in the city."

"In a hurry to go nowhere."

"I'm glad I don't drive," Emily said. "My nerves would be shattered."

"Pete, I can't thank you enough for driving," Daisy said. "I can't for the life of me imagine driving in this traffic."

Pete grinned and puffed proudly on his pipe. "The only thing better than one truck is two trucks, especially when one of them is out of commission."

"Is it far to go?" Daisy asked. "I'm beginning to get nervous. I'm not sure this was really such a good idea."

"Don't even go there," Pete said. "We're here now. You'll feel better once you see the guy and get the matter out in the open."

"Yes, but I don't even know what I'm going to say."

"You'll figure it out."

"Yes, Daisy, once you're face to face with Mr. . . . Mr. . . . Mr. who? Who are you going to see anyway? Where are we going? I never thought to ask."

"Luigi Rocco is the man's name. He's an old friend of Michel Mercure. He came to the farm day before yesterday. On his card, he says he's the owner of La Bella Vista Social Club. That's where we're going. We're looking for an address on St. Laurent Boulevard. Pete, are you sure you know where we're supposed to go?"

"Well, I know where St. Laurent is. With a name like Rocco, we're probably going to end up in Little Italy."

"Oh, how exciting," Emily said. "It's just like travelling to a foreign country. What exactly is a social club anyway?"

"I really don't know. He said he was in construction and trucking, but I'm not sure what a social club has to do with anything. I didn't think to ask any questions," she said. "I was so rattled by him standing in my kitchen, after so many years since Michel died. I just couldn't think straight. He said something about a promise he'd made to Michel but he never explained exactly what he wanted. I must admit, I was not having a very good day. I've been pretty shook up by Friday's discovery and all that business with the police interrogation, and the body and the shock of it all."

The subject of police reminded Emily of her current investigation. "That reminds me. I have an update, but now isn't the time to get into it. I don't want to spoil our adventure with bad news. Don't let me forget. I'll tell you on the way home about a conversation I had with Inspector Allard."

"I don't need any more bad news," said Pete. "Let's just relax and enjoy ourselves, shall we?"

"Here, here," said Daisy. "We're off to see the Wizard, the wonderful Wizard of Oz."

"What fun!" said Emily with a wiggle.

Pete took the turn off the Metropolitain onto St. Laurent Boulevard. As they drove along the Main, the ethnicities of the stores were like signposts from afar.

"Look at all those stores. Languages in Arabic, Hebrew, Spanish, Italian. It's like we're in another country."

"Many other countries. It sure is different from home."

They knew they were in Little Italy by the archways over the broad boulevard. The signs on the stores were in Italian. A grocery store featured all Italian specialty items. Nina's Clothing Store offered custom-made styles to suit all sizes. Banners on the street lamps, decorated in the red, white and green Italian flag, clearly indicated "La Petite Italie."

"There it is. La Bella Vista."

"I can't decide if I'm glad or scared to death that we really found it." Daisy's voice trembled. "Now I really don't know what I'm going to say."

"Take a deep breath," said Pete, using his gentle-but-firm approach to soothing Daisy's agitation. "You'll figure it out. We'll let you off here."

A large neon sign for La Bella Vista Social Club was turned off, but a small notice on the door announced they were open for business. Tall tinted windows gave the impression to passers-by the restaurant was black and empty, like a dungeon.

On the street, a round table with two chairs provided a smokers' refuge, which seemed odd given that the weather was cold and rainy. Nevertheless, the table was occupied by a young man, looking impervious to the weather. He wore a black jacket. His long legs were crossed, highlighting pointed black boots of Italian leather. He cradled his chin on one elbow on the table while tapping with long thin fingers a cigarette on the edge of an ashtray. His black hair was slicked back, accentuating his broad forehead and black moustache. He had an aquiline nose and high cheekbones. His eyes surveyed the street like a hawk looking for mice in a field.

"Go on, Daisy. We'll meet you at the Caffée Internationale up the street."

"Emily?" Daisy looked imploringly at Emily, but Emily stared straight ahead.

"You'll do fine, dear. Just pretend you're me, and you'll know exactly what to say."

Obviously flustered, Daisy forgot to hesitate before crossing. A horn blared and tires screeched. The farm-girl-in-the-city gathered her sweater around her and rushed across the street. She nodded to the man in black as she disappeared into the restaurant.

"Why does she always look so frumpy?" Emily did not try to mask her arrogance.

"She couldn't dress up even if she tried."

"Leave her alone. Why are you so down on her? She does the best she can with what she's got. Give her a break."

"It's just that she's always been so unambitious. She could have done something with her life. Sold the farm, moved on . . . lived life. Instead she just hides away out there and never challenges herself to be anything other than a little old lady, living alone, going nowhere."

"Seems to me you could learn something about being content with what you've got, Em. None of us have figured it out all that well, if you ask me."

Pete found a parking space down the street and manoeuvred the truck into place. Together they identified their parking spot by the number on the meter, bought the ticket at the nearest pay station and placed the receipt on the dashboard. They sauntered along the sidewalk taking in the sights and smells of the city.

# Chapter Twenty-Six

The interior of La Bella Vista Social Club was like a dark cave. Daisy paused just inside the door to let her eyes adjust to the dim lighting. Tables and chairs filled the room, a bar ran the length of one side and at the end of the long hall was a platform for bands or dancing. The room was painted black, with a geometric pattern of diamonds/squares, like a giant backgammon board on the tiled floor. Posters depicting photos of Italian sports cars such as Lamborghinis and Ferraris, and Ducati motorcycles lined the walls. Glasses hung upside down from the ceiling over the bar, and bottles of liquor lined the shelves.

The most remarkable thing about the décor was how drab and unimaginative it actually was. Daisy had the impression she had slipped into a dream world of darkness with no details, only shadows of absent figures milling about, acting out rituals of drinking and dancing in silence.

A voice from behind the bar startled her. "May I help you?"

She stammered, "Ah, yes. I'm . . . I'm looking for Luigi Rocco," she said, consulting his business card as if she were reading it for the first time. "I wonder if he's here."

"Do you have an appointment?"

"No . . . no, I don't. I was hoping to speak to him briefly. I didn't phone ahead."

"Just a moment," the waitress said.

Daisy was alone again and wondered if she had done the right thing dropping in on Rocco unannounced. Her fingers fidgeted. She anxiously tugged at her sweater, glad no one else was in the room.

She caught a glimpse of herself in the mirror behind the bar. Her long hair strayed across her cheeks. Sad and winsome eyes stared back. She tried to remember what she used to look like when she had considered herself somewhat attractive. She had lost the habit of dressing up and making herself pleasantly presentable. The stranger in the mirror looked homely. Worse than that, she appeared frightened and nervous. She forced the corners of her lips into a poor attempt at a smile to cheer herself up. Perhaps she could summon a good dose of self-assurance just by sheer willpower. However, she realized she was only fooling herself. No one would believe Daisy Blossom was a confident woman.

"Well hello, beautiful lady. What a pleasant surprise!"

Surely the large man striding across the room toward her was not really speaking to her. He could not be addressing her directly.

Daisy looked over her shoulder to see whether someone else had entered the club when she wasn't looking.

"Miss Blossom, I never expected to see you here!" Rocco said.

Daisy took a step backward. She gauged whether she could escape his enthusiastic greeting now that she was actually meeting him again face to face. He pinned her arms down with huge hands and kissed her on both cheeks.

She began to stammer uncontrollably. "I . . . I . . . I came to see . . . I got a ride with some friends . . ."

"Sally, bring us two special coffees, on the house. This is an occasion to celebrate. I really never expected you to accept my invitation quite so soon."

He guided her to a table at a booth in the darkest corner and indicated she should sit in an upholstered sofa-bench. He pulled up a chair next to her so he could face her and be close to her at the same time.

The dim light softened Luigi's features. His eyebrows did not look quite so bushy. His eyes twinkled from the shadows, and his jowls were less flabby than Daisy remembered. He smelled of aftershave and toothpaste. His shirt was unbuttoned at the collar and revealed a tangle of black hairs on his chest. His teeth gleamed in a flashing smile. Luigi wore charm as part of his pinstriped wardrobe.

Daisy's fingers fidgeted. He reached across the table and folded his large hands over hers. His gaze latched onto hers.

"Tell me," he said, "how are you? This is a long way outside your comfort zone, to come to the big city, to a strange place, to meet a person you hardly know."

"Well, not really," Daisy said, feeling her strength rushing back to her. "I needed to speak with you. There are some questions I need to ask you. When you came to the farm, you took me so off guard I wasn't ready. I didn't know what to say. Now I've been thinking, and I realize I shouldn't let the opportunity pass me by."

"I'm glad you've come to see things from my point of view." Rocco leaned back in his chair. His eyes scanned her face as if he were reading her like a book. "I wasn't sure you'd see what I was getting at."

"There were too many things that went unsaid the other day. Lots of years have passed . . . lots of unanswered questions."

"How can I help you understand?"

Sally appeared with two tall glasses of coffee topped with generous dollops of whipped cream. A distinct aroma of brandy wafted over the table. Daisy realized "special coffee" served in a bar inevitably involved liquor. Although she knew she should refuse, she welcomed the calming effects of the first delicious sips. She began to relax.

However, when she tried to explain her purpose for coming, Daisy once again felt awkward and ill at ease. "I don't really know where to begin."

When she hesitated, Luigi knew just what to say. "Why don't you start at the beginning? Tell me about yourself."

Daisy flushed. She found it quite necessary to study the patterns of foam around the rim of her glass of coffee. After what seemed an endless hesitation, she was able to gather her courage to speak. "It's been so long since anyone asked me that question, I'm not sure what to say that won't sound either too trite or too revealing."

"Tell me everything. I'm a good listener."

Daisy ignored the little demon in her head whispering that this man was far too understanding. She plunged in as if she had nothing to lose. "Well, my sister-in-law would tell you I'm an unambitious daydreamer who has squandered her life living on a farm in the boondocks, going nowhere."

"Frankly, I'm not interested in your sister-in-law's opinion. I didn't ask her. I asked you. How would you describe your life thus far, in the grand scheme of things?"

"I am a dreamer, that part is true . . . and an idealist, I guess. I've never really been good at following the status quo. I work hard on the farm because that's what I believe in. I love being close to the earth with animals as my best friends. The stars say goodnight, and the sun wakes me in the morning. Why would I want to live anywhere else?"

Luigi stirred uncomfortably, but Daisy continued blithely on. She believed what he had said: that he really wanted to know about her. "The world is a crazy place these days. So many things just don't make any sense: big corporations control governments without conscience; people go to war based on lies and power struggles, rather than ideology; millions starve while others think nothing of consuming and wasting precious resources. The whole planet is in danger because of our stupidity. I figure all humankind is going to hell in a hand basket. Eventually we'll pay one way or another."

Rocco took a deep breath and whistled through his teeth. "Those are pretty big thoughts for a beautiful woman. You mean to say that's what you think about when you're out there in the middle of nowhere? Don't you get scared living all by yourself? Especially if you think things are so bad, and people are so messed up?"

"Because I live alone, I can't afford to think about the worst things that can happen to me. I figure I'm probably safer in the country than I would be in the city among a million other people, all desperate and frustrated."

"What about all the work? Surely you get tired. You won't be able to go on forever. You may look young, but eventually you won't be able to care for all those animals all by yourself."

"I'll deal with that when the time comes."

"But what happens in the meantime? Don't you think you should plan ahead?"

At this point of the conversation, Daisy became suspicious. She didn't like his tone of voice. She sensed he was being pushy and domineering. "Mr. Rocco, why are you asking me these questions? Tell me about you. What do you believe in?"

"Sally, two more coffees, please," Rocco called over his shoulder.

"Sir?" Sally said, appearing from the back room.

"We need a couple more specials," he said impatiently. Then he turned back to the conversation. "Well, frankly, Miss Blossom. A lot of things happening around here have got me thinkin'. Guys are getting shot. My friends are disappearing. What's the point of it all? I'm not the kind of a guy who second-guesses himself. Don't get me wrong. But what about my family, the wife and the kids? What's it all for? That's when I thought of you."

"Me?"

"I should say, I thought about what Michel told me about you."

The mention of Michel's name sent a shiver through Daisy, like a shock directly into her heart. She remembered why she had come here in the first place. "What *did* Michel tell you about me?" she asked. She was glad he brought up the subject, the reason she had come to see Rocco.

"He told me about a beautiful woman he knew, who lived out in the country. He told me about your farm and how much he loved being there, being with you."

"If he loved me so much, Mr. Rocco, why did he leave? I believe he was working for you at the time. The last time I saw him, he told me he was quitting—that he'd leave the city and come back home for good. He was going to change his ways. We were in love. We were going to make a life together. But I never saw him again. I need to know. What happened?"

The question burst out like a gushing spring no longer contained by the weight of the earth. Her eyes filled with tears, but she refused to acknowledge them. This was her chance to hear the answer she had been seeking for so many years. She wasn't going to hide behind her pain any longer.

"What happened on the night that Michel Mercure died?"

Luigi Rocco seemed used to crying women. He was slick and cold and calculating. Whether or not Daisy deserved to know the truth, he had to tell her something that would satisfy her. Even in her desperation, Daisy realized that if he gave her the answers she craved, he thought she would be beholden to him. She did not know what he wanted from her, but she sensed she had something he considered worth his while.

He waited until Sally had served the second round of special coffees and had returned to the kitchen before he answered.

"Miss Blossom, let's make a deal."

Daisy took a large swallow of the brandy-laced coffee. She savoured the heat as it travelled from the tip of her tongue to her stomach. She waited.

"If I tell you what really happened that night, you must promise me to try to understand the situation from my point of view. I'm not a killer. It's not my fault where I was born, who my father was and who his father was before him. We didn't ask to be who we are; we ain't got no choice."

Daisy cupped her hands around the heat of the glass she held.

"You understand?"

"Go on."

"We didn't ask to be born. None of us got no choice who our parents are."

Daisy noticed that his speech had changed. He no longer tried to polish his words and phrases. He had reverted to the language of his roots, speaking from the back of his tongue, with an accent and grammatical intonation of Italian immigrants. She held her breath, eager to hear what he would tell her, afraid to know the truth.

"In this business, nobody gets out. You're in for life. Michel wanted out. He came to me that night hoping I'd understand. He told me he was in love with you. He wanted to make a clean start. He said he bought a ring and wanted to ask you to marry him. He wanted to move to the farm, get his hands dirty, work the land and make an honest living. It was a real pretty picture, what he said he wanted."

Rocco had ceased looking into Daisy's eyes and stared at the table. He whispered, as if by speaking softly he could somehow dampen the harshness of what he was about to tell her. When he looked at Daisy's face again, he was pleading for her forgiveness.

"In this business, nobody gets out alive."

"Michel never would have hurt anybody. He never talked. Not even to me."

"He saw too much, and he knew too much."

Daisy felt sick to her stomach. She heard what she wanted to hear. Michel did love her. He hadn't lied. But she hadn't bargained for the whole truth. She hadn't been prepared for the consequences of knowing. She was familiar with the deep, gut-wrenching sadness that had torn her heart to pieces, but the anger, the desire to murder in revenge, was totally foreign to her.

"How could you?" she gasped in horror.

Luigi shrugged like a small boy caught with his hand in a cookie jar. "There was nothing I could do. It's the law of *omertà*, the code of honour. I'm not a murderer. I didn't do it. But things happen."

Daisy reached for her purse and slid out of the booth. "Thank you for telling me," she said. "I'm not sure 'thank you' is the right thing to say at this point, but if I don't leave now, I may say something I'll regret later."

Rocco put his hand firmly on her arm and forced her to sit again. His eyes glimmered, and his jaw flexed. "Miss Blossom, there are two sides to our agreement."

"I don't remember that I agreed to anything."

"I did say you must try to understand my point of view, if I told you the truth."

"Ah," she said, finally realizing that, of course, he had his own motives for speaking to her.

"I am interested in the future—protecting my investments, shall we say. Your farm would fit quite nicely into my plans. I want you to consider giving me a first option to purchase. I'm willing to make you an extremely generous offer—a cash offer."

This time, Daisy was not impressed by his condescending smile. She stood up again.

"Mr. Rocco, I am not for sale."

"Don't be too hasty, Miss Blossom." He stood over her, blocking her flight toward daylight. "Take my advice and think about it. We wouldn't want you to suffer the consequences of any rash decisions."

This time she brushed past him before he could block her escape. "Goodbye, Mr. Rocco."

Daisy clutched her purse and politely offered to shake his hand. He took her palm in his two hands. She heard the click of his heels when he kissed the back of her hand.

"I'm sure we'll meet again, Miss Blossom."

She rushed for the door, desperate for a breath of fresh air.

# Chapter Twenty-Seven

The daylight blinded Daisy. She swayed uncertainly, realizing the brandy had gone straight to her head. Shivers ran up her spine in spite of the warmth of her sweater she clutched around her. Looking around, she was surrounded by a strange, noisy world of traffic, of people's faces, of smells and hard concrete. Nothing was familiar. She couldn't remember where she was or what she was supposed to do next. In shock, Daisy felt lonelier amidst the unfamiliar faces passing her by than she ever had before. She had no idea where to turn or what to do. She was utterly cold. Tears soaked her face. Confused emotions made her feel like a homesick child longing for the warmth of her cozy kitchen and the comfort of her animal companions. All she wanted was to see familiar faces and be with her friends; all she saw were strangers with blank eyes staring straight ahead.

"Lookin' for somethin'?" the man seated at the smokers' table said. "Maybe waitin' fer yer pals?"

Daisy turned around and was surprised to see him almost smiling. He didn't look like someone who knew how to be kind. Daisy assumed he was a bodyguard or a bouncer. She could even discern a bulge in his waist where his gun would be.

"My friends. My friends dropped me off, and I can't remember where I was supposed to meet them, or when."

"What do they look like? A short, scruffy guy with a skinny old broad?"

"You might say that."

"They was here a couple of minutes ago. Said they'd be back. Went to the cigar store up the street."

"Oh, thank you so much."

Sure enough, Daisy spotted Pete and Emily sauntering happily together toward her. She recognized Pete's rolling gait, enhanced by cowboy boots worn at the heel. The cuffs of his blue jeans scuffed the sidewalk. Emily almost skipped along beside him. Her elbow was hooked through his, and she leaned, just a little, on his arm. Emily's expression was unguarded and casually gay. She was obviously enjoying Pete's company.

Pete was studying the end of a cigar. His hat was pulled low over his face so only his moustache was visible. He put the cigar in his mouth and drew it through his lips to moisten the tobacco so it wouldn't burn too fast. Then he bit off the tip, spitting out the leaf. He tested by drawing air through the pruned end before striking a match to light up.

Daisy recognized the familiar gestures with a twinge of affection.

"Told you it was them, didn't I? A scruffy guy with an old broad."

"You're right. A perfect description. Thank you."

Daisy felt the urge to fly into Pete's arms and feel the warmth of his comforting hug. She wanted him to soothe away the loathing and terror that flipped her stomach into knots. She wanted his jokes to override the sombre conversation she'd just had with Luigi Rocco.

Instead, she realized Pete and Emily were more enthralled with each other than they were concerned with her problems. Instead of joy, she welcomed that familiar, heavy sadness she donned like a cloak. Despair was Daisy's way of validating herself.

"Daisy, Daisy," Emily said. "Such a face! Must have been a difficult conversation. You came a long way to make yourself so sad. I thought you were trying to resolve some issues, not make them worse. You look terrible."

"Thanks, Emily, I can always count on you to make me feel better."

"You look perfectly befuddled."

"No I'm not. I did find out what I wanted to know. I just didn't expect the whole truth. I guess I knew all along what really happened and didn't want to accept the implications of it all."

"Let's find the truck," Pete said. "We can talk about it on the way home. We don't want to get caught up in rush hour."

"Let's get out of town and then find some place for poutine. That'll make Daisy feel better."

"I know just the place," Pete said.

Daisy let herself be guided to the truck. Pete helped Emily in first and then offered his hand to Daisy. She hoisted herself awkwardly into the passenger seat. Pete relit his cigar before starting the motor. Emily was so content she didn't even complain when the truck cab filled with an overwhelming smell of burning, rotten leaves.

"I told the man at the smoke shop we wanted a really good cigar, as long as it didn't stink too badly. Daisy, you should have seen the humidor.

It was as large as your kitchen, all filled with cigars from all over the world. I'm sure most of them were pretty pricey. Did you see the guy who came in after us, Pete? He looked just like Al Capone."

"How do you know what Al Capone looked like?"

"Oh, I don't really. I'm just talking jumbo mumbo, rambling on and on."

"Mumbo jumbo," said Pete.

"That's what I said," Emily answered. "I'm just rattling on to make Daisy feel better."

"It's the truck that's rattling," said Daisy. She lay with her head cushioned against the window with her sweater. She closed her eyes, pretending not to be involved in the conversation. "It's your brain that's rattled, and your mouth that's rambling."

"That's good, Daisy," Emily said generously. "You're not as dumb as you look."

Daisy opened one eye as if to consider whether the comment warranted defending herself but thought better of it and closed her eyes again. She was asleep before the truck pulled onto the highway, heading west, toward home . . . toward safety.

# Chapter Twenty-Eight

Pete negotiated the truck through the city traffic as if he were driving a huge transport instead of a rundown, rattling pickup. He bullied his way through the congested, busy avenues. He even drove the wrong way down a one-way street.

"You're driving down the wrong way."

"Yeah—so?"

"Yeah—but . . . this is a one-way street."

"They'll get out of my way."

A taxi coming the opposite way honked its horn, flashed its lights and then pulled into the parking lane. The driver with bushy pinched eyebrows hunched his shoulders and showed palms up. His lips mouthed vociferous comments. Pete drove onto the sidewalk to pass the taxi. The astonished taxi driver followed the pickup's progress in the rear view mirror.

"The biggest thing in traffic is just to keep on goin'," Pete said. "If you hesitate, they drive all over you. You just gotta push your way through. You never back down. You never slow down. In Quebec, the taxi drivers drive with their horns, not with their brakes."

"You drive just like them. You just keep on moving."

"Other people will back off. That's how it works." Pete continued along the alley and turned down another side street, taking a shortcut to get to a major intersection. He seemed to know his way around, as if it were second nature.

"I wonder if we're going to beat rush hour."

"Montréal is the only city I know where you have to cross four lanes of traffic to get onto a major highway, which, believe it or not, exits on the left. Who designs a road like that?"

"And all the signs are in French, no less!"

Pete pushed the pedal to the floor as he negotiated four lane changes in order to take the ramp for the westbound highway. The truck shuttered, sputtered and sighed as it reluctantly leapt forward, passing the more cautious drivers, and then ducked between bumper-to-bumper vehicles that were stopping and starting for no apparent reason.

"Aren't you only supposed to pass on the left?" Emily asked, curling her fingers around the edge of the seat. She gripped the torn upholstery with her nails until her knuckles turned white.

Once on the highway, Pete carefully stubbed out the cigar so he could resume smoking it later. Then he pulled his pipe out of its holder and banged the bowl on the ashtray until it was cleared of tobacco. Pete slouched against the door with one hand on the steering wheel, and the other, holding his empty pipe propped between his lips. His hat was perched low over his eyes, limiting his range of vision.

"Everybody passes on the right if the cars in the left lane are moving too slow."

The traffic flowed slowly but steadily forward, gradually thinning as they left the downtown congestion. The city began to transform into suburbia, with low-slung industrial buildings sprawled along the service roads.

Pete propped his elbows on the steering wheel to refill his pipe. He struck several matches, carefully negotiating the flame to the tobacco while still steering through the river of vehicles rushing headlong in a race to beat time itself. The flame leapt with each puff; his eyes were crossed to see whether he had succeeded in getting a thorough burn in the pipe bowl. Spent matches landed in an overflowing ashtray, sometimes bouncing onto the floor littered with old papers and oily rags.

The truck meandered from lane to lane, almost of its own free will.

"Would you open your window?" said Emily, whose patience was wearing a bit thin.

"Yeah, yeah." He lowered the window just a little.

The fresh air revived Daisy. She opened her window wide enough to ride with her head perched against her elbow. The sounds of the blaring traffic and bustling city rushed in with the cold air. This worked for about a minute, until all three passengers were too cold for comfort.

"It's not as warm as it looks, is it?" Daisy asked as she rolled up her window.

"Doesn't his bad driving make you nervous, Daisy?" said Emily.

"Bad driving? Watch what you say. Have I hit anything yet?"

"No point in complaining," Daisy said. "I couldn't negotiate this traffic. I haven't got the reflexes for it. I'd rather he didn't dent the truck, but it's got enough bangs and scrapes that one more here or there would hardly matter."

She hesitated, getting her bearings after her nap. "The truck does seem to be running kind of rough. The engine doesn't sound right. Does it feel all right, Pete?"

"It's the pavement. There's a lot of construction on these roads. They're always working on the potholes in the spring. So much so there's even a contest to see where the worst one is in the city."

"Seems like they're always fixing—and then fixing the fixes," said Emily.

"That's the Mafia," said Pete. "There's been a lot in the news lately about the extortion and corruption in the construction industry. Even the politicians are involved. Makes a lot of people, including the Premier of Quebec, very nervous."

"I wonder if Luigi Rocco has anything to do with what's going on," said Daisy. "He mentioned he was in construction, but the Bella Vista Social Club doesn't look much like a construction site to me."

"With a name like Luigi Rocco, living in Little Italy," said Emily, "I wouldn't put it past him."

"Haven't there been a lot of gang wars and some pretty nasty shootings in Montréal lately?" said Daisy.

"Oh, yeah, they're not fooling around. The traditional Italian Mafia is getting challenged by other underworld gangs fighting for territory."

"It's not just construction. The drug trade and trafficking are big business too," said Emily.

"Wherever there's dirty money to be made," said Pete, "the Mafia gets involved somehow. Extortion, embezzlement, smuggling, prostitution—you name it, they've already thought of it. The newspapers imply that even the politicians are being paid under the table. It's a serious game."

"It seems awfully complicated—like out of the movies," Daisy said.

Emily told a story she'd heard about the Mafia wars. "On Halloween a few years ago, in a really nice neighbourhood, one guy was giving out candies to the neighbourhood kids. Two thugs, dressed in Halloween costumes with black masks over their heads shot the Mafioso boss in the face at point-blank range, right there in front of his wife and kids."

"Oh that's horrible," Daisy said. "That doesn't sound good at all."

"There have been some assassinations of the big guys just lately," Pete said.

"You mean the Risotto family?"

"Risotto? That's a good one, Em."

"Risotto is rice. I have a good recipe for mushroom risotto. It's in my Italian cookbook," Daisy said.

"What's their name then?"

Pete said, "Rizutto. The Rizutto family. The father was shot, and then his grandson. Only one son is still alive and is doing time in Colorado. They've nearly wiped out the whole family. There was a huge funeral at the Notre Dame Cathedral not long ago."

"I wish I could have been there," Emily said.

Pete laughed. "Oh yeah, you would have fit right in. I can see it now. All the limousines with the guys in black suits and their wives with diamonds and gold—and little ole you, sitting in the pews right next to them."

"I'm sure that's what Rocco was talking about. I think that's what happened to Michel."

Emily asked, "Is that was what that was all about? Did you ask Rocco about Michel?"

"Yes. I had to find out for myself. Michel never talked about what he did for them. Strangely, Luigi seemed to know things about Michel that nobody else knew: that he was in charge of security and transporting goods. I can only imagine that he had to carry a gun and use it on occasion. He must have been witness to some very nasty settling of accounts. I felt sick to my stomach when he started to talk. I really believe he knew a lot more than what he did admit."

"What did he say?"

"He told me Michel wanted to get out but said nobody gets out. That's why he had to die. Omertà. That's the word Rocco used. When they take care of their own. But Rocco said he didn't do it."

"Well, those guys never actually do the work themselves," said Pete. "They have hit men who do all the dirty work for them—if they're at the top. According to the papers, things are getting pretty hot for those big guys too."

"That must be why Luigi wants to get out of the city," Daisy said. "He mentioned there were things happening that were making him very nervous, especially for the sake of the wife and kids."

"I would be too, if I were him," Pete said.

"Oh," Emily said, as if she just realized a connection in the conversation. "I wonder if this has anything to do with our murder victim. I wonder if she tried to get out."

"Whoever did her in wasn't fooling around either," Pete said. "You don't just go and kill somebody, saw up the body and throw it in a ditch unless you mean business."

"But why so far from the city?"

"Precisely," Emily said. "There's a connection here that we're not getting."

"Speaking of saws," Pete said, slapping his head as if to wake himself from a deep sleep. "I just remembered . . . oh, I didn't think of this before . . . oh no."

"What's the matter, Pete? You sound as if you're in pain."

"Now you are making me nervous," Daisy said. "He always makes me nervous."

"No, no really. We've got a problem. I bought something at the flea market today, Em. I was going to show it to you. I figured it might have something to do with the case."

"What, Pete, what?"

"Well, this guy had a chainsaw. He was peddling a chainsaw. He described the man who sold it to him, and when I asked him more details, he described the place where you guys were this morning too, where you went to look after that dog. There was something about the chainsaw that made me suspicious. When I asked him the price, he threw it in with some other stuff he wanted to sell. It's in the truck, and the truck is in the impound yard. If the cops find it, then I could be in deep doo-doo."

"Oh, you're already in big trouble," Emily said. "I wasn't going to break it to you. I wasn't going to make a big deal of it. I was going to wait until . . . until we had a bit of a break. But I guess I'd better tell you both now, while we're on the subject of bad news."

"What's the matter?" Daisy said.

"Well, I had a talk with Inspector Allard when I went to the police station. He told me you're the prime suspect of the murder investigation."

"Pete's the prime suspect?"

"Daisy's the suspect?"

"Well, you're both suspects. In fact, he's trying to get a warrant for your arrests, both of you."

"No, that can't be."

"Oh, no." Pete groaned. "I don't need that."

"I think I convinced him to hold off. I really had a serious heart-to-heart talk with Allard. I told him there was no way . . . there was no way you had anything to do with that murder. All you did was find the evidence. But you know, the cops . . . they like to come up with some kind of a solution pretty quick so people don't panic. I mean, they don't want to have rumours of a serial killer running around loose. When a body gets found sawed up in pieces and tossed out into a ditch, well, they don't want that story to get out without having a suspect already arrested. Unfortunately, you guys are front and centre . . . the finger points pretty clearly in your direction."

". . . but we're not."

"We wouldn't ever think of doing such a thing."

"Yeah, well, Allard doesn't know you like I do. He doesn't care about you personally. What he cares about is saving his job."

"We've got to come up with a solution," Emily said, "before Allard does. I've got some ideas, some good ideas. I want to follow up a lead I discovered while Daisy was looking after Roger's dog. I think those guys at Spring Valley are suspicious characters. What was wrong with the chainsaw you picked up, Pete?"

"Well, we're going to have to go and get it."

"Get it? Your truck was impounded."

"Yep, I know where the impound yard is. We're going to have to go and get it, so you can see it, Em. Then you can tell me what we're going to do with it."

"Well, I think it should be returned to its rightful owner."

"Rightful owner?" Daisy asked. "How are you going to find the rightful owner?"

"I think we already know who that is." Emily imitated Sherlock Holmes talking with Dr. Watson. "Pete, tell me exactly what that man said."

"Well, he said he bought it off a guy from Spring Valley Road who was covered with snakes and devil tattoos and metal in his ears. The guy said he had some milk bottles to sell. He tossed the chainsaw into the deal. I picked up the saw to look at it 'cause I always pick up chainsaws. I've already got three or four at home, and none of them run."

"That's because you buy them at the flea market," Daisy said. "You don't really expect people to be selling perfectly good chainsaws at the market, do you? If they worked, they wouldn't be for sale."

"Well, you never know," Pete said. "A bargain is a bargain. Sometimes they work, and sometimes you can fix them."

"Well, I'd say you're probably doin' more fixin' than workin'."

"Get on with your story, Pete," Daisy said.

"Be that as it may, I bought the chainsaw. Well I didn't really buy it—the guy was selling it with some other tools, some old tools. I thought maybe Emily would want to see it, that she might have something to say about it. Looked to me like there was some evidence in the teeth of the saw."

"Um," Emily said, her detective's curiosity in full bloom. "What kind of evidence?"

"Looked to me like there was some flesh and hair caught up in the chain guard. Some blood on the blade was still visible. I don't know too many people who cut up bodies with chainsaws, do you? Even if you were cutting up meat for the freezer, it wouldn't have hair and skin on the carcass. Hunters generally clean their meat before putting it away for the winter."

"I'd like to see this saw," Emily said in her most professional detective's voice.

"I can't believe this would all fall together, that we would be able to track down the criminals who might actually be people we know," Daisy said. "It's just too much of a coincidence."

"Nonsense," Emily said. "It's a small town. There's not that many choices."

"You never know who lives on the fringes in this county," Pete said. "We have a pretty regular life, but around the edges there are a lot of shady characters."

"Roger Major isn't a shady character," Daisy said. "I know he's a very good man at heart. He just has a hard time because of his handicap. Living in the country is hard on people who are different—who are challenged."

"We're not talking about Roger," Emily said. "I met the characters who live downstairs. Those men are sticky."

"What d'ya mean, sticky?" Pete asked.

"Let's just say they're not the cream of the crop."

"Emily, you're getting your metaphors mixed up."

"Never mind that," Emily said. "I have reason to believe they're probably involved in dope dealing."

Daisy asked, "How does that work? Where does the Mafia come into it?"

"The Mafia," Pete said, "is everywhere where there's money to be made, but they don't do the work themselves. They hire people."

"Well, I think those men I met are the hired thugs. I think they're dealing drugs and running a grow-op to boot. I'll bet our young girl with the tattoo just got in the way. Maybe she saw too much."

"Well, I do know they don't fool around," Daisy said. "Michel was a nice guy too, and look how he ended up."

"I never did understand how you got tied up with him," Emily said. "You're a little too innocent. Naïve is putting it mildly. You always think the best of everyone."

"Yes, well, there's not much point in seeing the worst. If you think people are no good, they meet your expectations. If you see the best, sometimes you can save people, the same way you can save animals. If you treat an animal like an animal, it's going to be an animal. If you treat an animal with respect, then you'll have a friend forever. Look at Friday."

"Friday is a good dog," Pete said.

"Friday's a good dog?" Emily said. "I'm not so sure. He's lucky to have you, that's for sure, Daisy."

"Now don't go picking on Friday. He's only a dog."

"Yes, that's the point precisely," Emily said. "He's only a dog. He's not a human, and he needs to learn to behave like a dog. He hasn't got any manners."

"Emily, you're one to talk," Pete said. "You've got a cat that doesn't have any manners either."

"Charlie's beside the point. We're not talking about Charlie."

"Okay. We're not talking about Charlie."

"We're talking about gangsters," said Daisy.

"And hoodlums," said Pete.

"And criminals," said Daisy.

"And murderers," said Emily.

"Can't get much more serious than that," said Pete.

"Look, guys," Daisy said, "on the subject of serious subjects, I really need to eat something before too long. It's been a long time since breakfast."

"Actually," Pete said, "my stomach thinks my throat's been cut."

"There's a good chip stand just off the highway. We could stop there. It's not far out of our way," Daisy said.

Pete nodded. "I think poutine is lookin' better all the time. We could take a break, have a rest. We've got time to stop in and get something to eat before we go to the impound yard to take our chainsaw back."

"What about my animals?" Daisy asked. "I've been gone all day. I've got to be getting home."

"Your animals will look after themselves," Emily said. "We've got some important things to do. Besides, if something happens to you, if they arrest you, for instance, your animals will have to look after themselves anyway. If my hunch is correct, we can solve this murder. I hope I'm right because you can't afford to be arrested."

"No, I wouldn't even know how to start."

"You don't have to. Allard's an expert on the subject of arresting people."

Pete groaned. "I think I'm suddenly feeling rather sick to my stomach."

"No, no, no," Emily said. "It's just because you're hungry and tired. We've been going all day, and you've been up since four o'clock this morning."

"It has been a crazy day—a really crazy day."

"So let's stop and get something to eat, and then we'll discuss our plan afterward."

# Chapter Twenty-Nine

Once off the island of Montréal, the countryside stretched out into agricultural fields and rolling purple mountains. Dirty patches of snow stubbornly persisted in sheltered ditches and along wind breaks separating rural properties. The dark earth of ploughed fields lay in wait for the warmth of the sun to dry up in time for planting.

Though the truck motored more slowly along the highway, Pete, Emily and Daisy were not concerned. The more they thought about food, the hungrier they became.

"Okay, what makes a chip stand a *good* chip stand?" Pete was prone to reducing quality to a range of measurement. "On a scale of one to ten."

"Well, you have to have good French fries," Emily said. "Frites stand or chip stand, it all comes down to the potatoes."

"The potatoes have to be fresh cut and then soaked in ice water. They're fried once, cooled off, and then fried again." Daisy specialized in the finer details of good cooking.

"They have to be soft on the inside, crispy on the outside and steaming hot." Pete was a connoisseur of texture in spite of his missing teeth.

"That's good for the French fries. What about the poutine?"

"Oh," Daisy said, "I'm the expert on poutine. The French fries have to be so hot that when you put the cheese curds on, they immediately melt."

"Fresh curds of course. Mild cheddar in small chunks, can't be just any cheese—has to be fresh cheddar curds."

"And definitely not grated cheese. That would never do."

"The gravy has to be boiling hot," Emily said, refusing to be outdone when it came to poutine expertise. "It's got to be brown gravy, and not homemade but from a can."

"Even my gravy doesn't really taste right," Daisy admitted.

"The gravy has to be so hot that it makes the cheese go soggy."

"Squishy, the word is squishy—so that it squeaks when you bite into it."

"But the French fries still stay crispy."

"That's almost impossible to find."

Suddenly the truck jerked them to attention. The engine gave one last gasp and completely shut down. The power steering failed when the engine quit. Pete gripped the wheel with both hands on one side and guided the rickety vehicle onto the gravel shoulder with considerable effort.

"What's wrong, Pete?"

"The engine's not getting any gas."

"What does the gas gauge show? I filled it up this morning. There should be enough to get us back home with some to spare."

"As long as we're off the highway so we don't get rammed from behind, we'll have a chance to figure out what's wrong."

The truck rolled to a stop a safely. All three travellers alit from the cab. Pete heaved the hood open. They peered inside.

"Watch while I try to start it," Pete said. "See if anything's wrong."

"How will we know?"

"Watch for misfiring, sparks or broken hoses."

Emily kept her distance in case something exploded, but Daisy climbed up onto the fender and peered into the dark innards of her favourite machine. Pete tried several times. Although the motor turned over, the engine refused to catch.

While Pete and Daisy were preoccupied with discussing all the possible causes for misfiring, Emily glanced around at her surroundings and vaguely watched the passing cars as they whipped by, whooshing and spraying water into their faces.

All of a sudden she began to whoop and holler, gesturing and jumping up and down excitedly. "Look, look, there are my friends! Stop! Stop!" She jumped in front of an oncoming cube van, waving her arms and gesturing madly.

"Emily, get back here," Pete said, grabbing her by the sleeve and pulling her out of the traffic lane. "Are you crazy? You're going to get yourself killed."

"No, no, it's them! They'll stop to help us. I know they will."

Daisy gasped when she saw the two guys in the approaching van. The driver had a bandana on his head, with long straggling hair and gold earrings. His passenger was more frightening. His whole face was covered with tattoos; his mouth twisted into a horrid grin, with fangs and filed canines.

In the instant when the van approached and passed the disabled truck, one could read the interaction between them in a split second. The faces of the two men appeared stunned and curious about the odd little lady hopping up and down by the side of the road. Then they both stared in recognition when they realized she was pointing directly at them. They looked at each other, spoke, and pulled off the highway several hundred yards beyond where Pete, Emily and Daisy stood watching them pass by. Then the hazard lights flashed, and a backup siren sounded as they reversed.

"I knew they'd stop when they recognized who I was. I met them today. That's B. Man and Fatso from the Spring Valley house."

"Your prime suspects? That's them? And you just waved them down to help us? Emily, are you out of your mind?" Pete cried, whipping his hat off; he slapped his leg with the brim in exasperation.

"It's all right, Pete. Calm yourself. They might hear you. I know they're a bit strange, but we'll just ask them for a lift to the next exit, where we can hire a tow truck."

The van, with Bella Vista Transport marked in large red letters, parked in front of the truck. Both doors opened simultaneously. The men lumbered toward the stranded travellers with an unspoken assumption of authority and competence.

Pete whistled under his breath and murmured, "Tweedle Dum and Tweedle Dee in Technicolour."

"Pete, that's not nice," Emily said.

"No, and I'd bet they aren't either."

Ignoring Pete's comments, Emily gushed, assuming B. Man would consult her for an explanation. "I'm so glad you stopped. I told my friends here that I was sure you'd help us out. Thank you so much."

Instead, they walked right past her. A bond formed automatically between the men.

Pete took the lead. "Thanks, for stoppin', man."

They shook hands with a swagger. Then the three approached the broken-down truck as if they had known each other for years. They proceeded to poke and prod underneath the hood as Pete tried again and again to start the motor. The battery began to weaken before they gave up. Emily and Daisy stood by without any help to offer. After some consultation, B. Man announced their diagnosis.

"Probably gas starvation. Maybe a broken hose or carburetor problem."

"Look," Pete said. "I don't carry credit cards, but I've got one for CAA. If you give me a ride to the gas station at the next exit, I'll get a tow. They should be able to fix it in their garage."

Emily caught the glance that flashed between B. Man and Fatso.

"No room for a passenger, man. Truck's full. You stay here with the ladies."

The word "ladies" rolled off B. Man's tongue as if from some other world. The term was oddly out of context yet so pleasing to Emily's ears that she took it as a compliment. She smiled flirtatiously. Daisy, on the other hand, paid no notice.

"We'll stop on our way and tell the guy to come pick you up."

"Sure, man, whatever you say. That'd be great. Appreciate it."

Without saying another word, the gangsters got back in the van, spinning their tires on the gravel as they pulled out onto the highway.

"Do you really think they'll do what they say?" Daisy asked, unusually suspicious.

"We'll know soon enough," Pete said.

When the van veered onto the exit ramp, Emily breathed an audible sigh of relief.

"I knew I could trust my instincts. If you give a man a chance to do good, usually he'll rise to the challenge."

"Yeah, well we'll see if the tow truck really shows up," Pete said. "In the meantime, where were we? Cheeseburgers—what about the cheeseburgers?"

"A cheeseburger has to be made from fresh meat." Daisy took up the thread of conversation as if it had never been interrupted. "It should not be frozen, and should never be a premade patty."

"Fresh hamburgers are hard to find anymore."

"The burger's got to be big enough to fill the whole bun. Not just a roll with a dab of meat in the middle. We're talking about a cheeseburger, all-dressed."

Pete had to correct the diction. "All dresssss," he said, stressing the esses, tongue between his gums.

"That means burger, slab of cheese, lettuce, tomato," said Daisy.

"Onions, don't forget the onions," said Emily.

"Lots of onions," Pete said.

"Then you can put mustard and ketchup—" Daisy was still listing the all-dressed ingredients, when Pete interrupted.

"Ketchup? Americans use ketchup, not Canadians."

"Well, technically, you can put everything on if it's really all-dressed," Emily said.

"Mustard, relish, sauerkraut and *oignions cuits*," Daisy said.

"*Cuits*, not *crus*, cooked onions not raw. You have to have fried onions—a whole pile of them," Pete said. "They've got to be just right."

"A little tiny bit crunchy," Daisy said, "but mostly caramelized."

"Caramelized?" Pete said. "What's that?"

"Sweet, so they're crunchy and chewy at the same time."

"What about a chunk of raw onion?" Emily asked. "Pete likes raw onions."

"That's right. It's an insult to a good onion if you cook it," Pete said. "But if you cut it too thick, that would take at least one full point off the score on your scale of one to ten."

Emily spotted the tow truck heading east along the service road, toward the on-ramp accessing their lane.

"They did it! They actually stopped and convinced the guy to come for us!"

"He's not here yet," Pete said, putting a damper on Emily's enthusiasm.

"You know," said the detective Mrs. Blossom, "I think that truck was full of drugs. That's why they wouldn't give you a ride."

Pete cocked his eyebrows. Daisy stared in disbelief.

"Do you really think so?" said Daisy.

"They must have left the farm soon after we did. They drove to Montréal, picked up the stuff and now they're headed for delivery," said Emily. "The timing's right."

"Why did they stop then? They didn't have to. They could have driven by," said Daisy.

"With Emily out there jumping and carrying on in the middle of the highway, they would have had to explain a hit-and-run," Pete said.

The tow truck approached, lights flashing, engine roaring.

"Knights in shining armour come in strange costumes these days," Emily said.

The mechanic wore overalls covered in grease. He had large hands with black fingernails, dark eyes and swarthy skin. His hat was turned with the visor pointing backward. A day's growth of whiskers outlined high aboriginal cheekbones. An ample moustache sheltered large lips.

He addressed Pete in French through a toothless grin. "*Eh b'en, le truck ne marche pas?*"

"*Marche pas, cour pas . . . le truck va pas du tout,*" Pete replied, fluently but with a strong English accent. "*J'croix qu'il n'y a pas de gaz.*"

"*Sans gaz, ça va pas loin.*"

"*Oui, j'sais. C'est pourquoi on est ici, et pas chez toi deja.*"

"What are they saying?" Emily asked Daisy. Her French was not as colloquial as Daisy's.

"The mechanic asked if the truck wasn't working, and Pete said it wasn't running either. Pete thinks it's out of gas and the mechanic said, 'If it's out of gas, it won't go far'. Pete answered that that's why we're stuck here on the road and not already at the gas station." Then Daisy continued with her own comments. "I know it's not out of gas. I filled it just before leaving and we should have plenty. It must be something else."

Emily and Daisy stood by patiently while the men went through the routine of trying to start the unwilling truck, until the battery was completely drained, all to no avail. They considered various solutions, which neither woman could follow. Finally they concluded there was nothing to do but tow the pickup to the garage for a closer analysis of the problem.

The mechanic manoeuvred his towing trailer into place. With little fanfare but a great deal of noise and clatter, he attached a chain to the bumper and winched the vehicle onto the carrier.

Then Pete escorted his companions to the passengers' side of the tow truck and offered to help them onto the running board and into the cab.

Emily took one look inside the cab and balked. "We're going to ride in our own vehicle, thank you very much. There's too much smoke and debris in here."

She quickly turned, jumped nimbly onto the trailer ramp, and proceeded to open the door to Daisy's truck. "C'mon, Daisy, hop in!"

"*Ah, non, non, madame! On n'est pas capable. C'n'est pas permis.*"

Emily looked at Daisy for a translation. "He says we're not allowed to ride in the truck while it's being towed."

Without flinching or changing her mind, Emily replied, "*Pas capable est mort, son frere s'appelle.* 'Watch me'. I don't understand the word 'can't'."

With that, she took Daisy by the arm and hoisted her into the truck on the towing platform. Then she settled into the driver's side behind the wheel and cocked her elbow on the window, obviously preparing for another glorious adventure.

Pete knew better than to argue. He winked at the mechanic and reached into his pocket for two cigarillos. Handing one to the driver, he leapt into the tow truck, glancing back over his shoulder with a grin. "*On ne change pas les femmes avec les têtes dures. Nous pouvons fumer, sans qu'elles chiallent et briaillent. Elles peuvent se battre, sans que nous soyons au milieu.*"

"What did he say about us, Daisy?" Emily asked.

"He said, 'You can't change women with hard heads'. He said they were going to smoke in peace without us yelling and scolding them about filling up the cab with smoke. He said, 'They can fight and we won't be in the middle'."

"Well, he's perfectly right," said Emily. "We're much better off riding back here than we would be stuffed into the cab of that truck. And he certainly couldn't leave us alone by the side of the road, now, could he?"

Emily and Daisy perched primly in their seats viewing the countryside passing by, as if they were tourists on a double-decker bus. Emily's head barely looked out over the door sill, but she created a large appearance, with smiling eyes and flying feathery hair. Daisy was like a large, woolly pillow, her ponytail disobedient, her round face worn and rustic.

"Look how clever we are," Emily said. "We get fresh air and a beautiful view, and they can puff away to their hearts' content."

Daisy was not so sure. "What happens if the poor man gets into trouble?"

"Daisy, that's your problem: you always think of the other person first. Why can't you just sit back and enjoy life? If other people don't care, why should you?"

By this time, Daisy was tired and cranky. Her usually gentle nature was at its limits. "Why can't you mind your own business, Emily Blossom? You're always bossing other people around, as if you're better than everyone else. I get pretty sick and tired of you always picking on me. Why don't you lay off and look in the mirror once in a while? You might see that you're not as superior as you think you are."

She hesitated in her tirade, but not long enough for Emily to comment. She was on a roll. "On second thought, you probably wouldn't see your own faults if you did look in the mirror, would you? You'd be too busy admiring yourself. You go along in life claiming to be some kind of clever detective, when all you really are is a snoop with a fertile imagination. You pretend you're so attractive, flirting with men half your age. Do you honestly think they really take you seriously? What they see is a funny, delusional old broad. You go around making friends with all kinds of weirdos. Don't you know they would just as soon wipe you off the face of the planet as look at you? You've got a rude awakening in store for you, Emily Blossom, and I don't want to be around when you find out that you're really old and frail and approaching the end of your life real fast."

Emily watched the scenery, barely listening to her sister-in-law. She scanned the horizon for signs of spring. "Daisy, you take life far too seriously."

Daisy rarely allowed herself to vent her emotions, but she didn't miss this opportunity to tell Emily exactly what she thought. "I've only got one life to lead. Unlike you, I'm not going to squander it playing games and deluding myself that I'm somebody I'm not. Life is too short. You seem to think you can parade around butting into other people's lives, that it doesn't matter who you hurt in the process. You treat Pete like he's some sort of puppet on a string, at your beck and call whenever you need somebody to get you out of trouble. He's too good-hearted to tell you what he really thinks. He just goes along with your pranks and suffers the consequences. He could end up in jail. You know that, don't you?"

"You know, spring's just around the corner. The geese are feeding on corn stubble waiting for the ice to break up on the river."

"We could both end up in jail. You know that, don't you?" Daisy was shouting, but Emily refused to look at her.

"I'll visit you both regularly. Don't think I'd just abandon you, just because—"

Emily's words were hurtful. She was irritating Daisy on purpose, but she didn't care. On the contrary, she was enjoying herself immensely.

"There, I told you so!" Daisy's voice had reached a desperate pitch of agitation.

"That's exactly what I mean. You always go making fun of me when I'm trying to have a serious discussion, when I'm trying to tell you you're being a fool. Just watch out, Emily, because you're going to push me once too often! Then I won't be around when it's time to pick up your pieces. I'm warning you! Someday you're going to need friends, and you'll look around and find out you haven't got any. You've snubbed them all so often, they'll be long gone when you need help."

"There, there, Daisy, don't get yourself all worked up in a snit fit. I was only kidding."

"Kidding? Kidding? Well, I'm not. I don't need you to tell me how to live my life. And I'm not interested in following your example, thank you very much."

*

The truck slowed and pulled into the only gas station in the village, which straddled the border between Quebec and Ontario. The mechanic pulled around behind the garage so that no one would notice the two women riding in the cab of the pickup he was towing.

Pete opened the passenger door and offered Daisy his arm for balance. He sensed the women had been arguing and breathed a sigh of relief he had not been involved in their spat. "Enjoy your ride, ladies?" he asked cheerfully.

Daisy's cheeks were damp. She looked away, wiping tears with the back of her hand. Emily did not wait for his assistance. She stepped adroitly onto the trailer and hopped to the ground.

Pete may have interrupted a heated argument, but he carried on as if he did not notice the tension between them. "Our friend here is going to check the gas line. If we're lucky, it's a plugged gas filter. He should be able to fix that in a jiffy. Just long enough for us to have a good feed."

Emily sidled up to Pete, leaving Daisy far enough behind so she couldn't hear their conversation. "Daisy's having a bit of a meltdown, Pete. We need to get some food into her."

"It just so happens, our Frites stand is just across the street."

"An extra-large poutine should do the trick."

"Well, actually, I like the places that have a lot of different kinds of poutine," Daisy said, catching up with them as they crossed the street. "There's a place in Hamilton Mills with seafood poutine, Italian poutine (that's the one with tomato sauce and hamburger meat), chicken poutine, Chinese poutine . . ."

"What's that?"

"That's the one with stir-fried vegetables and brown gravy on top."

"That's too fancy for me," Pete said. "I might go for a parasol though."

"What's that?"

"You get the poutine and the cheeseburger all together—French fries, cheese curds, hamburger meat and the brown gravy all in one."

"Ugh. That's too much," Emily said.

"How about a pogo?" Pete asked.

"Too much pastry around the hot dog."

"Don't forget the Pepsi—poutine and a Pepsi with a Mae Wesss for deeesssert. That would be the Quebecois version of a balanced diet."

They approached a converted school bus permanently parked in a lot overlooking the river. The faded sign at the road was a wood cutout depicting a giant box overflowing with French fries.

"This place pretty well suits the bill," Pete said.

"I'm so hungry right now," Daisy said, "I could eat even a bad poutine."

"Well, I'm so smug right now—and hungry," Emily said, "I'm going to splurge. Dinner's on me."

"Whoa," Pete said, "I'm not saying no to that."

"I figured as much," Emily said.

"Well, thank you, Emily, it's really not necessary," Daisy said. "It was my idea to come to town after all, wasn't it?"

"It's all right; you've given me lots of meals. I'm buying. Who knows when you'll get another chance to indulge in such gourmet cooking?"

"Emily, don't talk like that."

"She's just teasing you. Let it go."

**Frites Stand**

# Chapter Thirty

The frites stand didn't disappoint them. Soon they were sitting down to a delicious meal. The food was so good, there was no time for talk. Juice ran along Pete's moustache and down his chin. Daisy's cheeks were full of poutine. Emily delicately dabbed the edges of her mouth to make sure she didn't drip any ketchup on her outfit. When they finished, there was not a scrap, not even a French fry, left on the paper plates.

"No doggy bag for Friday today," Daisy said.

"I guess we were hungry, all right."

"I'm going to leave you two ladies to clean up," Pete said, rising from his chair. "I'll go for the truck."

Daisy and Emily sat for a while in silence, surveying the empty plates. After eating, they had no energy for squabbling. They cleared the table and threw the papers in the trash. Emily made sure to place the cans in the recycle box.

By the time they spotted the truck in the parking lot, they could see Pete's boots crossed on the dashboard, but no head was apparent. With his seat reclined, he was stretched out; a *Journal de Montréal* newspaper covered his face. His unlit pipe hung at an awkward angle from his lips. Snores emanated from underneath a blaring headline: La Chute D'un Empire du Crime. The headline featured the downfall of the Criminal Empire in Montréal. A gory photograph of a slain mobster was featured on the front page.

The passenger door creaked loudly when they opened it, but Pete didn't budge. Emily climbed into the truck and settled in next to Pete. Daisy pushed the seat back and put her feet up on the dashboard as well. Soon all three were snoozing in the sun, basking in the warmth of the truck.

After a good twenty-minute nap, Pete stirred. He put his feet back on the floor, lifted his seat, opened a slit in the window and lit his pipe.

Emily opened her eyes, sat up and yawned.

Daisy put her feet down and raised her seat into place. Then she leaned her elbow on the window, resting her head against her arm to catch a few extra stolen moments of sweet slumber.

"Well, I guess it's time to be on our way," Pete said. "It must be around closing time over at the impound yard. We should be able to get in there and scope out the place. We'll figure out how we're going to get that chainsaw back."

He turned the key, and the truck obediently roared to life.

"Well, I guess we're on our way to another stage of our adventure," Emily said. "Isn't it all so very exciting?"

"I could do with less excitement and more sleep," Daisy mumbled, still with her eyes squeezed shut, trying to avoid the inevitable waking. "I wish I could go back to last week. Everything seemed so simple then."

"Yes, but think how you'll feel once this is all over," Emily said. "You'll appreciate your ordinary life so much more once you've experienced an escapade."

"I don't need to appreciate my life more than I do, thank you very much. I'm too old for adventures."

"Old? Old? Don't say that, Daisy. A person should never use age as an excuse not to do something. You're only as old as you let yourself be."

"Emily, how about if you have enough excitement for the three of us? Then you can come back and tell us all about it."

"What fun would that be? Without you, I'd be on my own."

"Exactly."

"Precisely."

# Chapter Thirty-One

Wally's gas station and restaurant was just off the main highway between Ottawa and Montréal at the exit for Emerald Hill. Wally had the primary towing contract for the region. He also had a liking for small airplanes. On the lot was room for truck parking, as well as a large garage for heavy equipment repairs. As a result, Wally's Place was a repository for vehicles of all sizes and descriptions, from large transports to single-engine airplanes to tractor trailers and passenger cars. Long-distance drivers stopped for gas and a bite to eat; truckers could shower and buy girlie magazines and beef jerky; broken-down vehicles and crashed cars were stored behind the garage. The impound lot was tucked in a corner behind tin walls, surrounded by a chain-link fence.

Wally's parking lot was a hive of activity, with vehicles coming and going at all hours of the day and night. Bright lights illuminated the gas tanks and restaurant entrance, but at the edge of the property, crippled tractor trailers and empty cube vans loomed in the shadows like abandoned dead monsters.

By the time Daisy's truck rolled up Wally's drive, the sun had disappeared behind the trees on the horizon. An orange hue highlighted skeletal lace along the edges of sky fading into night. Most drivers had switched on their headlights. Vehicles twinkled along the highway, like passing sparks. Cars stopped under the lights of the station as if the travellers wanted to arrive before dark swallowed them into uncertainty.

Pete drove slowly up the drive and veered purposefully toward the truck lot.

"Is that the impound yard?" Emily whispered, as if by keeping her voice down they would have less likelihood of being noticed.

"Yes, there's the gate at the front with a padlock."

"It looks like barbed wire runs all the way around the top of the fence," Daisy said, defeated before they had begun.

"That's no big deal. Pete will figure it out."

"I can see my truck parked over there in the corner," he said, recognizing an old friend among a crowd of strangers.

Pete kept the truck moving very slowly past the yard so they could study the situation without being seen. He drove around the back of the garage, across the restaurant parking lot and then made another pass, as if searching for a mechanic at the garage.

"How will you ever get in there?" Daisy asked. "The fence is much taller than you are, and you're liable to get your pants hung up on the barbs."

"It'll be a piece of cake," he said. "Look at the back corner. There's a van parked right up next to the fence on the outside. The wire doesn't go that far around the back. I can climb up on the van's roof and hop over to the other side."

"How will you get out?"

"I'll figure that out when I get to it. Emily, you get out here and scope out the front gate. If anybody comes, keep him busy. Daisy, you come with me and help me climb. If we get caught, you'll drive the truck while I hide. Nobody will suspect you. Pretend you're a confused old lady who took a wrong turn."

"I can do that."

He stopped in the shadow of a trailer to let Emily out. She had to pass over Daisy's knees and underneath the dashboard to exit. The truck door creaked like a haunted house when Daisy lifted the lever.

"Shh. Not so loud!"

"I can't help it!"

"Close it softly."

"I can't!" Daisy's voice, by this point, resembled a ewe caught in a fence at night when coyotes were howling in the distance.

"Shh! Don't tell the whole world we're over here!"

Pete inched the truck, with its motor purring and the muffler rumbling into the dark shadows at the back of the lot. In the meanwhile, Emily hiked her purse onto her shoulder and disappeared along the wall toward the gate.

When she reached a good vantage spot, she hesitated and glanced around to see if anyone had noticed her.

*In the line of duty, a detective must be creative . . . sometimes to the point of stretching the truth beyond recognition.*

Then she began to search the ground as if she had lost something. She listened for the sound of the pickup idling behind the fence. Out of the corner of her eye, she scanned the parking lot for approaching strangers. An eternity passed as she waited.

Then she saw him. A twentyish-something fellow in a mechanic's uniform ambled in her direction from the garage. He had dark, curly hair and a friendly twinkle in his eye. His cheeks were childlike, shaded with an attempt at a moustache.

"Lose something?" he asked casually, as if her presence were an everyday occurrence.

"Yes, yes, I believe I have," Emily said in her most shaky and frail tone of voice. "I've misplaced my house key. My daughter will be very upset with me."

The young man took up the search with her. "Where did you lose it? Around here?"

"Yes, I dropped it when I was fumbling in my pocket for a handkerchief. I was just getting a breath of fresh air. I think I heard it fall onto the pavement."

Emily continued aimlessly searching, walking in circles. The young man took up the hunt as well.

"My daughter will be so angry when she finds out."

She bantered on, filling the air with noisy chatter. As a master of deception, Emily made the most of her chance to perfect the art of make-believe. "I know I'm clumsy, even though I try to be careful. I'm always causing some sort of trouble. She gets so tired of me sometimes. You're so kind to help me. I hope we can find it before she comes back. She's inside having a coffee. Actually, she's probably talking on her cell phone. She always talks to her friends while she leaves me sitting in the car. I just didn't want to sit any longer waiting for her to come out."

Emily heard a loud thump coming from the back of the impound yard. She cleared her throat and sneezed vehemently. She manoeuvred her circle so that she could face the lad and at the same time see inside the yard over his shoulder.

Emily looked at the fellow to see if he had heard anything unusual. He was scanning the ground for the lost key. His pocket bore the name Serge.

"Did you say your name was Serge?" she asked, imposing herself on his attention. "Are you from around here?"

213

The mechanic interrupted his search and smiled, flattered that she called him by name. "Yes, how did you know?"

Emily was well aware that everyone liked to be recognized as someone special.

"Are you my friend's son? The one who works at Wally's as a mechanic."

"You mean my mom, Mrs. Carriere? Are you friends with her?"

"Yes, yes, I know your mom quite well. Mrs. Carriere. And you're Serge, the one she talks so fondly of."

Over the mechanic's shoulder, Emily saw Pete's shadow flying across the back of the impound yard toward his truck. She made sure her eyes did not follow his movements but fixed her gaze on Serge's face, demanding he focus on her.

"She talks about you all the time. She's so proud of you."

"Really?" Serge said. He knit his forehead in surprise so that his ample eyebrows nearly met just above his nose. "That's funny. She never tells me that. She's always complaining that I never went to university."

"Oh, no, young man, don't believe that drivel. All mothers pretend their children have to be better than they are. It's their way of encouraging you to be the best you can be. But don't you worry; your mother is very proud of you."

Serge's face portrayed a range of emotions from pleasure to puzzlement and back again. Emily always did have a soft spot for people whose expressions were like an open book. At the same time, behind Serge's back, she watched Pete's crouching figure hightailing back across the yard, carrying a bulky object that encumbered his progress.

She fumbled in her pocket and produced a single key. "Now, look at that! There's what I was looking for! It was in my pocket all along. It must have fallen into the lining." She smiled broadly. "Thank you so much, Serge, for helping me find my key."

She reached for his arm and gently guided him toward the garage. "Now, I'll just go on back and sit in the car until my daughter comes. Please give my best regards to your mother."

"What did you say your name was?" Serge asked. It had suddenly occurred to him he didn't have a clue who she was.

"Mrs. Duval," Emily said with a nod. "She'll know which Duval family. We're all related, actually. She'll figure it out. The Carrieres always do."

Serge smiled and returned to his work in the garage while Emily made her way toward the restaurant. She waited until she was sure he was no longer watching her before she circled around to where she thought the truck would reappear.

Sure enough, out of the shadows came the faithful Chevy, its two passengers basking in the glow of a mission accomplished. This time no one cared when the door clanked and slammed. Emily slipped into her place behind the dash, and the three drove confidently toward the next stage of their plan.

# Chapter Thirty-Two

"How did you do it?" Emily asked, quite pleased with her own cleverness. "I think I've been holding my breath the whole time you were gone."

"Nothing to it," Pete said.

"Just don't ask him to get out of the truck," Daisy said, chuckling.

"I can't believe you were so fast."

"How long does it take to get something out of the box of a truck?"

"Yes, but what about the fence?"

"You're worried about whether I hurt the fence?"

"No, how did you get over the fence?"

"He nearly had to stay there overnight."

"Lucky I had my pocket knife."

"C'mon. Tell me what happened."

"Just a little glitch in the plans," Daisy said.

"You did get the saw though, didn't you?"

"Oh, yes, no problem on that score," Pete said.

"Are you keeping me in suspense on purpose?" Emily was beginning to get a little perturbed. She did not like being kept in suspense, especially after she so efficiently waylaid the interference. "What did I miss?"

"Well, everything went exactly as planned."

"Right up until the very end."

"The tail end, you might say."

"Okay, okay. Out with it. What happened? Stop fooling around."

"We are telling you," Pete said.

"You go," Daisy said. "Tell her the whole thing, and I'll put in my two cents' worth."

"Well, everything went well. Daisy gave me a boost up onto the cube van, which was parked next to the back fence—so far, so good. The barbed wire was missing from the brackets, and it was pretty easy to climb over the top. Luckily, there was a back hoe on the inside, and I was able to climb onto the bucket and lower myself down to the ground from there. Then I ran across the yard—"

"Yes, I saw you do that," Emily said. "I was keeping the kid busy, but I could see you from where I was standing."

"I picked up the chainsaw, carried it back across the yard and climbed up, one-handed, onto the back hoe. That's where Daisy comes in."

"I had to climb up onto the cube van from the inside. Pete reached as far as he could while balancing on the fence. I had to reach as high as I could to grab it."

"Got her in the weak spot; hit her in the hands."

"Well, I didn't drop it, did I? Everything was good so far, but when Pete went to jump down onto the van, he caught his pants on a steel post, and he was literally—"

"Don't tell me," Emily chimed in. "Hanging by the seat of his pants?"

"Yes, that's it exactly," Daisy said, no longer able to contain her laughter. "You should have seen the look on his face!"

Pete was laughing so hard he hunched over the steering wheel and could hardly keep the truck on the road.

"Go on! It couldn't have been that bad!"

"I'm telling you," Daisy said with tears rolling down her cheeks, "it was that bad!"

"I must have been over at the garage at that point," Emily said, a bit miffed that she had missed all the fun. "I didn't hear a thing."

"We didn't dare laugh out loud," Daisy said. "I practically peed my pants. There I was, hanging onto the saw, tears running down my cheeks, sniveling and snorting and trying to hold it all in."

"Just don't ask me to get out of the truck," Pete said. "You'll have to look the other way."

"Gee, I can't wait," Emily said.

"I can," Daisy said.

As they told the story, the truck seemed to drive itself automatically toward Spring Valley Road. Before they knew it, they were at the foot of the hill, at the laneway of the farm where Roger Major lived. The lights of the farmhouse glowed in the distance.

"Wait, wait," Emily said. "We don't have a plan."

"I do," Pete said. "We're just going to drive on up there, put the chainsaw in the shed and drive away."

"Don't we have to tell them what we're doing?"

"Why? We're simply returning the saw to its rightful owner."

"Are we sure we know this is where it belongs?"

"If not, no one will be the wiser, and we'll be rid of it," Pete said. "I really don't want to get caught with that thing in my possession."

"How will I know if it's valuable evidence?" Detective Blossom said. "I haven't even had a chance to examine it closely."

Pete's patience was running short. "Look, Em. Take my word for it. The cops will put two and two together when the time comes."

"I guess you're right. We don't want to get caught red-handed."

"I'm glad you see my point of view. Let's get on with it."

"I'm anxious to get back to the farm. The animals aren't used to being out after dark."

Pete put the truck into gear and headed up the driveway, negotiating the ruts and potholes. Approaching the farmhouse, they could see through the curtains figures moving around in the kitchen. A dark silhouette loomed at the window with cupped hands, looking down the laneway, as the truck approached the crest of the driveway. Pete drove straight past the house and turned around in the barnyard.

The headlights, scanning the buildings like spotlights, revealed doors on broken hinges, gaping holes in the barn walls, the rusted Chevrolet in the middle of the yard and a flash of Poochie's green eyes. The little brown dog watched them from the safety of his dog house. He didn't bark but cowered at the end of his heavy chain.

Pete put the truck into park. He got out, went to the back, reached for the chainsaw and swung it effortlessly out of the box. Then he deposited the heavy saw into the shed and light-footed back to the truck. From the cab, Emily and Daisy tracked his every move.

"I know it's illegal, but we're only returning the saw to its rightful owner," said Emily smugly. "Pete, you did say that the man told you it came from a farm on Spring Valley Road, didn't you?"

"That's what he said. There's no other farm on this road that I know of."

"Don't forget the fingerprints!" Emily said. "Go wipe the fingerprints off the handle."

"Here's a rag," Daisy said. She reached under the seat and produced a grimy cloth she used for checking the oil.

Pete ran back to the shed and vigorously rubbed the handle.

"Nobody's coming out," Daisy whispered.

"Good. Let's hope they don't."

No one appeared at the door. Pete slid behind the steering wheel. He put the truck into drive and veered around the corner of the house to descend the laneway.

They all gasped at the same time when they saw what was approaching the farm from the road.

Five police cars, with lights flashing and sirens blaring headed up the hill toward them, blocking their only escape route.

# *Chapter Thirty-Three*

Pete slammed the truck into reverse, spinning tires backward, throwing gravel at the windows of the house. He drove straight back, slamming into the abandoned Chevrolet parked in the middle of the yard. Their short flight ended with a thud and crunch of collapsing metal.

"I've always wondered what it was like to be in the demolition derby," Emily said.

"But not with my truck." Daisy moaned, her voice on the edge of despair.

Pete slumped with his head on his hands on the steering wheel, hiding his face under his hat as the beacons of the first police car racing over the top of the hill shined, full force, into the cab. The three fugitives were like deer in the headlights.

Emily came to her senses and began to scramble. She reached past Daisy's broad bosom for the door handle, crawling across her sister-in-law's lap to get out of the truck.

"You guys stay here! I'll look after this!"

She flew out of the cab and tried to shut the door, but it refused to latch. Daisy automatically gripped the handle to keep the door from swinging open.

The five cruisers filled the barnyard. With screeching tires, they parked at all angles. Spotlights flashed beams into the shadows and upward to the night sky. Sirens wailed into the air. Car doors slammed all around them, as constables, with guns drawn, leapt out and began searching for evidence of criminal activity.

Mrs. Emily Blossom stood erect, her scarf jauntily flung over her shoulder, her hand on her purse as if she were out for a stroll. She recognized Inspector Allard and glided toward him with her head held high and a smile illuminating her face. She willed the crow's foot wrinkles around her eyes to cast their magical spell. A disobedient lock of hair strayed over one eye, creating a seductive impression, carefree yet competent.

"Allo, Allard! Fancy meeting you here," she said in her best most elegant greeting. "I see you decided to follow up on my lead and track down the real suspects in our murder investigation."

"Mrs. Blossom, what the hell are you doing here? Who tipped you off?"

Emily cocked her head, grinning mischievously. She raised one eyebrow and winked. "Now, now, Inspector, you don't really expect me to reveal my sources, do you?"

"What are they doing here?" Allard asked, tipping his hat in the direction of Pete and Daisy.

The police were pointing guns at the two of them, sitting in the truck with their hands held high, wide-eyed and motionless in the midst of the commotion. Hoards of police officers scanned and poked into sheds, barns and out-buildings.

"Have you forgotten I don't drive?" Emily asked. "I wouldn't have missed your arrival for all the tea in China. I needed a lift so I could be here to help in your raid. Pete drove, and Daisy let us use her truck. Naturally we had to bring her along as well, didn't we?"

"Leave them in the truck, but keep them under surveillance," Allard said to the policeman holding them at gunpoint.

At that moment, Constable Wilson approached but waited at a correct distance, until he could interrupt the conversation.

"Why, here's my favourite constable," Emily exclaimed. "How nice to see you this evening!"

Allard signalled to him to step forward.

"How were the BTs?" Emily whispered.

The constable looked puzzled. She'd caught him off guard.

"Butter tarts?" she prompted, as if their little secret was safe with her. Constable Wilson blushed.

"What's up?" the inspector said, indicating that Wilson could speak freely in Emily's presence.

Emily happily assumed he meant to include her as a member of the force.

"We're ready to enter the house, sir," Wilson said. "We think there are at least four occupants."

"Be careful. They may be armed."

"And dangerous," Emily added, "especially the tall, thin one with the moustache."

Allard glanced at her sideways, questioning her knowledge.

She shrugged. "I told you about him this morning, didn't I? I believe I gave you a description of the men whom I'd met here—or did that slip your mind?"

Allard pretended he knew what she was referring to.

A group of policemen crowded onto the entrance of the porch.

"Police! Come out with your hands up!" one shouted. "You're under arrest!"

"Did you have any trouble getting a search warrant?" Emily asked Allard as they watched the proceedings from a safe distance.

"We followed your leads and leaned on the fellow who told Pete about this gang," he said. "After investigating our sources, we came up with enough proof to get a search warrant. I'm expecting to collect enough evidence to convict these guys."

"Yes, Inspector, I told you: there's a grow-op in the back of that barn, drugs in the house, and don't miss the sketch of the viper's nest on the wall. The design matches the tattoo on our victim's ring finger. There's also a suspicious chainsaw in the shed over there."

There was a pounding on the farmhouse door, and the constables all disappeared inside the house. Presently, four men emerged with their hands on their heads, followed by a policeman with a gun pointed at their backs.

Emily surmised that the pianist, B. Man, and his companion Fatso had recently returned from their drug run to Montréal. She recognized the other two, Snake and the Kid, from her bathroom visit that morning. In contrast to their surly attitude that morning, the gang members all looked sheepish and powerless in the custody of the police.

"Guilty by association," Emily said, walking away from Allard toward the motley group of four. Then she directed her comments to them. "Hello, fellows, fancy meeting you here."

Snake glowered at her. Fatso looked away. The Kid regarded her with soft blue eyes, as if he wasn't fully aware of what was happening to him. Only B. Man met her gaze as an equal. The hooded skull on his T-shirt created an eerie impression that it too was staring at her eye to eye.

"I figured you were snooping around this morning," he said to her, his hands clasped behind his head. "You were just too polished for a little old lady. But after seeing you on the highway, in that broken down truck, I wasn't so sure. You put up a good front."

Emily decided to be flattered. "Why, thank you. I do have a good undercover."

The policeman escorting the suspects lowered his gun and began speaking to his partner. "Better get them into the cruiser. Hey, Wilson, bring us the handcuffs."

All eyes were on Wilson for one instant—the nanosecond Snake was waiting for. He lunged at Emily and threw his arms around her, pinning her arms to her sides. With a powerful thrust, he dragged her backward towards the house, shouting, "Get back, all of you! Fatso, Kid—in the house!"

To the police, he yelled, "Stay back or I'll slit her throat!" The flash of a switchblade confirmed that he had been concealing a weapon in his belt.

A hush descended on the farmyard when all the police officers froze, afraid that any move toward the hostage would result in Mrs. Blossom's murder.

The simple word *shit* dropped in the still air like the sound of a shot. Allard was otherwise speechless.

\*

Pete's fingers clutched the steering wheel, where he watched helplessly as the drama unfolded in the achingly bright lights of the police cars.

"Shit!" He echoed Allard's comment from the inside the cab of the truck.

Daisy was sobbing; tears rolled down her cheeks and dropped from her chin onto her tattered sweater. She did not bother to brush them away.

# Chapter Thirty-Four

"What the f-k!"

"What the hell're ya doin'?"

"How the hell you think we're gonna get outta this alive!"

"What the f-k?"

The gang of four spoke at once as they crowded back into the kitchen. Snake threw Emily onto a seat beside the kitchen table. "Gimme a rope!" he shouted.

Fatso produced a rope from the broom closet, and they tied Emily's hands behind the back of the chair. They tied her legs together so tightly that her toes became numb almost instantly.

"Could you loosen those a bit?" she said, trying to sound helpless and friendly at the same time. "Just a little. I promise I won't try to escape—and I always keep my word."

Kid looked at B. Man, who nodded. He slackened the ropes enough for her to retrieve some feeling.

"Thanks so much, young fellow. There's a fine boy."

Suddenly a voice blared over a loudspeaker from the farmyard. "This is Inspector Allard. Come out with your hands over your heads. Give up immediately!"

A hush in the room accentuated the sound of a clock ticking and the tap dripping. The hostage-takers' eyes flitted from one to another, as if trying to read each other's minds. None of them dared move.

The kitchen smelled like stale beer and smoke. The walls were dingy and stained. Dirty dishes and coffee cups were piled in the sink and on the counter. Tattered lace curtains were out of place; whoever had hung them had long since abandoned the scene. Dust and spider webs nested in the corners of the snake pit sketch on the wall.

"We can make a deal as long as this doesn't drag out," said the megaphone voice.

"Like hell," Snake whispered.

B. Man returned again and again to the window, watching the cops from behind the curtains. A gun leaned against the wall, butt end on the floor, half hidden by the drapes. One of the guns on the gun rack in the living room was missing. The gang leader stood, back to the wall by the gun; he flicked the curtain sideways, studied the activity in the yard and then let the curtain fall. He paced from room to room. He walked around the table, into the living room and back, staring at the ceiling as if to find answers written in the cracks of the plaster.

"I thought those lights from the pickup were the fellas comin' for the shipment. That's why we never made a move." He muttered under his breath, thinking out loud. "When they find the stuff in the van, we're done for. The other guys better not show up. They'll see the cops and hightail it back to Ottawa. On the other hand, maybe they could help us out, distract the cops and put up a fight to get us free. No good usin' a cell phone. They'd tap into us sure as shit. We don't really stand a chance, though. There ain't no way outta this mess."

Searchlights scanned the walls as if they were in a disco bar. From his dog house, Poochie barked and howled mournfully, alone and bewildered. Other sounds of gravel on the laneway, cars coming and going up the laneway. The mutterings of walkie-talkies were not loud enough to reveal the details, but sufficient to transmit the urgency of police on the hunt.

Fatso stared at the table, puffing on a joint. The kid drummed his fingers to the rhythm of Jimmy Hendrix. Snake glared at Emily with his darting eyes as he sniffed a line of white powder up his nose. They waited for their boss to come up with a plan.

Emily was unusually silent while she considered her predicament. She suddenly felt extremely tired. Her energy drained out of her. She almost felt like giving up.

The stinging cut at her throat, which she had sustained from Snake's switchblade, reminded her these men were perfectly capable of committing extreme violence. This gang was well beyond anything she had ever experienced. She had never met anyone like them before. Even her husband had never actually hit her; his aggression had tended more toward psychological abuse. The thugs she had come across during her last murder investigation had been bumbling idiots. She had outsmarted them with relative ease. But these culprits were another story altogether. Plus, they were fighting for their lives. If it came down to her life or theirs, she was pretty sure she knew who would come out on top—and it wouldn't be her.

She knew, in hostage taking, the trick was to play a waiting game. The cops would be as patient as possible, waiting for the kidnappers to break down. However, they could be in for a long wait. There was no telling how much food these men had in the fridge, or how long they could hold out before their nerves cracked. They acted as if they were used to waiting, for hours at a time, with nothing better to do.

*Detectives never give up.*

Emily decided to make the best of the worst situation. Talking had always been her most effective weapon. Besides, she could rarely be quiet for long, and she did love to chatter. She would take advantage of her captive audience.

"You know the first time I met you fellows this morning, I knew you were fine, upstanding young men, just gone a little crooked. After all, you're all friends, and there's honour among the . . . ethical treatment of your fellow gangsters—like pirates. Did you know pirates have the most democratic self-government of any group of the . . . Even Robin Hood was considered a hero, even though he was a the . . . He stole from the rich to give to poor folks. He had noble intentions. Who knows? Maybe you'll be famous, like Bonnie and Clyde, or Al Capone. They do make movies about gangsters. Can you imagine a movie about you guys? How you took a little old lady hostage, and how you spared my life, and were heroes in the end? Happily after ever and all that."

"Shut the f-k up!" Snake yelled at B. Man. "Make her shut her f-king mouth, Baldy! I'm sick of her f-king face!"

"Baldy? Is that what they call you?" Emily asked. "I had no idea! We've never been introduced formally. My name is Emily, Emily Blossom. Emily, meet Baldy, Baldy, meet Emily. Somehow I would have imagined you with a name like Glenn, as in Gould, or Arthur, as in Rubenstein. Wasn't he a wonderful pianist? Mind you, your version of the *Moonlight Sonata* this morning was perfectly brilliant. How on earth did you ever learn to play like that? You must come from a fine outstanding family, Baldy."

"Shut her up, Baldy! I'm warning you now! If she doesn't shut the f-k up, I'm gonna do it for her."

B. Man continued pacing the room. The fat man lit another cigarette, propping it between his slit lip and his canine teeth, as if he would eat it rather than smoke it. The Kid popped open a Coke. Then he began drumming on the table. His fingers were thin and bony, with long dirty fingernails.

"And they must call you Jimmy, for Jimmy Hendrix, eh? Wasn't he one of the best drummers ever?"

"Jimmy Hendrix played the guitar."

"What about the Grateful Dead. Are you a Dead head? Did they have a good drummer?"

"The who?"

"That was a good band too. As you can see, I'm not really up on my drummers. But I can tell your drumming is quite good. You have a great sense of rhyme and reason. I can see you practice a lot."

The Kid's fingers beat the table intently, encouraged by her enthusiasm.

"I've heard that real drummers might become obsolete. They say automatic drumming machines are just as good as live percussion. But I can tell, when I listen to you, it's not the same thing at all. No machine is going to replace the talent of a young drummer like you, Kid. You skip to the rhythm of a distant beat."

His upper lip was adorned with a small gold ring. The glimmer of a smile tickled the edges of his lips, making the ring quiver. His sky-blue eyes gazed vacantly as he concentrated on rolling his fingertips on the table, maintaining a steady beat for an imaginary band.

"The broad's nuts," Snake said. "She's f-n' off her rocker. We're surrounded by cops in the middle of the night, and she's f-n' talkin' about drumming."

"I'm quite curious about your tattoos, Mr. . . . Mr.? What did you say your name was?"

"Snake. We call him Snake," the Kid said without missing a beat.

Snake glared at the Kid. "Who asked you?"

Emily continued babbling. "That makes sense, because of his tattoos—and wonderful snakes they are too. I can see those are very intricate designs. Does it hurt to get that done? Is there any danger of getting poisoned by the ink? Do you take drugs to mask the pain? Those needles must hurt. You must have a very good tattoo artist. You might say your tattoos are actually a work of art. Did you ever think of yourself as an art form? I'm an expert in art, you know. It's my specialty. I recognize a good design when I see one, but I must admit I've never actually had the chance to study someone like you up close. Without being too intimate, could I ask you personally, is there anywhere you don't have them? Tell me, why, actually, did you pick those particular designs? Some people would be afraid to have snakes all over their body, even if they are only tattoos."

"It's the gang we belong to, the Vipers," the Kid said. "You gotta have a snake tattoo to be a member."

"I'm warning you!"

"I see Snake has one on his ring finger. Does that mean something special?"

Before the Kid could answer her, Snake's chair squealed as he shoved it backward, slamming it down onto the floor. He leaned over the table and grabbed Kid's shirt at the nape of his neck, lifting him out of his seat. "Shut up, Kid!" Snake yelled. "Don't you f-kin' tell her nothin'!"

The Kid stared coldly back at him, wiping spit from his cheek. He yanked his shirt free from Snake's grasp and sat down. He didn't take his eyes off Snake's menacing glare. His expression hardened into anger and hatred. He changed in that instant from a boy into a bitter young man. He extended his hands on the table and resumed drum rolls.

The ring in his lip quivered as he spoke through clenched teeth. "You tell her then," he said, his words like hot steel on ice. "You tell her about your dear, sweet wife."

The Kid continued, now speaking to Emily. "Rosie was the artist. She's the one who drew that sketch on the wall you've been lookin' at. She's the one who did every one a them pictures Snake's got on his body."

"Wife? You must be kidding. I never married her! You crazy!"

"What's the rings for then? Those tattoos that never come off? Sign of eternal devotion or just stupidity?"

"Shut the f-k up, Kid. I'm warning you."

"You tell the lady here about how she was only a stripper. A whore, you said, who happened to be at the wrong place at the wrong time. Eh? Rosie had feelings too. She deserved better than you. She actually loved you. She told me so. I warned her, but she wouldn't listen. She thought you loved her too. Poor thing. You never loved nobody.

"She wouldn't've talked. No more than anyone else who saw what you done. F-n' robbery gone wrong. Wasn't her fault. Y're the one who botched the heist. Y're the one who pulled the trigger. She didn't even see what happened. She was standing at the door, watchin' to make sure nobody come in. But you did her in. Y're a addict; that's what you are—hooked on killing. You enjoyed her pleadin' with you, beggin' you not to do it. I heard it all through the walls. I didn't have the guts to face up to you then, but I do now—now that it's too late. You f-n' bastard!"

"That's enough!" Baldy shouted. "I can't think. I'm trying to figure out how we're gonna get outta this mess, eh?"

"I reckon we're done for, boss," Fatso said without moving or shifting his gaze from the butt of the reefer he held between his finger and thumb. "Those cops ain't gonna leave us alone. Takin' the broad hostage might keep 'em back for a while, but eventually we gonna have to give up."

"I'm not getting' outta here alive," Snake said. "And she's not either."

"If y're goin' down for one murder, you might as well go down for two—is that it?" the Kid asked. "The more the merrier?"

"What the f-k do you know? You ain't got the brains of a cockroach."

"Cockroaches are survivors, actually," Emily said. "They say that even if all the humans in the world were destroyed, cockroaches and ants would take over the planet. They live in colonies, you know, and they have designated duties for the sake of the survival of the fitting. Not like humans, who kill members of their own species."

"We need a plan," B. Man said. "Some kind of strategy."

"Somebody goes out the door shootin' and covers for the rest, who hightail it out the back when nobody's lookin'."

"Yeah, and then what? We're up here on an f-n' hill in the middle of nowhere with no cover. What makes you think we can make a run for it?"

"A bullet in the back, that's what you'll get."

"I tell you, we gotta give ourselves up. They ain't got no proof of no crimes; and even if they do, the case'll get tied up in court for years. Some guys never go to jail."

"When they arrested all those Hell's Angels a couple a years back they let half of 'em go. There wasn't enough judges to bring 'em all to trial in less than ten years. The court system's a joke. We could give ourselves up and still be out on bail for years before they can take us to trial."

"If we got a good lawyer, we could still get off scot free."

"Rocco's got good lawyers. He'll stand up for us."

"Rocco?" Emily interrupted their planning. She couldn't help herself. "Luigi Rocco?"

"Let's just say we know somebody, okay?" Baldy said.

# Chapter Thirty-Five

"Can I talk to you in private?" Emily asked. "I think I may have a suggestion, but I can't say it out loud."

"Can't say it out loud? The f-kin' bitch is loony. Don't listen to her, Baldy! She don't know what she's talkin' about."

"First you have to untie my feet. I can't join you in the other room unless I can walk."

B. Man nodded to Kid. The lad gently untied the ropes at Emily's ankles.

"You might as well untie her hands as well. If she tries to make a break for it, she'll end up with a bullet hole the same as us."

"I won't leave without you, fellows. I promise. And my word is good as diamonds." She motioned Baldy to the living room. She whispered, holding her fingers over her mouth to garble the sound. She wanted to create the impression that their conversation was secret and confidential. She wanted to convince Baldy to trust her with his life.

"Look, I have to ask you, where did you come from to get yourself in this mess? You're not the type to get caught up in a shootout. You're too good for this gang."

"What do you mean? How can you tell?"

"Everything about you is polished and sophisticated. You're not from trash stock. You have an aristocrat's fingers, not working hands. Your accent is articulate and educated. Even by the way you watch the others, I can tell you're not like them. What are you doing way out here in the boondocks?"

"What's it to you?"

"I've got pull. If I know something about you, I can put in a good word for you with Inspector Allard."

The loudspeaker blared again, startling them both. "James Winston, we know you're in there."

"James Winston? Is that your real name?"

Baldy looked away from Emily's penetrating inquiry. He sneaked up beside the window by the piano, looking out over the fields as if sending his thoughts beyond his immediate surroundings. The darkness of the night outside intensified the darkness of his eyes, searching for an escape.

"I don't know how they found out I was here. Who ratted me out?"

"Could they have traced the license plate on the van, or maybe on your motorcycle?" Emily moved close and spoke over his shoulder in a soft, confiding manner. "How on earth did you end up in this godforsaken place?"

Before he could answer, the megaphone interrupted their conversation. "Winston, we've got your mother on the phone. She wants to talk to you."

"Damn!" Jimmy snapped. When he heard the plaintive voice echoing across the barnyard and through the walls of the old farmhouse, his face twisted into a kaleidoscope of emotions: anger, sadness and resentment.

"Jimmy, the police contacted me. They say you're in trouble?" She ended her sentence like a question she would never hear the answer to. "They want me to ask you to give yourself up. Please, Jimmy, please. I love you always, no matter what."

At this point the words became broken and incoherent. They faded into a throaty whisper, but everyone listening could hear her final message clearly through the hush of tension.

"Your father sends his regards."

The loudspeaker ceased crackling and fell silent. Emily hardly hesitated before she resumed her interrogation into Jimmy's background. "I knew I recognized good breeding when I first met you. The Winston family? You're from a good family."

Emily walked over to the battered piano and began to tap out the first chords of the *Moonlight Sonata*. The notes, clear and slightly out of tune, filled the air, like starlight in a deep night's sky. She tried several times but couldn't get past the first measure without making a mistake.

"I can never get it right," she said. "Jimmy, would you play it again for me?"

Jimmy Winston, alias Baldy, approached the dusty piano in the dingy, shabby room. The magical harmony of *Beethoven's Sonata No. 14* floated from his fingertips into the crisp, evening air. Jimmy lost himself between ebony and ivory and became one with the keyboard. The music rose and fell and meandered: soft, then louder, tumbling alive with hope and defiance and then fading into trickles, teardrops from broken hearts of a composer from centuries past and a musician who relived his anguish. As the melody wound its way through lyrical progressions, tension dissipated, replaced by a promise of eternity. The chords repeated over and again, like ripples on a lake glistening under a full moon. The world held its breath until the last note faded into a mere echo of itself. The earth hesitated, hushed, in silence for an instant before resuming her inexorable orbit.

"How is it that music can take you so very far from reality?" Emily asked. "Doesn't take long for it to all come crashing down around you though, as soon as the last note disappears."

Emily cleared her throat. "Yes, well, where were we then? How did you get yourself into this mess? That's what I was asking."

"Rocco. I was dating his daughter, and he offered me a job. I always had everything I wanted. This was different. It was exciting. It pays well, and I get to use my brain."

"But the people you work with? Why would you want to associate with these hoodlums?"

"Not everybody's born with a silver spoon. They've got their hang-ups; everybody does. At least these guys don't pretend to be somebody they're not."

"But you could have anything you wanted."

"When you've got all the money you need, and all the opportunities, people expect you to be like everyone else. At least they expect you to pretend just like everyone else does. They put on a good show, but they've got their dirty underwear too. Only they think their shit doesn't stink. I'm not real good at faking it. I didn't play the games real well either. I never liked their rules. I was never good enough to please my father."

"But what about the people you hurt? The drug deals? The violence? Don't you have a conscience? Don't you know that what you're doing is wrong, that there are a lot of people who are innocent victims?"

"Nobody said the world was fair."

"What makes you think Rocco will stand up for you? He's got nothing to gain by helping you guys out."

"Luigi will stand up for me. He said he would if anything went wrong."

Emily shook her head, clicking her tongue against her cheek. "Aren't you being a bit naïve? There's nothing in it for him. At this point, they've got nothing on him. You guys will take the rap, and his hands are clean."

"He's not like that."

"No, and your mother doesn't give a damn about you either."

"The old man would just as soon see me rot in hell. 'Sends his regards'? You know what that means? 'Piss up a rope'."

"You honestly think Luigi Rocco is more likely to defend you than your own father? Don't get me wrong. I'm not saying your dad will help you out—but I'm saying that I doubt whether Rocco has any better ethics than your father, and he's no blood relation either.

"Frankly I think you're in big trouble, and I think you're more naïve than you should be. You've got some sky-eyed vision that, for you, everything will work out. I'm afraid, in the scheme of things, you're one of the few people who really live up to what they say they'll do. Now you've got yourself out on a limb, and you don't know how to get down. I'm betting nobody out there is going to help you if you don't help yourself."

"Have you got any other great news? I thought you had a suggestion."

"If you get out of this alive, you can make a plea bargain. Disclose the identity of the big bosses, give the courts proof. You'll turn provincial witness."

"Provincial witness? What's that?"

"That's the Canadian version of state's evidence."

Jimmy Winston hesitated, as if he might accept her proposal, but then he frowned and reconsidered. "What's in it for you? Why should you help me out when nobody else gives a damn?"

Emily looked at the gangster, sizing him up as if deciding whether to be straightforward or to manipulate his emotions, as she had been doing up until this point. His question hit a chord with her. She opted for honesty.

"Jimmy, every one of us can go through life like a fairy tale. We can convince ourselves we're the hero or the villain, the lover or the sceptic; but at some point we have to look in the mirror."

"So?"

"So, there's one person looking back at you. You've only got one life to live."

"What's that got to do with me?"

"Who is it you want to see when you're staring at yourself in the mirror? You haven't got too many chances to get it right."

"What makes you think I want to? What does it matter?"

"Who are you kidding in the long run?"

"Why should I care?"

"Why shouldn't you? It's the only thing that gives life meaning."

"Gimme a moment to think about it."

# Chapter Thirty-Six

When Emily returned to the kitchen, Snake was disturbed and anxious. The lines of powder on the plate in front of him were gone. His eyes were glassy and darted from one face to another, blinking rapidly, unable to focus. His tongue constantly searched out his lips beneath his straggling moustache, where beads of white foam collected at the corners of his mouth. His hands were shaking. Fingers were constantly in motion, first wiping his pants, then his sleeve, and then brushing his palms together, as if by fierce rubbing he could engage his thoughts.

"You're gonna turn me in, aren't you?" he muttered. "That's the plan, ain't it?"

Emily knew instinctively she must tread very softly. He appeared about to strike. She sat on the edge of her chair with her hands folded in her lap and her feet clamped together. She tried to summon her crow's feet wrinkles, but her face muscles felt leaden and uncooperative. Her smile pinched into sour crookedness.

"No, no, turning you in was definitely not part of the strategy. What good would that do? We're all in this together," she said, trying to control her tone of voice, to soothe and calm his edginess.

"Shut the f-k up," he yelled, spit flying at her across the table. "I ain't talkin' to you! Baldy, you're the boss. Don't let her tell you what to do."

Jimmy lost his cool. "What're ya doin' blowin' yer brains out through yer nose? Ain't we in enough shit without you bein' out of your f-kin' head on coke? We all need to think clearly if we're gonna get outta this alive."

"I commit crimes when people piss me off," Snake said.

Emily wondered whether he was merely stating a fact or whether he was warning them about something he intended to do.

She was annoyed when the police megaphone blasted through the night air again.

"You're surrounded. We've got snipers and tear gas. You're outnumbered. This is your last chance to save yourselves. Let Mrs. Blossom go and come out with your hands up!"

"Apparently they're trying to pressure you into taking action," she commented over her shoulder to Jimmy, who was still contemplating his best course of action.

"Fat chance!" Snake sneered. "Let Mrs. Blossom go? And then what? They blow our f-kn' heads off when we walk out that f-kn' door."

Snake grew more and more agitated. Then he suddenly seemed to reach a breaking point. Losing all restraint, he stood up and threw his chair across the room. In one leap, he grabbed Emily out of her seat. Holding her by the neck, he jerked her face to within an inch in front of his.

"It's all your fault. You waltzed in here this morning like some innocent old broad. 'I have to go to the bathroom', you said. Like f-k you did! You were snooping around. You tipped 'em off, didn't you? You're gonna wish you'd never laid eyes on us.

You and your creepy innocent look. I'll burn your head in the furnace just like I did hers. Close them staring eyes forever."

Emily felt the knifepoint at her throat. Snake's hand holding the switchblade twitched and shook violently. She could smell his bad breath. She willed herself to smile as if he was making a joke, but he didn't waver.

*Detectives never flinch.*

"Kiss your last breath goodbye."

Everything happened so fast at this point, that afterward Emily could not remember a single detail.

Snake suddenly fell to the floor. Apparently Jimmy was an expert in karate. A chop to the neck felled Snake and paralyzed his knife hand at the same time. But the effect was only temporary, long enough for Emily to dash for the living room. She saw Jimmy Winston stabbing at Snake, writhing on the floor. Blood spurted across the room. She expected to see her saviour victorious, standing over his quarry in triumph.

Instead, Jimmy sprawled out over the motionless body beneath him.

When the Kid nudged his boss with his foot, Jimmy flopped over, face up, the shock of horror in his eyes. Snake's switchblade stuck vertically out of the eye of the hooded skull on his T-shirt. A pool of blood collected on the floor.

His eyes rolled in their sockets, searching for focus on Emily's face. With a final, foaming breath, he uttered his last words. "I'm not a bad guy, really. You're right. Just a bit misguided."

# Chapter Thirty-Seven

When Emily, Kid and Fatso stepped outside with their hands over their heads, a gust of fresh, sweet air greeted them. Emily energetically waved a piece of tattered curtain as a sign of truce. "Yoo hoo, it's us! There's only three left! We're unarmed. Don't shoot! Don't shoot!"

Emily was blinded by searchlights. All she could see were shadows of three figures: fat, thin, thinner, like ghosts emerging from the netherworld. A din of activity buzzed in the dark beyond her field of vision.

"Move in! Grab those guys! *Appelez l'ambulance!* Call in the ambulance! Where are the other two?"

Police officers, guns drawn, crept behind them in the darkness onto the porch and into the farmhouse. Emily tried not to imagine the scene they would come upon: the bodies, the blood, the gaping mouths, the vacant, staring eyes.

As soon as the glaring lights were turned off, she could discern the yard full of police cars, flashlights, people milling in all directions.

Pete and Daisy waited by the truck. Pete leaned against the hood, a pipe in the corner of his mouth, his hat pulled low over his eyes. Daisy paced back and forth, her grey hair straggling in all directions. Her full lips were slightly parted, as if paused in the middle of a sentence.

Emily moved toward them, drawn by a promise of safety and comfort. They were the only people in the world she wanted to be with.

"Mrs. Blossom, we'll need a statement from you," Allard said, approaching from behind.

"Can we do it tomorrow? Surely you have a lot to do to wrap up the case. I've had a rather long day."

"I'll send a constable by your house tomorrow morning."

"That'll be fine. I'll be waiting."

She shook his hand and headed toward the truck. All of a sudden, every muscle ached.

*Detectives put one foot in front of the other.*

"Mrs. Blossom?" Allard said again.

She turned, wobbling, afraid of losing her balance. Her smile was forced and tentative.

"Good job," the inspector said.

Emily was so tired she could hardly revel in his compliment. "Thank you, sir."

"Are you okay? Shall we take you to the hospital?"

"Goodness no, I'll be fine. I just need a good cup of tea and a warm bed to lay my head."

"Go on home then. Constable Wilson will pick you up in the morning."

"Yes, sir."

Allard returned to his duties. Several officers were waiting for him to give them instructions.

Emily was left on her own. When Emily concentrated her efforts on reaching her friends, they seemed farther and farther away. She felt faint. Her legs turned to lead.

Daisy ran forward and enveloped her in a comforting hug. The next thing she knew, Pete had scooped her into his arms and placed her gently into her seat in the truck. He tucked her and Daisy together under a blanket, which he had borrowed from the first aid responders.

Emily managed to mumble, "This isn't a very dignified way for a detective to exit the scene."

"Most detectives would already be retired for twenty years," Pete said. "You're just getting the hang of it."

As he fussed with the blanket to make sure it completely covered them, Emily continued. "I was afraid you might try to save me."

"Not a chance," Pete said. "I'm no hero."

He slid into the driver's seat and packed his pipe full of tobacco. Then he puffed until the truck was filled with smoke before turning the key to head for home.

Emily snuggled down into the warmth between her two friends as the pickup rattled down the laneway. "I'm so glad you're both safe."

# Chapter Thirty-Eight

The day could not have been better for a parade. After the dreary cold of winter and relentless rains of early spring, a warming sun broke through the clouds, glittering like a giant jewel. The townsfolk emerged from their homes to line the length of Main Street. Children wore Irish top hats. Little girls' cheeks were painted with shamrocks. Boys on bicycles and skateboards wore green helmets and waved flags. Grandmothers took photos, and fathers carried toddlers on their shoulders. Little dogs were dressed in green blankets and booties with ribbons and bows in their fur. Even the stately Victorian brick homes took on a festive air with their architectural gingerbread decoration and dancing tulips in spring gardens.

The O'Reilly Family Band specialized in Irish ballads and tunes: father played guitar; daughter sang the lyrics; brother played the fiddle; mother corded on the keyboard and the littlest child, with copper bouncing curls, danced jigs.

The parking lot of the tavern was cordoned off, where customers drank green beer and ate pizza and poutine.

In the middle of all the activity, one leprechaun stood above the crowd on a platform. The MC was none other than Pete Picken dressed as an Irishman, a crumpled emerald top hat perched at a precarious angle on his head. His hair billowed from underneath the brim in all directions. He had an unruly moustache, several days' growth of whiskers, ruby cheeks and twinkling eyes. His clothing, hat, vest, shirt and pants were all varying shades of green, except for scruffy, mud-stained cowboy boots.

Emily had just arrived. For the occasion, she had chosen her green felt bowler hat. She arranged her favourite peacock feathers into the hat band with a shamrock pin to hold them in place. She wore a soft green scarf around her neck to hide the wounds from Snake's knife. Feeling quite dapper, she was looking for familiar faces when Pete spotted her.

Quicker than a wink, he left his platform and ran through the crowd to meet her. His enthusiasm was palpable. "Emily, you won't believe what happened this morning! The funeral home was broken into. The Underhills were going in to work. When they got there, they realized the glass doors had been smashed, and the place was trashed. They called the police. The cops came, investigated and left to write their report."

Emily heard what Pete was saying, but she was distracted by the angle of his hat. Every time he began a new sentence, the floppy brim descended a bit further over his eyes, defying gravity. His bow tie was so large, he had it tucked beside his chin, off to the side, beneath his ear so he could speak. Overall, he looked quite lopsided, but the story continued nonetheless.

"Then Mr. Underhill went around to the side entrance because he wanted to check the basement where the urns were stored. He walked downstairs in the dark. When he flicked on the light, he saw a guy sound asleep in one of the coffins. They called the cops again. The constables came back, woke up the fellow and charged him with breaking and entering. The cop had somebody in the back of the cruiser when he stopped to say he'd be late to lead the parade, but I couldn't see the guy's face. We're waiting for Constable Wilson to get back so he can escort the parade through town."

Emily could feel the giggles jiggling in her belly, just before they welled up, bursting into gales of laughter.

"The guy was sound asleep in the coffin, snoring away."

"I can't believe it! Only in Emerald Hill! How funny is that?" She struggled for control, but Pete's earnest expression made her laugh even harder. "Do they know who it is? How he got there? Or why?"

"Apparently he told the cops he was from out of town. He had been drinking at the tavern after a hockey game at the arena. Because he was too drunk to drive, he went to his friend's house. When the guy wasn't home, he put a bench through the window to get in. That's all he could remember."

"I wouldn't want his hangover this morning."

"Look, I gotta run. See you after the parade." He turned and disappeared into the crowd of green. Cheerful leprechauns surrounded the platform. Then Emily saw his crooked top hat above the crowd.

"Good morning, everybody! *Bienvenue à tout le monde!*" His voice rang out over the village from a loudspeaker. "Welcome to Emerald Hill, where everyone is Irish on St. Patrick's Day. *Même qu'on parle français, on est vert aujourdhui.* We're glad you've all turned out to see our parade, which will be arriving shortly. We have fabulous entertainment for you today. We hope everyone has a great time. Enjoy your day!"

Emily wandered down the street looking for friends with whom to watch the parade. The would-be mayor, mousey Dora and Marie Cartier stood in a cluster on the shady side. Emily stayed in the sun.

She ducked behind Alan, a tall, long-haired and bearded man from the British Isles and his pretty Canadian wife, Julie. They were standing with another friend who sported a lavish handlebar moustache whom she knew from the auctions.

*Good people to be with . . . no complications or implications . . . no gossip or criticism.*

Two small boys sneaked up behind the men with long hair. One tweaked the beard; one tugged on the moustache to see if they were real. They ran away laughing, jumped on their bikes and sped down the street. Everyone chuckled and chattered merrily, waiting for the show to begin.

The loudspeaker blared again. "So, folks, while we're waiting for the parade to begin: Does anybody know what's the difference between an Irish wedding and an Irish wake?"

"Green icing," someone shouted from the audience.

"One less drunk," Pete answered.

The crowd groaned in response.

"Okay, okay. Here's another one that's funnier." Pete was obviously enjoying his captive audience. His efforts to imitate an Irish accent were adequate, if not accurate.

"Paddy and Murphy were driving on the wrong side of the highway in Canada, and Murphy swerved to miss a moose. The car ended up in a ditch. The two Irishmen didn't know what to do.

"'Maybe we should pray', Paddy suggested.

"Murphy answered, 'It's been a long time since I said a prayer. I don't know how to begin'.

"'Let me handle it', Paddy said. 'I lived across from the church. All the people would go inside. I listened to them praying every week. I know what to say'.

"'Okay', Murphy said. 'Tell me how it begins'.

"Paddy puffs himself up and gets ready and says, 'Under the B 5!'"

Pete paused to let the punch line sink in. There was not a peep from the crowd—not even a groan—for a full thirty seconds. Only the birds were chirping.

"Ay, c'mon folks!" came Pete's stricken complaint. "Don't any of you have a sense of humour? Nobody plays bingo in this crowd?"

"Boo, hiss," yelled the "green icing" man from the audience.

Quickly everyone joined in, hissing and jeering good-naturedly at the bad joke.

Pete was saved by the sounds of bagpipes coming from the other end of the street.

"Here it is, everybody! The moment we've been waiting for," Pete shouted. "Here comes the parade!"

The crowds lining the streets rustled and repositioned, crooning their necks, hoping for the first sight of pipers leading the parade. Fathers lifted their children high on their shoulders to give them a good vantage point. Mothers moved their strollers into position. Grandmothers whispered to their little ones and pointed in the direction of the sound of the band. Emily and her friends stepped farther into the street. Mrs. Seguin and her buddies, who were gossiping as usual, hardly paused to pay attention to the approaching commotion.

As the sound grew louder, everyone strained for a view of the first pipers. In the distance, the Quebec hills created a purple backdrop for the marching band. Their pipes appeared bobbing up and down just as they cleared the crest of Emerald Hill. The pompoms of their plaid hats bounced to the rhythm of the march.

Dabbing at his eyes with his shirttails, Alan the Englishman, said, "I always get tears in my eyes when I hear bagpipes."

"Oh, no, here we go again," Julie said. She had obviously experienced her husband's sentimentality many times before.

The wailing of the bagpipes grew louder, like a giant, moaning freight train. First the pipes, then the hats, and then the whole band with their matching plaid skirts and white stockings came marching into view to the beat of the drums. The musicians' puffing cheeks and dancing fingers could be seen playing the melody, while the drums thundered out the marching rhythm. Tartans flared and silver buckles sparkled. The bandleader strode majestically ahead of them all, twirling his gleaming baton high into the air.

"I can see why the enemy fled from the battlefields when they saw bagpipers approaching across the countryside," Emily said to Julie. "They send chills up my spine just watching them marching. The drums make my heart throb."

"I think that's the idea."

Alan dabbed at the tears streaming down his ruddy cheeks.

When the band neared the corner next to Joe's Convenience Store, the baton twirler stepped sideways to lead his band down the side street. The whole troupe began to follow him.

"Whoa! Whoa!" Pete shouted. "Not that way! Come back! Come back! The parade comes along Main Street and turns at *this* intersection!"

The pipers fell out of step, regrouped without missing a beat and redirected their marching back onto Main Street where the crowd waited. They never skipped a note of the music. Everyone cheered. The bagpipes blared, joyfully announcing the arrival of the parade.

Following the marching band came the float of the rival town of Scotsdale. A pickup truck pulled a hay wagon decorated in shamrocks. The mayor of Scotsdale sat on a bale of hay, waving to the crowd. Wearing a farmer's cap and with a stalk of straw between his teeth, he gave the appearance of a down-home boy made good. One of the town's councillors and the publicity coordinator smiled and greeted the audience with smug confidence.

"Our gold sponsors are our neighbours down the road," Pete announced. "They bid you welcome from the lovely town of Scotsdale. You're cordially invited to visit their shops and businesses waiting to serve you."

Next came Farmer John driving his antique John Deere tractor. The motor was so loud the children cupped their hands over their ears as he passed. Daisy Blossom's truck followed, decorated with Irish green flags and clover decals. Daisy wore a bowler cap decorated with feathers from her farm roosters, and Robin waved from the passenger seat. Green-clad riders rode three paint horses with green leg bandages. Their manes and tails were braided with flowing emerald ribbons. They were followed by a scruffy pony, whose whole body was dyed a neon shade the colour of Granny Smith apples. Barefoot belly dancers flounced in Hawaiian grass skirts, with hips swaying and bellies bulging. They wore plastic flowers in long hair cascading down their backs and gestured to the tunes of invisible ukuleles. Long-legged dogs with necklaces and ankle bracelets dragged their owners behind them, carrying a sign supporting Great Dane Rescue. Car dealers drove demos. Boy Scouts camped in tents on a flatbed trailer. Green-clad real estate agents handed out candies to the children. The town's sparkling red fire engine brought up the end of the parade, with sirens blaring and lights flashing.

As the last entry rounded the corner, Pete announced an added feature. "Don't go away, folks! The parade's coming back again."

Sure enough, a few moments later, bagpipes could be heard approaching.

Alan the Englishman began to cry again. "I hope they don't come back a third time," he sobbed, dabbing furiously at his tears. "I couldn't take another round."

The crowd cheered for every float the second time around, almost as enthusiastically as the first.

This time, when Daisy's truck passed the place where Emily was viewing the parade, Daisy stopped her Chevy in the middle of the street. She was signalling frantically.

Emily ran over to the truck, and Daisy rolled down the window. "Emily, Luigi Rocco's in the crowd down by the general store! What's he doing here?"

"I'll take care of it, Daisy. Don't you worry. Don't hold up the whole parade on account of one fly in the milk."

Daisy drove off to catch up with the rest of the parade, and the belly dancers had to run to keep up with her. Emily sauntered down the street toward Joe's Depanneur. She immediately spotted Rocco even though she had never actually met him before.

Luigi Rocco was dressed in a grey, pinstriped three-piece suit. His hair was slicked back, gleaming in the sun. The woman holding his arm wore spiked heels, a hip tight skirt and bright red lipstick. Her hair was butter blonde with black roots that matched her eyebrows. Two very obvious bodyguards flanked them on either side.

Emily strode up to Luigi Rocco. The guards stepped forward to intercept her, but she shouldered her way between them as if she hadn't noticed their attempt to block her advance. She proffered her hand while looking the Mafia boss straight in the eye.

"Mr. Rocco, I believe," she said. "Welcome to Emerald Hill."

Rocco tucked his chin into his neck, like a turtle in retreat. Caught off guard, he eyed her quizzically. "I don't believe we've met."

The hand he offered in return to Emily's firm handshake was weak and tentative.

"Mr. Rocco, in Emerald Hill, everybody knows everybody else. We know all about you."

"Is that so?"

Mrs. Rocco was following their conversation with a glint of fear on her face. She could not read the tone, but she knew there was an undercurrent of meaning that she could not decipher.

Emily began to chatter. "Oh, yes, Mr. Rocco, I'm actually so pleased to meet you in person. I've heard so much about you."

"Is that so?"

"I've never met a mobster before. I understand you're quite high up in the scheme of things. You all are having quite a time of it these days, what with people being dumped in the river; fathers shot in front of their families; bodies beheaded and chopped up into little pieces. You must be getting a bit nervous. The politicians blame the Mafia. People mysteriously resign their important positions in the cabinet for personal reasons. Things must be very hot where you live."

"Is that so?" By this time, Rocco's eyes were flitting through the crowd, looking for escape. His wife was tugging at his sleeve, and the bodyguards pretended not to be listening to the gist of Emily's discussion.

However, Emily was on a rant. She spoke as she did in the Country Kitchen when she wanted to make sure that Maria, in the kitchen, could hear every word of the news she was spreading.

"Oh, Mrs. Seguin, there you are! Perfect timing. Mr. Rocco, may I introduce you to our would-be mayor. Mrs. Seguin makes it her business to know all about famous visitors to our town. She makes sure everyone knows everything about everyone."

Followed by her trusty sidekick, mousey Dora, Mrs. Seguin was giggling and rubbing her hands together excitedly. The would-be mayor was about to burst, so happy was she to receive such wonderful information to spread around town.

"Mr. Rocco here has come to our little town to savour the peace and quiet of the country life, I imagine," Emily said, whose tirade continued unabated so that no one could get a word in edgewise. "Isn't that right, Mr. Rocco? It's a far cry from the city. Here everyone knows everyone else's business. We have no secrets here, Mr. Rocco. Some people think living in a rural area is safe and private because everyone is so spread out, but really it's the opposite. We specialize in knowing all the details about our neighbours. Just ask our friends here; they are experts in spreading the town gossip. Why, before you know it, the whole town will be talking about our important visitor, the famous gangster Luigi Rocco—and of course we'll not forget to mention his lovely wife. Well, I must be going. My friends are waiting down the street. It's been such a pleasure to meet you, Mr. Rocco."

Emily shook hands again. Then she, Mrs. Seguin and Dora scuttled off to spread the word around town.

Luigi Rocco and his entourage escaped to their black Mercedes Benz and headed back to the city before the parade had finished its second trip around the village.

When the final fire truck disappeared around the corner, everyone was reluctant to clear the streets and return to normalcy. Green beer flowed in the tavern until evening, and Irish songs became more harmonious as the afternoon wore on.

Meanwhile, on the grounds of the nearby gallery, the memorial service for Janet English was just getting underway. Some of the parade watchers made their way over to the service to pay their respects. More than 100 people gathered on the lawn. Mourners shared a glass of wine and told their favourite stories of Janet's wit and special talents.

"English may have been her name, but today even Janet would have been Irish," Jack said with a tear in his eye. "She always loved festivals and celebrations. In her heart, Emerald Hill was her forever home sweet home."

As the copper sun disappeared below the horizon in the valley, the streets of the town on the hill settled into peaceful hush. Lights in the windows began to come on, one at a time, across town. Rooms glowed golden. The inhabitants in silhouettes performed their evening chores: supper, dishes, TV, bedtime. A soft breeze rustled the tender leaves. A sweet fragrance of hyacinths wafted on the air. Night descended, and the village drifted into sleep.

# Chapter Thirty-Nine

Every Thursday morning two copies of the *Hill News* arrived on the doorstep of the Country Kitchen. Some clients came to the Country Kitchen just to catch up on the latest gossip and the headlines. All the regulars were in for morning coffee. The would-be mayor, mousey Dora and Marie Cartier occupied their favourite table by the window. Constant Black was debating politics with Burton Barton, while Cecilia refreshed her makeup after eating. Suzanne and her mother discussed what type of muffins they would have. The Women's Institute ladies sipped tea and planned their next meeting.

One person sat alone at the corner table with his feet propped on a chair beside him. The newspaper hid his face. Its headline was bold and defiant: Murder Mystery Solved, Suspects Arrested.

The din in the restaurant muffled the tinkle of the bell on the door, announcing the arrival of new customers. Emily Blossom and Inspector Allard entered, paused and made their way toward the corner table. She looked tiny in a grey knit sweater and slacks to match. Her only flash of colour was a bright red scarf around her neck. Allard, in his imposing uniform with hat pulled low over his face, was a giant next to Emily's excited elfin bundle of energy.

"Speak of the Devil," Pete said, looking up from behind the paper. He lowered his feet, put his hat on the floor beside his chair and made way for his guests to be seated.

"I thought we might find you here," Emily said, fairly gushing. "We wanted to fill you in on the latest developments in the case."

"With all due respect, Inspector," he said to Allard and then to Emily, "thanks but no thanks."

"You and Daisy are going to get honourable discussion."

Pete shook his head.

"Mention, honourable mention."

"Yes, that's it, exactly. That's what I said."

"Emily, you don't get it."

"Yes I do. Daisy's on her way here too. We need to discuss the details."

At that moment, Daisy appeared in the doorway, escorted by Constable Wilson. There was a scraping of chairs and rearranging of tables to make room for five at the small table intended for two. By this time, most of the customers in the restaurant were eavesdropping, hoping to be the first to be able to spread the latest news of the village.

Ilsa brought coffee.

With a flourish, Emily made the order for all of them. "Butter tarts all around, please, Ilsa. Maria makes the best butter tarts in the whole world. Doesn't she, Constable Wilson?"

*Wink. Wink.*

"Now, where were we? Oh yes, Daisy, you're in on this too."

"Look, Em, you're the one who's superwoman. Me and Daisy, we're just ordinary folk. We ain't got nothin' prove. And the next time you decide to save the world, why don't you just leave us out of it?"

"Pete, Emily didn't mean to get us mixed up in all this."

"That's the thing about Emily, Daisy," Pete said as if Emily were not actually sitting between them. "She doesn't think about anybody but herself. In fact, correction—Emily doesn't think, period. She reacts."

"To put the blame where it's due," Emily said, "the whole thing is Friday's fault."

"You can't blame a dog for what happened, Emily, and you know it."

"Now, now, ladies," Allard said. He spoke with the authority of a person with an argumentative mother, a person empowered to negotiate between squabbling women. "Let's get down to business."

Allard extracted a notebook from his breast pocket and placed his glasses on the tip of his nose. He licked his fingers and stretched out his arm to adjust his sleeve. Only then did he begin to flip through the pages to read his notes on the case.

"Emily, would you please summarize exactly what happened over the past few days? What led you to the conclusions you came to? Please describe the details of the crime against the missing and murdered person, whose pieces were discovered and retrieved at Blossoms' Corners on Sunday past, by Daisy's dog, known as My Dog Friday."

Emily took a deep breath, as if about to embark upon a long monologue. Until now, she had not considered exactly how she would approach the subject. "Daisy called, and I found Pete, and together we came up with suspects, and—"

"Whoa, whoa, *tabernac*!" Pete cursed. "It wasn't like that at all."

Then she reconsidered her approach and began again. "No, you're right. I'll make a long story short. I'll tell you what I think happened, not how we figured it all out."

"We've filled in the blanks," Allard said. "You tell us what you know."

"A gang of motorcycle thugs were running several illegal operations out of the farm on Spring Valley Road."

"That's where Roger Major lives," Daisy said. "Did he know what was going on?"

"No, Roger happened to live there, only because he could afford the cheap rent. He could store his tractors on the property. He had nothing to do with the actual criminal activity going on there. In fact, when the raid took place, Roger hid in his apartment upstairs until the whole thing was over.

"The gang consisted of four men. Their immediate leader was a man they called Baldy, whose real name was Jimmy Winston. They were armed robbers, ran a grow-op in the barn and delivered guns and drugs between Montréal and Ottawa, using the farm as a base for their operations. One of the men, known as Snake, had a girlfriend. She was a prostitute and a tattoo artist. Unfortunately for her, she happened to witness a robbery in Montréal where the shopkeeper was killed. The only way to guarantee she wouldn't talk was to do her in.

"Snake murdered her, froze the body, cut it up with a chainsaw, stashed it in trash bags and threw the pieces into the ditch by Daisy's place, where the dog recovered one of her hands. The only missing body part, the head of the poor girl, was burned in the outdoor furnace on the farm.

"In the end, during the hostage-taking, Snake wanted to kill me too, but Jimmy Winston saved my life. During the knife fight, Jimmy killed Snake, but he also got fatally stabbed in the process. That left the fat man and the kid, who are now under arrest."

"Well done," the would-be mayor said, contributing her two cents to the discussion from across the room.

"We can all go home and sleep well at night," said Peter, the singing Presbyterian minister.

"If it only ended there, everything seems fairly simple. That would be the end of it," Dora said hopefully.

"Nobody operates in a vacuum. There's a lot more to it. I just bet," Constant Black said.

Emily continued. "This is where it gets complicated. I can guess at some of the bigger implications."

"Go on," Allard said. "I can't tell you anything that has not been substantiated, but I'm interested in knowing where you're going with this, Mrs. Blossom."

"Be careful, Em," Pete warned. "You're one small person in a very big world."

"I do know that Jimmy worked for Luigi Rocco. In fact—"

"The Luigi Rocco who knew Michel?" Daisy asked.

"I knew that guy looked suspicious," Pete said.

"Jimmy was a go-between. He was employed to manage the gang. They did some of the dirty work for Rocco's less-than-savoury enterprises. Of course there's no actual proof. Rocco would never leave a paper trail. The Mafia never does."

"You could never prove it," Allard said. "Besides, we have strict orders from higher up not to get involved beyond our jurisdiction."

"Exactly," Emily said. "And they know that. Even if you caught them in possession, you'd never be able to prove who actually sourced those drugs, provided the cash and organized the sales. All those details would be made verbally, in private."

"What about Bella Vista Transport?"

"You know what? Dealing and delivering guns is not illegal," Emily said. "The man up on the hill with an arsenal of weapons and artillery can get away with it because there's no law against manufacturing and selling guns. There are no records of gun owners in Canada. How are the cops going to control who buys them and where they end up?"

"Go figure."

"That stinks," Black said.

"Kind of like the construction industry in Quebec."

"Rocco is in construction," Daisy said.

"Precisely," Emily said. "But there's no law against construction, now, is there? Quebecers pay more than anyone else in the country for their roads and bridges, and the infrastructure is still falling apart, even though the government spends millions of dollars of taxpayers' money for repairs. There's no way of proving that the people are being ripped off."

"I'm glad we live here in our little village," Mrs. Seguin said. "We don't have to worry about all that."

"Amen," the minister said.

"Speaking of our little village, who was the man in the coffin on St. Patrick's Day?" the would-be mayor asked.

"Depends on who's telling the story," Pete said. "Everyone has a different version."

"A man in a coffin?" Old Mrs. Duval said to Suzanne. "Who died?"

"No one died, Mother. He was sleeping." Suzanne knew it was fruitless to explain. She regretted the mention of it as soon as the words escaped her mouth.

"Sleeping? Why was he sleeping in a coffin? We don't have homeless people in Emerald Hill."

"Apparently he was from out of town, but he wasn't acting on his own," Allard said. "His so-called friends took him to the funeral home after a drinking party at the tavern. They were playing hockey at the arena and went for a few drinks after practice. They decided to play a prank on their pal, who was so out of it he didn't know what was happening to him."

Constant, who rarely smiled and never told jokes, said, "Now the Underhills can start a new business. They could call it a Dead and Breakfast."

"Did anybody notice that the council members from our village of Emerald Hill were suspiciously absent from the parade?" Pete asked, addressing the room full of locals.

"Come to mention it, I did notice there was no village float. Why was the Scotsdale mayor looking so smug?" Dora asked.

"Apparently there's been a running feud between the town councils. Our council looked pretty short-sighted and unimaginative, didn't they? As it turned out, Scotsdale businesses were apparently booming the next day."

"Speaking of the parade," Franny said to the Women's Institute members. "I signed us all up for belly dancing lessons. That's our activity for the next meeting."

Ethel and Betty blushed, but their eyes sparkled just the same.

"Maybe we could take photos," Betty said. "We could make calendars and sell them to raise money for our scholarship fund."

Ethel was the most practical of the three at the Women's Institute table. "Wait a minute, Betty. Don't you think we should see if we can actually do it before we go planning to take photos?"

"We can do it," Franny said. "What have we got to lose? It would be good for us all. Who knows? Maybe we'd get some new members."

At this point, the customers in the Country Kitchen began to shuffle. The gossipers were eager to spread the word.

Robin and Cassie came in giggling. Robin whispered to Daisy in a hug. "I met a man. We have a date."

Cassie said, "Emily, the secret's out. It's a girl. We're so excited."

Pete stood up, reaching for his hat. "Well, I'll be on my way. Now that I have my truck back, I've got some picking to catch up on."

"Wait, Pete," Emily said. "You haven't heard the big news. We've been nominated for an award, for courage in the face of danger."

"You keep it, Em," Pete said. "You deserve it."

"But, but—"

Daisy put her hand on Emily's sleeve. "Don't push him, Emily. He needs his space."

"What about you, Daisy? You're on the list too."

"Emily, darling, you keep your awards. We're all proud of you." Daisy followed Pete out the door, which left Emily sitting with Inspector Allard and Constable Wilson.

Emily sat for a moment, her two hands wrapped around her cup. "We humans do have a way of complicating things then, don't we?" she said to the reflection of one questioning eye staring back at her from the surface of her tea. "Nothing is ever black or white, good or evil."

Then she looked at Allard with an unusually pensive expression. "It's never all that clear, is it?"

"What's that?"

"It seems to be more about survival than justice."

Thus challenged to defend himself, Allard leaned back in his chair and cleared his throat. "I hope there's more to it than that."

**FIN**